To Chri[...]
with best i[...]
bright & happy future
all the Best.
Lorene

MW01609508

No Malice Intended

One Woman's Journey
From The Depths Of Despair To Acceptance & Surrender

LORENE ALBERS

outskirtspress
DENVER, COLORADO

No Malice Intended
One Woman's Journey From The Depth Of Despair To Acceptance & Surrender
All Rights Reserved.
Copyright © 2013 Lorene Albers
v3.0

Cover Photo © 2013 Christian Laue. All rights reserved - used with permission.

Outskirts Press, Inc.
http://www.outskirtspress.com

ISBN: 978-1-4787-1744-7

Library of Congress Control Number: 2013904803

Outskirts Press and the "OP" logo are trademarks belonging to Outskirts Press, Inc.

PRINTED IN THE UNITED STATES OF AMERICA

Acknowledgements

In any literary endeavor, one never stands alone.

There are always people in the background, cheering you on, believing in you and your work and so I wish to thank only a few of them.

My gentle reader, Heide, who believed in the story from the onset.

My close friend and editor extraordinaire, Dawn, who gave so much of her time and provided invaluable input.

My dear friend Rick Pyman, who always believed in me as a writer. You are deeply missed.

And my son Christian (Mike). You complete my life.

I thank you all.

Prologue

If it weren't for my friend, Antonia, I wouldn't be sitting here on this warm, sunny beach, thinking about my life, trying to figure out exactly what happened and why. And trying to make sense of it all.

Without my friend Antonia, I wouldn't have the luxury of staying at a posh condo at Boca's seashore. I'd be stuck in my apartment, trying to ignore the icy Canadian winter.

The condo belongs to Antonia and she insists that I use it for as long as I like. Except for the housekeeper, Maria, I'm completely alone here and it's like being in paradise.

As I said, if it weren't for Antonia, I wouldn't be here. Sitting on this endless beach that stretches for miles and miles, watching little brown birds dodging the waves, running for their lives. Back and forth. Running.... Running...... Running.

You would never have thought, when we first met, that Antonia would become my friend. My best friend, actually. In fact, when we first met I didn't like her all that much. It was at one of Mark's schmooze-with-clients parties at an upscale hotel.

Mark had come home early that Friday, a week before the party.

He walked up behind me in the kitchen, wrapped his arms 'round me and kissed my hair.

"I want you to go out and buy a nice dress, a really nice dress. Spend as much as you like. It doesn't matter how much it costs."

"Ok, sure, if you like. I'll go. I'll go on Saturday. What's the occasion?"

"Well, we're having a soiree-type of thing next week for a potentially huge client. The guy is a publisher of some sort and we've just taken on his account, so it's important. And it's important that you look good. Not that you don't always look good. So go in the morning and buy yourself something really special, ok?"

Now, that was exciting because I didn't get to go shopping for myself much. One thing, when you live in a small town, you don't dress up very often. It's usually jeans or shorts, depending on the season. Looking after the kids, shopping at the local market, gardening – not much need for cocktail dresses.

So yes, I was excited. And I went to the mall with my friend Melanie and we had a great time. We left the kids with the sitter and we checked out all the stores, especially the really expensive boutiques.

And that's when I saw the dress. The perfect dress. Slinky and sexy, with ruffles at the bottom of the skirt that swished softly 'round my ankles. It was black with silver threads woven through and it shimmered like moonlight on dark water. And I looked slim in that dress. Slim and sexy. And I was happy.

We went to a bunch of other stores and I bought strappy silver sandals and a glittery little purse to go with the dress. And then we had a really expensive lunch at Panini's. Melanie laughed because I only ordered a salad and mineral water.

"You're not going to lose any weight in a couple of days," she teased.

But I kept looking at my shopping bag with the magical dress inside.

"Well, it can't hurt, can it?" But then I ordered a glass of wine anyway. To celebrate.

Mark's eyes lit up when I modeled the dress that evening.

It showed a lot of cleavage, and had I put on the teardrop diamond necklace and diamond studs that Mark had given me when the twins were born.

"You look amazing, Puss. You are going to be the best-looking babe at the party. Do something with your hair though, will you?"

It was such a typical response. That's what he did best: he built you up and took you down. What the hell, I should have been used to it by then. And I did something with my hair alright; I went and had it cut. Short and bouncy with shimmering highlights. I knew Mark wouldn't be crazy about that because he liked my hair long, but I didn't care. I loved my new look.

The party was at the Hyatt Hotel in Richmond. Mark's firm always had their parties at big hotels. Always big and splashy and expensive. I took the commuter train into the city to meet Mark.

The kids were at Melanie's. I had packed my little overnight bag. We were going to stay at the hotel and drive home Sunday morning. Like a mini holiday. I looked forward to it. My gorgeous new dress, my new hair. I was happy.

And it was a really nice night out. I mean, really, really nice. Lots of people. Lots of women, dressed in fancy gowns and men in dark evening suits. And I looked good. I could tell that Mark was proud of me as he introduced me 'round the room:

"My wife, Stephanie," he said. "Mother of my children and the love of my life."

And then I met Antonia.

Antonia was Ken's wife, the publisher they were courting this evening. She was from Italy, born and raised there. Typically Italian.

Gorgeous, in a Sophia Loren kind of way. Her eyes a warm brown, flecked with gold, and reddish hair dancing 'round her face like flames. I guessed her to be about five or six years older than me.

"So you're Stephanie?" she shook my hand. She was wearing the biggest diamond I had ever seen, and in the soft light, it threw sparks all over the place. I thought it a bit ostentatious. Antonia caught my look and sighed.

"It's big, isn't it? Too bloody big. But Ken gave it to me and he is so proud and happy, I don't have the heart not to wear it. In any case, it's so goddamned big, it looks fake. It's good to finally meet you," she smiled. "Mark talks about you all the time."

He does? Why? But then who knows what they talk about at their meetings. Mark always likes to become friendly with his clients. Have them over to the house. Play golf. That sort of thing.

"I like you, Stephanie, I really do like you," Antonia said in her direct way. "You must come over for dinner. With Mark of course. We actually don't live that far from you, on Grosvenor Drive. Do you golf?"

"Oh yes. If I love anything, I love golf. I'm not very good at it, but I'm hopelessly in love with the game."

"Great, me too. Let's play, just you and me. We've just joined the country club and I don't really know too many people yet. Anyhow, I'm not crazy about most of the women there. Too bloody snooty, if you ask me."

Like I said, I didn't really like Antonia that much at first. She was a little too much. Too glam. Too cosmopolitan. Too European, I guess. Yeah, that's it, too European. But something inside me said 'this woman is going to play an important part in your life one day'. Something said that inside me but at the time I didn't know what that could possibly mean.

Before she turned 'round to join Ken, Antonia smiled, "Don't forget: golf. I'll call you, ok?"

I simply nodded and went in search of Mark.

"What did you talk about?" he asked. "Isn't she nice? Do you like her?"

"Well, yeah, sort of." I wasn't going to commit.

"So what did you talk about?"

"She wants to play golf, and have us over for dinner, that kind of thing."

Mark was pleased. He put his arm around my shoulders and kissed my forehead. It was a condescending little gesture, like when you pat a kid on the head in passing. And I felt small, like a little girl that had done good. And I resented Antonia for it, even though it wasn't her fault.

So, yes, I was a little overwhelmed when I first met Antonia. But as I got to know her, I realized that there was nothing phony about her. Nothing.

Sure, her husband was rich, very rich, but that didn't mean a thing to Antonia. She treated everyone with kindness and respect; the waitress, the guy at the gas station, the girls at the supermarket, the mayor of our little town and his snooty wife, even though she made faces as soon as those two turned their backs.

But then I forgot about Antonia, and we had a lovely, lovely evening, with champagne, a superb dinner, and melted chocolate flowing over little strawberries for dessert. And we stayed in a suite at the hotel and we made love half the night. And it was just like when we first met. Feeling free. So free. Not a care in the world. Not a single care.

On the drive home, Mark started up again about Antonia.

"So she really likes you, hmm?"

"Well, I guess, but she probably doesn't mean anything by it. She's just saying that to be nice. They'll never invite us. She's got better things to do than to spend time with a boring housewife."

But I was wrong. I was as wrong as you can possibly be. Because a week later I got a card. A little card that smelled ever so faintly of an expensive perfume.

And the little card said: 'Would you and Mark come to dinner on Sunday, like we talked about? Very informal, ok? Wear jeans. I will. We'll have a little dinner, a couple of drinks, and get to know each other better.'

I can't say that I was overly happy. Not really. But the note was cheery and inviting and, of course, Mark was thrilled. Absolutely thrilled. I had not seen him this pleased in a long while, and I was happy about that.

Ken and Antonia lived in a spectacular house. Spectacular, but not in a showy way. It was one of those old houses at the end of a cul-de-sac, with a verandah wrapped all around it and huge trees towering above. You couldn't see the backyard for the trees. It was like living in the middle of the woods. A little path led from the huge back porch down to a still, clear, shallow lake.

"Ken wants to build a pool," Antonia sighed, "but I won't have it. Imagine, a pool! It would kill the look of the house. I much prefer the lake. It's so calm and clear and not too deep, so you can always see the bottom. I don't like dark water. You never know what's beneath you."

I laughed and agreed. I have always had that same feeling. Ever since I was a little girl, I have hated dark waters.

The afternoon was sunny and mellow. Just as her note had said, Antonia was wearing jeans. With her brilliant hair tied back in a ponytail, she looked like a kid. Unsure of myself, I had settled for Capri's and a casual blouse. She had greeted us at the front door, holding a tiny black kitten while the mother cat rubbed against her leg.

And then there were the horses. And I love horses. There were two of them, in a small stable near the lake. The most beautiful creatures I had ever seen. Pitch black with long wavy manes and flowing tails and silky coats. Their clever liquid eyes and velvety nostrils reminded me of a passage I had read somewhere: 'They drink the wind and their movement is lighter than air.'

"They are Friesians," Antonia explained, "a gorgeous breed, very gentle and so affectionate. Magnolia and Ophelia. Sisters."

Antonia held out her palm and offered each a sugar cube.

"They are my best friends."

I had to laugh. "What about Ken?"

She smiled at me, but her eyes were serious.

"Stephanie, these two are my best friends."

It seemed an odd response coming from someone who so obviously had everything a woman could wish for. Looks, charm, money, a great relationship.

"Do you ride?"

"Well, yes, I used to, a long time ago. But I don't know..."

"You'll be alright. They are as gentle as lambs. We'll just go for a short ride."

And we did. After dinner. We went for a quiet ride along the path in the quiet woods. And it was magical, just magical. The horses knew the path well and walked along with a steady gait, bobbing their heads and snorting softly with the pleasure at being outside.

Antonia talked about Europe and how she missed her friends.

"Don't get me wrong. I love Ken, and I love America. But this whole lifestyle... It's not really me. I'm happiest out here with my horses or at the beach. I have a condo by the ocean in Florida, and I love it. We'll go there sometime, you and I. We'll have a good time, you'll see."

Back at the house, the two men sat on the porch, nursing brandies and smoking cigars. They seemed to be getting on great together, laughing at something or other and looking a bit like conspirators. I was happy for Mark. I knew how important it was to him and his firm to have a good relationship with Ken. Antonia wrinkled her nose.

"Oh God, that stench, I can't stand it. But Ken loves his cigar, so what am I to do?"

She flashed him a huge smile. Her flaming hair glowed in the sunset.

And then I knew that I liked her. I liked her more and more. I think the horses and the cats did it. Yeah. So that's how we became friends.

Antonia lived so close by that she visited quite often. Sometimes she'd come on her bicycle, or she'd show up in her Jag.

"I hate this car. I really, really hate this car, but Ken wants me to have it. I'd prefer something a little less showy, but one shouldn't complain, should one?"

Then she'd come bouncing into the kitchen and stroke the twins' heads. She'd always bring them something. Something different. Something other grownups didn't think of. Something like.. well, one time she brought a small music box for Bettina. Not just any music box, mind you. This was an antique she'd bought in Italy. It played the most beautiful, lilting tunes and Bettina took it to bed with her, she loved it so much.

And for Adam she once brought an old globe. You know, the ones that have the ancient names of countries and oceans on it, and he was so intrigued.

Other times she'd bring chocolates and tell the children that they were magical and that they mustn't eat them before dinner, otherwise the magic wouldn't work. And they'd look at her, wide-eyed and knowing. And they understood and set the chocolates aside and ate them slowly, one by one.

The kids have always loved Antonia because she is so totally herself and so totally Italian. And she can eat like a horse. You'd never know it looking at her. Pasta, of course, is her favourite.

"Pasta is good for you," she claimed the first time she came over for lunch. "It's good for your nerves and it puts you in a good mood and it keeps you slim."

"Yeah, right," I snorted. "If I ate that much pasta, I'd look like a blimp."

"Don't you worry, you're just right. Not too skinny, but with nice curves, the way European men like their women."

And we both laughed, and had more pasta.

And that's how it all started. That's how Antonia and I became friends.. Real friends.. Soul sisters, in fact.

But all this happened way in the future, way after I met Mark, way after life happened to me.

Not the way I had wished for life to happen or imagined it to happen.

But then, it never does, does it?

BOOK I

Chapter 1

Sometimes in your life you have to go back, way back, to try and figure out what happened. Why things turned out the way they did, why things changed and try to make sense of it all.

I've always known that I must have my father's looks even though I never knew him. Certainly not my mom's. Mom is blonde, petite, the Nordic type. And so is my aunt Elizabeth, Sissy for short. Both blue-eyed blondes. My grandparents emigrated from Poland, which goes to show you that not all blue-eyed, blonde-haired people come from Germany or Scandinavia.

My hair is dark, very dark, and so are my eyes. Dark, dark brown, and my skin tone is a little on the olive side. So I guess that's where my looks came from: my father. My father.....The man Mom never, ever talks about.

The only time she did, I remember, was when I was still quite little, maybe ten or eleven.

She sat at the edge of my bed and she said, "I cannot tell you anything about your father. Only that he was killed before you were born. It was very, very hard for me and I don't want to talk about it, ever again."

She brushed the curls back from my forehead and looked past me at the white muslin curtains, moving softly in the evening breeze.

"I'm telling you this now. I know you're still very young, but this is the only time I'm ever going to mention him. I loved your father very, very much. As much as any person can love another. And you are all I have left of him. And I am thankful for that. In you, I see him and you are now the most important person in the world to me."

"Ok mom," I replied. "Ok, I won't ask about him, but he must have been a good man for you to love him so."

She smiled, a quiet smile that never quite reached her eyes, and again she stroked my hair and looked far off into the distance.

She is good, my mom, the best. She does everything for me that you could possibly wish for. She never, ever makes me feel that it is a hardship for her. Mom works at a big legal firm downtown. She is the comptroller and I guess she makes good money. It can't be easy though, raising a little girl on your own. Making a nice home for us, a condo, mind you, but nice nevertheless.

But she is strict. Very, very strict. More than strict. I wouldn't say she doesn't trust me but she always wants to know where I'm going and with whom. When I do go out with friends, I'll have to be home at ten. Not twenty past ten, not even ten past ten. Ten. Not negotiable. Of course, my friends tease me, call me a 'mama's girl' but to be honest, I don't mind. Mom has her reasons and I respect them.

She insists that I get the very best education she can afford. And if that means going off to university and living away from her, so be it. Anyway, it's not all that far away, the university, only about an hour's drive north of the city.

I share a flat with my best friend, Nanette, and I try to be as responsible and grown up as possible. We didn't want to live on campus. so we found this great two bedroom flat in a very old neighborhood with giant trees lining both sides of the street and all the houses built more than half a century ago. It's perfect. Small living room, even smaller kitchen, a tiny bathroom and a tiny balcony. We totally love it. Mom likes the place too, even though it's not very spacious, but I think she mostly likes the fact that our landlady, Mrs Chenovski, lives downstairs and is, shall we say, a little nosy. So mom thinks that she might keep an eye on us, make sure we don't have wild parties and stuff

But overall, Mom doesn't pester me with incessant phone calls or anything like that.

Nanette always says how cool my mom is. Her parents are constantly dropping by, bringing baskets of food and clean sheets and towels, that sort of thing, as if we didn't know how to work a stove or a washing machine.

The fact that they live only about an hour away doesn't help, so every excuse they can come up with, will do. But they are nice, really nice. And they care, so that is important. And they have money, rich, I think they are.

Nanette's dad is a lawyer who handles mostly divorce cases and, as everyone knows, there's a lot of money to be made in divorce court. He doesn't look at all like a lawyer though. He is short and balding and looks more like a greengrocer. I don't tell Nanette that, of course. And you know what is really ironic? Even though he deals with couples breaking up, mud slinging, backstabbing and heartbreak every single day, he and Nanette's mom have the happiest of marriages. They are like two peas in a pod, literally. One won't go anywhere or do anything without the other.

Nanette's mother is very, very pretty, gorgeous actually. That's where Nanette gets her looks. Her mom has pitch-black hair, blue eyes, and a pale, pale complexion that makes her eyes sparkle like sapphires. Just like Nanette's. They both have these piercing blue eyes that stand in sharp contrast to their dark hair and is the first thing you notice about them. Irish looking, you know? Beauty and the Beast. That's what they remind me of, Nan's parents.

They both dote on their daughter. An only child, Nanette can do no wrong. She is a genius, the apple of their eye... that sort of thing. So they heap all their love and money on her. They buy her a car so she's able to get around; mostly to visit them, I suspect. They probably would have preferred for her to live in a posh apartment building, but Nanette won't have it. She loves our flat. We both do, and her parents are nothing if not pretentious. They treat everyone with kindness and respect, even some of our scruffier friends.

My mom, on the other hand, hardly ever comes to visit. She doesn't drive, so having to take a bus is a bit of a pain. But she calls at least once a week and she writes real actual letters with real actual stuff in them. Like what she is doing, about her job, about people at work, what movies she's seen, and how the cat is being his usual goofball self. I know it is her way of making me a part of her life, as if I haven't really left, and I love her for it. And I am grateful for my weekly letters. And I am saving them forever.

At nineteen, I am still a virgin. Would you believe that? I think I am the only one on campus. The only one among my friends, for sure. But I don't talk about it much. Nobody really believes it any-way and I almost… almost, went all the way once. When I was eigh-teen.

I was in love with the cutest guy on the tennis team. Actually, every single girl was in love with this guy. But he chose me. And we went out together.

I'd go to all the matches, I'd wear his sweater… you know, corny stuff like that. And of course, everybody, including my best friends, thought we were doing it. He was so good looking and so mascu-line.

But we didn't really do anything. We did make out, mind you. All the time. Heavy necking, groping in the backseat of his car … that sort of thing. And one day he took me to his parent's cottage. We had planned that that would be the day. The day I would lose my virgin-ity. And he his, as it turned out. But I didn't know about that then. He never talked about other girls. And I knew that I would have to do it one day, might as well be with a guy I liked.

And then, after a couple of glasses of wine, fresh sheets on the bed, candles on the dresser, that sort of thing, nothing happened. By that time I was ready, you can be sure of that. But he couldn't do it.

He simply could not. And then he started to cry and said that had never happened to him. Never, ever! And he said that he loved me and maybe he respected me too much, and on and on.

And you know what? Deep in my heart, I was glad. Glad it wasn't he who would be the first. I knew I wasn't really in love with him; I was in love with the idea of him. In love with the fact that all the girls wanted him and I thought I was hot stuff for landing him.

So I promised him never to tell anyone. Not even my best friend, Nanette. Only much, much later did I find out that this had happened before, and speculations were that maybe he was gay and that he couldn't admit to that.

So that leaves me a virgin still, at nineteen. And I don't mind; I know it will happen eventually. I will simply wait.

As it turns out, I don't have to wait too long because at the end of my nineteenth summer I meet Mark. My Mark.

You would think we'd meet at a party. Nanette and I never miss a party. We go to parties, we give parties, plenty of opportunity to meet guys. But no. I bump into him at the supermarket. Literally. Bump into him with my cart. I hit him with my cart just as he is reaching for some laundry detergent and the box flies out of his hand and he turns 'round with the most surprised look on his face. His mouth drops open and I have to laugh. I feel like an idiot but I can't stop laughing.

"Well, thanks a lot."

He bends down to pick up the box and I think 'nice butt' and stop laughing and start to apologize.

"It's ok, don't worry. You didn't do it on purpose. Or did you?"

He smiles. He has this peculiar smile; a funny little half grin that goes straight to my heart.

"No, of course not. I mean, I didn't see you. I was looking at my list, sorry."

"Ok, never mind then, but I think you owe me. While we're in this romantic aisle, can I beg your advice on what detergent to use? What's best for the environment and still cleans my sweats?"

"I can't believe you said that. I mean, please!"

"Yeah, neither can I, sorry. I just couldn't think of anything clever enough to start a conversation. Let me be more direct. Will you go out with me? For a cup of coffee or some such? My name is Mark, by the way."

He is tall. Much taller than I am. And his hair is dark and kind of unruly and falls into his eyes. And his eyes get to me; get to me right away. They are dark brown, like mine, with a warm, impish glow in them. He is dressed in jeans and a plain white shirt, but you can tell they are designer jeans and they fit him well.

I hold out my hand.

"Stephanie. And yes, Mark, I'd love to have a cup of coffee with you sometime."

His hand is warm and dry and he has a firm grip without hurting my fingers.

"What's wrong with right now? We can go to the donut shop across the street. You can always count on the coffee there being good, right?"

I hesitate for a moment, but not too long and after we've paid for our groceries we head for the donut shop.

I've never really believed in love at first sight. I've always thought it too romantic and a little silly. I mean, how can you fall in love with someone you've just met? No, I never believed in that concept, ever! Until now.

We're in this donut shop and I watch Mark standing in the lineup to get coffee. And I'm asking myself, what the heck am I doing here? Sitting in this donut place, waiting for a total stranger to get my coffee.

For a second I think of getting up and leaving, but that would just be rude, even if I'd never see him again. Out of the corner of my eyes

I watch him standing there. He is good looking, I mean really, really good looking.

An old man, leaning heavily on a cane, is standing behind him and Mark turns around and gestures for the man to go ahead of him. I can't hear the conversation, but it looks at first as if the man is declining and then he smiles and limps up to the counter ahead of Mark to place his order. It's a small gesture, but a gesture that is kind and considerate.

So I wait until he comes over with two cups of coffee and a handful of little cream containers.

"I usually drink coffee black, if I drink it at all," he sets the cups down and smiles at me and again his smile goes straight to my heart. It is warm and open and genuine and I feel my hand tremble just a little when I raise my cup to my lips. The coffee is hot, very, very hot, which takes my mind of the fact that he's brushed against my hand ever so slightly when he handed me the cup. Every so slightly, ever so softly, like a tiny bird in flight. I check myself sharply. What a ridiculous notion, a flipping bird in flight.

I take little sips of my coffee, trying to avoid looking into his eyes because I know if I do, I'll be lost, as silly as that might sound. He too sips his coffee and pulls a face.

"I don't normally drink coffee," he explains "I much prefer tea."

"Me too. Actually, I don't drink it at all. If I have two cups a year, that's about it. But I love the smell of fresh brewed coffee, just as I like the smell of chocolate but don't really like eating it."

"What?" he laughs "I've never ever met a girl that doesn't like chocolate and one so young. Wow, that's different." And he laughs again and looks straight into my eyes.

"What else don't you like, Stephanie? Or should I say, what do you like?"

I try not to return his gaze and look at the people in the restaurant instead.

"Being young has nothing to do with it," I reply a bit petulantly, "I just never ever liked chocolate or cake or candies. Even when I was a small child I asked for something spicy to get rid of the sweet taste. My mom thought it odd too. And anyway, I'm not that young," I add, as if it were relevant.

"Well, when I said young, I meant that in the nicest possible way. You're certainly much younger than I am."

"Why, how old do you think I am?" I wished I could take that question back as soon as it left my mouth. What an idiotic thing to say, oh man, I could kick myself.

He squints at me over the rim of his cup.

"Twenty two?"

"Close, I've just turned twenty."

"Oh", he pauses, "Well, as I said - young! I'm much, much older than that, I'm afraid. On my next birthday, I'll be thirty two. Shocked?"

"Not in the least," I reply although, truth be told, I think being over thirty is, well, rather on the old side. But he doesn't look it, not one bit.

He's tanned, fit, beautifully dressed, he's just - well, gorgeous.

"Ten years is quite a bit," he continues "especially when you're only twenty. Later in life it doesn't seem to be as significant.

We sit in that donut shop for more than two hours and talk. I've never met anyone who is so easy to talk to, so interested in what I have to say, so full of funny stories about himself, his cat, his job. I have no idea where the time has gone until I look at my watch and jump up. "Oh my God, I have to rush, I didn't even call my friend, and she'll worry,"

He escorts me to my car and helps put the groceries into the trunk. He takes my hand in his, warm, protective.

"When will I see you again? No pressure, it's just that I had such a good time, you're so easy to talk to, so easy to be with." He smiles down at me and blows a strand of hair out of his eyes.

So I give him my number, something I never, ever do with somebody

I've just met, but I am smitten; there is no other word for it. Smitten. And I have stars in my eyes when I come back to the flat. You may think that sounds silly, but I look into the mirror and I have stars in my eyes. Honest. Even Nanette says so.

"You have stars in your eyes. Where have you been? I've been waiting for ages for something to eat."

And that's how it starts. That is how Mark and I start.

He lives not far from our little flat, but the difference is like day and night. While our flat is on the second floor in an old house, he lives in a super posh condominium building, sitting on top of a hill and surrounded by park like grounds. His is a penthouse with a wrap-around balcony which you can access from the living room and the master bedroom. At night you can see the entire city. An endless carpet of light.

The living room has beautiful off-white carpeting and an actual fireplace and bookcases filled with all kinds of books. Mark's furniture is a little masculine. Dark shiny mahogany, glass tables… that sort of thing. But nice. Really, really nice. And you can tell he has a housekeeper. The place is always immaculate.

We spend a lot of time at Mark's condo. And at the golf club. And at restaurants, both posh and quaint. And we make love. Everywhere, it seems, but mostly in his king-sized bed. Mark is gentle. Gentle and sweet and tender. The best lover in the world, I'm absolutely sure of it. But then I have no one to compare him to.

Even though we spend so much time together, it doesn't affect my school work. If anything, Mark encourages my studies, helps me with them, in fact, and many evenings I pour over my books at his place while he reads some golf magazine or other. Never disturbing me, never even turning on the radio or TV. I don't have that long to go though, to finish university, that is. I will graduate in the spring and I want more than anything to become a vet.

"A veterinarian is a great job, sweetie," Mark says, "and you'll be good at it, very good indeed."

He loves animals, all sorts of animals. His cat, Sapphire, a blue point Siamese, has the run of the condo. She'll drape herself over the armrest of the chair and stare at nothing in particular...... the picture of perfection.

But in the end it never happens. I never become a veterinarian. And I always feel kind of sad about that.

I can never really be sure whether Nanette likes Mark. She's only met him once, mind you. He invited her to come along to a tiny Hungarian restaurant where I met him one evening after Nanette and I had been shopping. The three of us sat and talked for a while, but Nanette wasn't her usual self, you know, bubbly, outgoing, that sort of thing. In fact, she was pretty quiet and seemed a little ill at ease.

But anyway, she is so busy with her new boyfriend and I'm always with Mark, so I hardly ever see her. It makes me sad though. We have been friends practically forever. Since high school. Bosom buddies. There is nothing she doesn't know about me and I about her. But since I've met Mark she's become more distant. Maybe she thinks that he doesn't fit in with our friends, or has too much money, or is too old, or maybe she even thinks he's a snob? I don't know. It would be nice if they'd get on though.

Mark doesn't like parties too much, at least not the ones Nanette and I go to. He is more into the business crowd, executives, that sort of thing. And he loves playing golf with his friends, a sport I have always thought to be really, really boring.

"You must try it," he says one day when we wake up.

I sit on the edge of the bed with his shirt on. I like to wear his shirts. It makes me feel as if he is still part of me the way he has been part of me all night long. When we make love. When he holds me. When we fall asleep in each other's arms.

"Try what?"

"Golf, what else?"

"Golf, me?"

"Sure why not. I'll take you to the club this weekend. We'll hit a few balls. You never know, you might get to like it."

"Yeah, right. Golf is so boring. I'd rather watch paint dry."

As it turns out, I am wrong. The first few balls I hit on the practice range aren't too bad. I am actually beginning to enjoy myself. Of course, it helps that Mark has his arms round me to show me the proper stance. How to grip the club. How to swing down on the ball.

"You're a natural, Steph. We'll have you take a few lessons from our pro, and Bob's your uncle."

I am happy to see him so pleased but to be honest, I am bitten by the golf bug almost immediately. We spend every weekend at the club, where Mark is a member. I love the posh environment. I love being outdoors. I love the game. And, most of all, I love Mark.

Nanette just shakes her head. She doesn't want to hear about golf and she really doesn't want to hear much about Mark either.

"But why?" I whine one night when we are sharing a pizza. "Why don't you like him? You know what the problem is? You don't know him. You don't know him the way I do."

"I certainly hope not," she says, her mouth full of pizza. "Ok, Steph, maybe I'm wrong. He seems a little too perfect, a little too full of himself, but like I said, maybe I'm wrong about him."

Nanette pours a glass of wine. We like that. Pizza and red wine. Kind of takes the grease out of the whole thing.

"Tell you what," she swallows. "We'll have a party, here. Here in our apartment. Mark will come, we'll have a few of our friends, and if Mark wants to invite one of his friends, that's ok too. What do you think? We'll get to know each other."

"Well, our apartment is a little…" I hesitate.

"A little what?"

"Small. It's awfully small, Nan."

"That's never stopped us before. Nobody minds being a little crowded; most people hang out in the kitchen anyway, or on the balcony to smoke."

I don't want to mention that Mark lives in a posh condo, such as we could never afford, with mirrored elevators and plush carpeting in the hallways, and twenty four hour security and all. Why, there is even a real aquarium in the lobby. Huge. With tropical fish in all sorts of colours swimming about.

Our little flat is dreary compared to that. Don't get me wrong. I am not ashamed of it. I love our flat. It is cozy, in a hippy kind of way. Very clean and very colourful with bits and bobs of furniture and pictures from the flea market.

Mark has never been to our apartment so I have no idea how he will react. To hell with that, I think, if he doesn't like it, too bad. It's our place and we're happy here.

"You're right, Nan. We can't all live in a palace and our place is cozy enough, right?"

We have the party the following Saturday. Mark is late. Not a good sign. I'm nervous. What if he isn't coming? I keep looking out the bedroom window and altogether drive Nanette crazy.

"Instead of being glued to the window you might consider giving me a hand with these hors d'oeuvres. Whose idea was it anyway to make tiny smoked salmon pinwheels? Everybody is going to think we're nuts," she mutters to herself.

"Ok, ok, I'll help. You're right, he'll get here whenever."

After all, it has been my idea to make something fancy. Something Mark will like. Not chips and dip, that's for sure.

Mark arrives in the Beemer with the top down. It looks a little out of place, parked among all the Chevys and Hondas. He brings a bouquet of roses for me and a bunch of daisies and a box of truffles for Nanette. I must have told him that truffles are her favourite and he remembered. And he brings wine, of course. I am touched and very, very proud.

Mark keeps assuring us how much he loves the flat. It reminds him of his college days. He mingles easily with our friends, laughing, kidding, even having a toke on the balcony and engaging in serious conversations. You know the type of conversations that get deeper and more meaningful, or so you think, as the night wears on. Everyone seems to like him.

And Nanette noticeably warms to him. I watch from the hallway, they are drinking wine and chatting like old friends. In the kitchen, of course, just like she'd said. She's leaning against the sink and throws back her head, laughing at something he's said. It makes me happy, seeing them like that.

Months later that scene would come back to haunt me.

Chapter 2

I can't wait for Mom to meet Mark but she's gone on vacation. For Aunt Sissy's fiftieth birthday, Mom took her on a cruise. Not just one of those 10 day or two week cruises, but a month-long journey that starts in Scandinavia and threads all the way to the Mediterranean with stops in the most famous and exotic places imaginable.

She's been sending lovely postcards each and every day.

Sometimes they arrive in lots of three or four, depending on where they came from and she's emailing photos of Aunt Sissy and herself from aboard ship, both looking touristy, happy and relaxed. I'm glad for Mom, she's not taken a vacation in years and now she's going all out.

Still, I'm anxious for her to meet Mark. I know she'll like him, he's so, well, different from any of my boyfriends she's met in the past.

She's called a couple of times but that's always a bit iffy, depending on the location, and I haven't told her about him at all. I'd rather wait until she's back and tell her in person.

And then it turns out that the two never meet at all.

A week after her return I get a phone call in the early hours of the morning. Two o'clock. A phone call from my Aunt Sissy. She is hysterical.

"Stephanie, you have to come home. You have to come home now. Now!"

"Why? For heaven's sake, what's happened?"

"It's your mother. Please, please come now! Come home right away!"

Right away…. Echoing round and round in my head…. Right away…. Not tomorrow, no, right away.

"But what's wrong? You've got to tell me Aunt Sissy. What's wrong with Mom?"

"There was an accident. We came out of a movie theatre and she, and she..." sobbing at the other end of the line.

"She what? What?"

I can hear myself yelling and I see Nanette in her pyjamas, standing next to my bed, looking scared.

""She stepped onto the street and a bus.... she didn't see.... it was no one's fault, she just didn't pay attention," a little calmer now.

"How badly hurt is she? Tell me, tell me please!"

"They are still doing x-rays, all kinds of tests..."

"Ok, I'm leaving immediately. Which hospital?"

"St. Michaels, downtown. It was the closest."

Nanette has left; I can hear water running, and then rummaging in her room. She is throwing things into an overnight bag.

"I'm going with you. I'm driving. You're in no condition."

There is no arguing with her, of course. I just look at her, dry-eyed, grateful. We hug for a long time.

"Ok, let's get started. She'll be ok, your Mom, you'll see."

"Yeah. Sure. Thanks. Love you."

The drive to Toronto takes just over an hour. Nanette stops for coffee at an all-night donut shop and I gratefully sip the hot liquid that burns my tongue.

Let Mom be ok.... Let Mom be ok... Let Mom be... I can think of nothing else. Not even Mark. I will call him.... later.

Aunt Sissy has gone home to change because her clothes were covered in blood, the nurse at reception tells me. She looks at me strangely, the nurse does. Strangely, with sympathy in her eyes.

Nanette has dropped me off at emergency and is searching for a parking spot. I see a doctor come down the hallway, his lab coat aflutter. He strides down the hallway in slow motion, it seems, one step, another step, coat fluttering..... Like a bad movie.

"You must be Stephanie. Your aunt told me you would be coming. "

"Yes. Yes, I am."

He motions to the nurse at the desk.

"Please take Stephanie to the quiet room," he says, and, turning to me, "I'll be with you in just a moment. Have to make a quick call......"

"Come with me please." The nurse leads me into a small room next to a private office. This must be it. The quiet room. What the hell does that mean? Through a small window I can see Nanette, talking to the nurse who motions her to have a seat. Like in a silent movie, I see all that.

"Have a seat." The doctor has returned. He is fidgeting. I am scared. My mouth is dry.

"Could I have a glass of water please?" Stalling.

He walks over to the water cooler and fills one of those ridiculous little paper cones, which I drink in one big gulp. I get up and refill it myself.

"Ok, my mother. How is she? Can I see her?"

He clears his throat and does not look directly at me.

"I would not advise it. Your mother... you see Stephanie, your mother suffered severe facial injuries. Severe. You would not wish to see her the way she looks. Best to remember her the way you last saw her."

"Remember her? What do you mean, remember her?"

"She's dead, Stephanie. Your mother died about thirty minutes ago."

I stare at him. I cannot speak. It's a joke, it has to be. My sweet lovely mom, the person I love more than anything else in the world cannot be dead. It's impossible. I fall onto a chair and keep staring at the doctor. My mouth is dry; I have no tears, an icy cold feeling is creeping into my heart. A huge black abyss opens between myself sitting there and the rest of the world.

The enormity the doctors words, hanging in the room, is not something I am prepared to deal with. Not just yet. Maybe never.

The doctor picks up the phone and almost immediately a nurse rushes in with some sort of needle on a tray. And I see Nanette standing in the doorway, white. Ashen. Looking at me with huge round eyes.

And the needle somehow goes into my arm and that's all I remember.

I can't really say that. That's not all I remember. It's the immediate things right after I wake up that I don't remember. Don't want to remember. Can't bear to think about.

Yet, I remember sharply, in fact, I'll never forget, when they bring in my mom's clothes. You know, stuff she was wearing at the time of the accident. Her dress. Her coat. Her purse. Everything. And I look at that stuff. I scoop it up in my arms. And that's all I have left of Mom. That's all.

"Would you sign for this?" the nurse says. "You have to sign for receiving your mother's belongings. Things she had on her person at the time of admittance."

She holds out a piece of paper and a pen and her face is without expression, without any expression whatsoever. And I know that she probably has to do this kind of thing a lot. I feel like killing her. Right here and now. Killing her.

The days after Mom's death are a blur. I don't remember anything, as if I'm not even there.

It's unbelievable how much there is to do when somebody dies. Especially when they die unexpectedly, like she did. But it keeps me so busy; I don't have time to cry. Only at night, when I am alone, I cry.

The hardest part, of course, is going through her things; her clothes, her photos. She has kept every single card I have ever given her; birthdays, Mother's day, Christmas, all of them it seems. And every single photo that has ever been taken of me. Even the one from the hospital the day I was born, where I look like a Chinaman.

And there it is. Spread out on her dining room table. Her life. I have been her life. And no mention of my father, anywhere! No sign, no picture, no reference at all. 'Father unknown' it says on my birth certificate..... Unknown.

You get to know people when there is a crisis, get to know them real well. And I get to know Mark really well during this time. He takes time off work, he looks after all the legal documentation, and he arranges for the cremation. He says he'll make sure her ashes will be taken to a lakeside, as she had wished.

Mark does all that and throughout it all he keeps saying how much he would have liked to have met her, to assure her that her little girl was in good hands, that she wouldn't have to worry about my future. That he would look after me, always.

And during all this time, Nanette is strangely absent. She only drops by on the day of mom's cremation.

We have a get-together at mom's apartment, which was another thing she had wanted. No tears. No sadness. Just memories of all the good times she has spent with everyone. All of mom's friends show up. People from her office, her bosses, friends from her bridge club, Nanette and her parents.

But we don't have a chance to talk at all, Nanette and I. Not with all these people around. She just hugs me, hard, and looks into my eyes with a strange expression that I cannot interpret. Pity, yes..... but something else.

"How are you holding up?" she asks.

"Ok, I guess, but without Mark, I mean, he's been wonderful."

"I bet he has," sarcastically.

"Why, what do you mean?"

"Nothing. Nothing at all. We'll talk, but not today."

And she leaves shortly thereafter. And leaves me wondering.

After everyone has gone, Mark comes over to the couch, carrying a glass of brandy.

"Here, drink this. It'll do you good. You were terrific. You held up beautifully. Your mom would have been so proud."

"Thanks, but I don't feel terrific. I feel lost. I feel alone. I feel abandoned. I have to rethink my future. I'll have to leave college, of course, and find a job."

"You don't have to if you don't want to," he replies, and puts his arm around my shoulder. "You could move in with me. We could get married."

"Married? Are you crazy? Married?"

"Not quite the response I expected," he says quietly, holding me tight and leaning his chin on the top of my head, "but it's not the right time either, I'm aware of that. I only thought it might put your mind at ease. About your future. Our future."

"Oh Mark…" for the first time today I start to sob.

I look at Mom's pictures that are everywhere and I think, would she be happy? Happy for me?

"I would love to be your wife, Mark. And this is the saddest and happiest day of my life. Sad and happy all at once."

"We'll talk about everything in the next little while. We have all the time in the world. You'll stay with me tonight, ok? We'll get you into bed to get some rest. Heaven knows you need it."

I slowly walk around the apartment and shut off all the lights. Only a little nightlight stays on and it illuminates one of Mom's pictures in a silver frame.

I take Mark's hand and then we leave.

And I softly close the door on a life….. On her life….. On our life together.

I wait a few days before I call Nanette.

"Let's meet for lunch," I say. "I have something to tell you."

"Ok, where? Are you alright?"

"Yeah, as good as can be expected. Let's meet at Sardinia's."

"Sardinia's? That's rich."

"Oh, why not? I'm buying, ok?"

Sardinia's is one of the most elegant restaurants downtown and we only go there on special occasions. Very special occasions. You know the kind of place: candles, crisp white tablecloths, shimmering crystal glasses, silver cutlery, and a separate knife and fork for everything.

Nanette is already sitting at the table when I walk in. I do not wear black. Black does not suit me, and anyway Mom would have hated it. I have on a navy pantsuit and a white blouse.

"You look good, all things considered." Nanette gets up to give me a kiss and a hug, and another kiss.

"Thanks. Let's order something. Believe it or not, I'm actually hungry."

We study the menu for a few minutes. We always do that and we always end up ordering the same thing.

"Salmon?" says Nanette.

"Yeah, salmon. It's just too good."

And the salmon is fabulous: it always is. No surprises here. Slightly charred with a buttery basil sauce, tiny potatoes and grilled veggies.

The waiter stays discreetly in the background, not fawning, like in so many other places. We savour our lunch and talk about Mom. Mostly about Mom. Nanette has loved my mom, loved her a lot.

Finally over dessert she asks, "What are you going to do now? Are you coming back to college? Will you be able to afford it?"

"No, I'm not coming back. That's what I wanted to tell you. I'm getting married."

Nanette drops the fork with tiramisu she had raised halfway to her mouth. Drops it. Just like that. It clatters onto the delicate porcelain plate and takes a chip out of it. Nanette doesn't seem to notice. The waiter rushes over and takes the plate only to replace it almost immediately, with a fresh piece of dessert on it. Nanette hasn't moved.

"What's wrong with you?" I ask. "Your face is like thunder. I thought you'd be happy for me. I know that my mom just died, but we're not getting married until October and in the meantime I'm moving in with Mark."

"You're getting married." Finally, a response. "You're getting married to... Mark."

"Yes. What's so difficult to understand about that?"

"Nothing. Nothing at all. I'm sorry. Let's order a brandy with our coffee, ok?"

Nanette orders two double Courvoisier's. I am surprised; she normally doesn't like brandy all that much.

She lights a cigarette and we slowly sip our brandy and coffee. I wait. I know something is coming, but I am not prepared for what she says next.

"Stephanie, we've been friends forever. You know I love you and want nothing but the best for you, don't you?"

I nod and drag deeply on my cigarette.

"Mark, well, I don't quite know how to put this except come straight out with it. Remember our party a few months ago? Mark came on to me. I mean really came on to me."

I recall the scene in the kitchen. Nanette leaning against the sink, Mark saying something or other to her and her throwing back her head and laughing. It had looked pretty innocent to me.

"Stop it. Don't be ridiculous," I say. "Mark is not like that. He was just trying to be friendly. He simply wants for you to like him."

"To the point of asking me to go out with him? To the point of trying to kiss me? He wants me to like him that much? Stephanie, get real."

"Nanette, you're wrong. You're so, so wrong. I don't know what you're trying to pull, but it isn't working. I know Mark. I love Mark, and he would never, ever do anything to hurt me. He's not like that."

Nanette stubs out her cigarette and stands up.

"You know what you just did, Steph? You called me a liar. What reason would I have to lie to you? I'm sorry, I really am."

She rummages in her purse, pulls out some money and puts it on the table. I see pain in her blue eyes. Pain and pity. She turns round and leaves the restaurant.

I sit for a long while. Smoking another cigarette. Finishing my brandy. Not believing what I have just heard. All I know deep in my heart is that it can't possibly be true. And I try to figure out why she would say such a thing. She is my friend, my very best friend.

But it doesn't take long for me to find out the reason.

That night, after dinner, Mark and I sit in front of the fire. He has done the dishes and poured a glass of wine for us. He inches down onto the floor next to me and strokes my hair.

"What's wrong, puss?" he asks quietly.

"Nothing."

"Don't say nothing. Don't ever say nothing. I know something's bothering you. And you must tell me, ok? You must always tell me what's going on in that beautiful head of yours."

I swear, he sometimes says the corniest things, but he can get away with it. It doesn't sound corny coming from him. Just kind of sweet.

"I don't think I want to talk about it. I don't know. I'm too upset."

He cups my chin with his free hand and turns my head round so I have to look directly into his eyes.

"Don't say that. Don't ever say that. We're going to be married. You will be my wife. There is nothing, absolutely nothing that you can't tell me."

I see nothing but concern in his eyes. Concern and love. Nothing else.

"It's Nanette," I say after a little pause. "We had lunch today. At Sardinia's," I add, as if that's relevant.

"Ok? So you had lunch at Sardinia's, and...?"

"Well, I don't think she'll come to the wedding. I don't think she approves." I can hear myself stammering. Fishing for the right words. Wanting to stop and not say anything more.

"Ok? So she doesn't approve. May I ask why?" Sarcastic like.

"Oh Mark, it's so ridiculous. I mean, I don't believe it for a minute and I have no idea why she'd make up such a thing."

"Such as?" Cautiously. Hesitantly. Or do I imagine that?

"Well, she said," I take a deep breath and look straight into his eyes, "she said.... you, she, you..."

"Oh Steph, come out with it. She, I... what?"

"She said you had come on to her. At our party. Not just come on to her but tried to kiss her and get her to go out with you."

He doesn't say anything. Nothing. Just lets go of my chin and stares into the fire. I wish he would get angry. Shout. Deny everything. But not this. Not this silence.

"Mark?"

Without looking at me he stands up, pours another glass of wine and lights a cigarette. He doesn't smoke very often, so I am surprised and alarmed. Surprised and alarmed at the same time.

"Want one?" he finally says and hands me the pack.

"Yes, please. Thanks."

Inhaling deeply, sipping my wine, staring into the fire.

"Stephanie, you love me, don't you? Have you ever regretted that you agreed to marry me? To become my wife? Do you have any second thoughts about our future together?"

"Of course I love you. Of course I want to spend the rest of my life with you, but...."

"There are no buts. The only thing that matters is that we love each other. I would have never told you what happened between Nanette and me, not in a million years. I would never hurt you that much be-cause I know what she means to you."

I wait. Smoke my cigarette. Drink my wine. Wait. He sits down next to me.

"Let me tell you what really happened. It's going to hurt you and I wish I didn't have to talk about it. But, well, I guess she's asked for it. Steph, it was the other way around. Totally the other way around. I didn't come on to her. Even flirt with her. Nanette is the one who suggested we get together. Have a little fling, as she put it. Nobody needs to get hurt, she said, and Stephanie won't ever have to find out."

I look up at him. Disbelieving. Nanette? My Nanette? It is ludi-crous, the most ridiculous thing I've ever heard. She would never! Or would she?

"I don't believe it," I finally manage to say. "Not Nanette. I mean, why? She doesn't even like you that much."

"That's what she tells you, isn't it? What better cover-up is there? You know, Hon, at first I just figured she'd had a few drinks. People sometimes say or do stupid things when they're drinking. And maybe she was just joking. But later on in the evening…" he stops and lights another cigarette. He falls heavily into the armchair next to the fire-place.

"Later on?"

"Well, later in the evening I'd stepped out on the balcony and she came up behind me and, well, she wrapped her arms round me and pressed against me in a way that nobody could misinterpret. So I said, cut it out Nanette, this is not funny, not in the slightest. And she went back into the living room and just said 'your loss' over her shoulder. To say I was embarrassed would be an understatement and, if you remember, I left rather abruptly."

"Yes, I remember that. I thought you were mad at me or some-thing."

"Mad at you? Oh no, my darling girl, but I needed to get fresh air. If you know what I mean."

I move closer to his chair and put my head on his lap. Absentmindedly, he strokes my hair and I think I can see the hurt in his eyes. The fact that he has had to hurt me, I guess.

And I remember something Nanette had said to me a while ago, jokingly, sort of.

"We both like the same type of guys, don't we Steph? Who knows, there might come a time when we'll be fighting over a man."

My head hurts. I don't know what to believe. But I know I love Mark more than anything and if he says that's what happened, then that's what happened. I mean, nobody can look you straight in the eye and lie like that, can they?

"Of course I believe you, darling. I know Nanette can be a bit of a flirt. I just would have never thought she'd try it with you. Let's just forget about it, ok?"

I fall asleep in his arms. There is no nagging voice in my head doubting his words.

None whatsoever.

Chapter 3

It's a good thing that you don't know ahead of time what's going to happen in your life. If you did, you'd probably think that you would never be able to deal with it. The hurt -- the pain -- the whole life thing. The plans that have gone awry -- the dreams that will never come true -- the people that have left you. As I said, the whole life thing.

Just a few months ago there was no Mark, there was no gaping hole in my life left by Mom's death, there was no mourning the loss of my best friend. I was happy, you know? But then I think, would I want things to be different? Change them back to the way they were?

Now I cannot imagine a life without Mark in it, but I want Mom back, more than anything in the entire universe, I want my mom back -- and I know that's not going to happen and I hope in my heart that she can see me -- that she knows I'm happy with Mark -- that I'll have a good life with him -- I really, really hope she knows that.

After my lunch with Nanette I stay at Mark's place for a couple of weeks. I don't think I want to see her for a while. She has betrayed me. My best friend has betrayed me and that's hard to swallow on top of everything else that has happened.

I keep thinking back to what she'd said; "You're calling me a liar", over and over I think about that. But there is no way, no way in the world that Mark would lie to me and so, yes, I think Nanette is a liar. She lied to me because of what? Because she's jealous? Because she doesn't want to admit that she's made a pass at Mark? Why?

Mark has taken time off work to stay with me. He doesn't want me to be alone. He wants me to move in with him, and he wants me to quit university, which I find a little odd since he's always encouraged my studies.

We're sitting on the couch on a Sunday afternoon. There's a football game on TV and Mark loves football. I was surprised when I learned that, it seems so unlike him to be interested in contact sports. I mean golf, I can understand, but football? And even hockey?

"It's all about strategy, Hon", he explained, "but there's more to it than that. It's the team spirit, you know, hometown pride. I grew up with hockey and football, played in little league, got up at the crack of dawn and Dad would drive me to the local arena where he was the coach. I still remember getting into his van when it was still dark outside; remember the freezing cold and how we could see our breath before the car warmed up. Dad would stop at a donut shop and get steaming coffee and warm yummy donuts to eat on the way to the arena. And I remember how proud he was when our team won or when I scored a goal."

"What about your mother? Did she go with you guys to the arena?"

"No", Mark chuckles, "Mom didn't like the cold or getting up that early, but mostly she didn't like hockey or the people, you know, the other parents. She thought them to be commoners, and she wanted nothing to do with them."

"Oh, I see. But you had fun with your dad."

"Yes, we did, we had a lot of fun together. Wait until you meet my father, you'll like him, I know you will."

"Will I like your mother, do you think?"

"Well, she's a little harder to get to know, very reserved, but she will get to love you and anyway, they live in Virginia, so it's not that we will get to see a lot of them."

I change the subject, I'm not really that interested in whether I'll like his mother or not. It's more important that she likes me. But as Mark says, they live far away.

"I still don't understand why you think I should quit university? You know that I want to get my diploma, I want to work and. . . ."

"You don't ever have to go to work, Hon, never ever. I'll always take care of you; you'll have the best of everything. You can call me old fashioned, go ahead, you can call me that, but I've always wanted to have someone to come home to, to open the door when I get there...... like in my parent's marriage. There's something so comforting and reassuring knowing that someone is always there. Waiting for you."

"Ok, ok, I'll think about it.... but I really want to finish my education... and...."

"That's all I ask, darling, think about it and in the meantime we'll go get your stuff. We'll drive up to the flat right now. If we go together, it will be less awkward for you to see Nanette again."

He kisses the tip of my nose, turns off the TV and digs in his pockets for the car keys.

As it turns out, there is no awkwardness when we get to the flat. Turns out Nanette isn't even there.

"She's gone to Mexico for a couple of weeks," our landlady, Mrs. Chenovski, tells me, "with her boyfriend. And I'm really, really sorry to see you leave, you kids are such good tenants. I guess Nanette is going to look for another roommate?"

"I don't know, I suppose so, I haven't really discussed it with her." I'm trying to avoid specifics. Mrs. Chenovski has what you would call a heart of gold. She's from Poland and bakes the best, the absolute best, poppy seed cake. Over the years she's spoiled us with homemade perogies and the best goulash ever. But all that spoiling comes at a price. She wants to know absolutely everything about our lives and every time we come home, whether it's from school or from a party, we can see the curtains in her living room move ever so slightly, meaning she's standing there making sure she doesn't miss anything. So yes, you could say she's a bit nosy.

Now she's standing in the doorway, arms folded over her ample bosom, while I pack a couple of suitcases. I don't have a lot of stuff left to pack; most of my things are already at Mark's, what with going back and forth and all.

"I'll miss you, Stephanie, and I've heard you're getting married? Well let me congratulate you, he certainly looks like a nice guy".

"He is, Mrs. Chenovsky, he is. A very, very nice guy…" I smile and give her a quick hug.

The nice guy has gone down to the car only to return with his wallet. He scribbles quickly and hands her a cheque.

"Here's Stephanie's share of the rent for the next six months," he says and grins his crooked grin. "It's not your fault that things happened the way they did and we wouldn't want you to have a financial loss because of it."

"Well, thank you so much," she's actually blushing, "But it's not necessary, really… Not at all necessary," as she quickly buries the cheque in the pocket of her apron. "You are most generous.. Most generous.. Stephanie is a lucky girl."

I'm a little embarrassed by this generosity, and being called a lucky girl – I have my own money, Mom's seen to that, and I would have paid my share for the next few months myself.

"You shouldn't have done that," I say as we walk upstairs. "Done what?"

"Give Mrs. Chenovsky the rent money. I can take care of my own obligations."

"Don't make a big deal of it, Hon," he laughs, "what's mine is yours and vice versa. We'll be married soon and then we'll figure out who's better at handling the finances."

"Well, I guess, but"…

"No buts, we'll work it out, it's not important."

Mark walks into my room to pick up the last suitcase and I have a quick look 'round while he heads downstairs.

There's not much left up in the bathroom. Nanette has taken most of her stuff on her trip but she's left behind an unopened bottle of Enchante, her favorite perfume, and memories of our life together come rushing back. How much time we spent in this bathroom. It's one of those old fashioned ones, huge, with a window and a claw-footed tub that lets you take a real bath with the water coming all the way up to your chin.

And one of us would soak with bubbles floating all over the place and the other would sit on the edge of the tub with a glass of wine, smoking, and talking about God only knows what. How close we were -- like sisters. Closer than sisters. And our talks were clever and our hopes were high and our dreams were lofty and brilliant -- especially after a toke or two.

I step back into my room and take a quick look 'round and I try not to think any longer of the many, many months we've spent at this flat together, Nanette and I.

There's a print on the living room wall that we both liked so much. Van Gogh's "Starry Night." I think back to the day when we got it at the flea market.

"Too blue," Nanette had said. "But I like the stars and I guess for 20 bucks, with the frame and all, it's a pretty good deal!" So we both chipped in 10 bucks and took our treasure home. Now I look at it and I'm tempted. Tempted to take it with me. I take it off the wall and then I think of Mark's apartment and how it would look so totally out of place. And I leave it behind, leaning against a chair. And in my heart I hope Nanette will know that I've thought about our flea market trip, about leaving the picture for her -- memories of our life together -- of our friendship.

"That's it" I turn round and give Mrs. Chenovsky a quick kiss on the cheek. "Bye. I'll be in touch. I'll never forget how kind you've been to us – and I," But now I feel a lump in my throat and tears welling up and I quickly follow Mark down the stairs.

As the Beemer pulls away, I turn around for one more look and I see the slight movement of the curtains in Mrs. Chenovsky's living room for the last time.

Chapter 4

We had planned our wedding for the spring but I get pregnant way before that. Pregnant, just like that, totally out of the blue. I hadn't even considered that possibility. I'd used birth control pills most of the time but I must have slipped up somewhere along the line. And I'm not surprised that I had slipped up, really, with everything that has happened, all the turmoil, the ups and downs of the last few months.

Mark is ecstatic. Totally.

"I'll be the best dad a kid could ever have," he says when I tell him one evening after he comes home from work. "The best ever. Oh my God, darling, a child!" He's pacing back and forth, running his fingers through his hair and is altogether beside himself.

"It'll be a boy, I just know it, and we'll call him Max, after my father. We could… he could… I'll teach him how to golf and…."

I cannot believe his reaction. I expected him to be, well, happy, but not this excited about the whole thing.

"I never had brothers or sisters," he explains "not even a dog or a cat. Mother is allergic to most animals and, I guess, to most kids as well. Don't misunderstand, she loves me to bits, but altogether she's not the really the motherly type."

His tone is lighthearted, very matter of fact.

"But now we'll have our own child," he goes on, "Imagine, a baby. We'll have to move the wedding ahead a bit," he adds. "We'll have a quiet ceremony. My mom and dad will come up from Virginia, of course."

He takes me in his arms and kisses my forehead, soft and tender.

"I'm so happy, Hon, I'm only sad that your mom is not here to celebrate with us. It will be one of the greatest regrets in my life, not having had the chance to meet her. But my parents will love you, you'll see."

They do come up from Virginia for the wedding, as Mark had said. They are staying downtown at the Royal York hotel and they invite us for dinner the night of their arrival. I'm nervous, I don't know why, but nervous just the same. I guess everyone is when they meet their future in-laws for the first time.

We are late. Mark's parents are already seated in the elegant dining room when we walk in. Max, Mark's father, gets up, gives me a light hug and pulls out a chair for me. His mother does not. Get up, I mean. She holds on to a glass of wine and looks me up and down as if I were a cheap piece of merchandise from Wal-Mart.

Hannah is a good looking woman, a bit thin and gaunt, but handsome none the less. Her hair is perfectly done, nails manicured and she's dressed in an expensive flowing cocktail type of number. Mark bends down and kisses her on the cheek.

"Mother, this is Stephanie, I'm sure you'll get on famously once you get to know each other".

"I'm sure," she replies without a hint of sincerity and holds out her hand. I'm not sure whether I should kiss her hand or curtsy. It's altogether very uncomfortable. I can sense that all she can do is be polite.

She turns her attention to Mark. You can just feel how much she loves him; she hangs on every word he says, laughs at all his comments, whether they're funny or not. And she pays absolutely no attention to me. None whatever.

But Max does. He does pay attention to me, as if to make up for Hannah's snub. He pours a glass of wine, asks about university and will I miss it, is thrilled that we're going to be married. I guess Mark hasn't told them about the baby yet which is just as well because I wouldn't want his mother inspecting me up and down to see how far along I am.

Max is in his mid sixties, I guess, and even at his age he has that charm, that warmth about him, just like Mark, and he is the most un-affected man you'd ever want to meet.

"Mark tells me that you grew up without your father," he says and puts his hand on mine, "and with your mother - well, with your moth-er gone - I wonder if you'd allow me the honour of giving you away on your wedding day?"

I'm speechless. I look over at Mark who nods his head as if to say, see? I knew you'd love him.

"The honour will be mine," I manage to reply, "you are right, I never knew my father, so it will mean a lot to me to have you represent a man whom I never knew but who meant the world to my mother."

"Well, that's settled then." He raises my hand and actually kisses it, you know, the old fashioned European way of honoring a lady and I feel ever so special and ever so welcome.

Not so with Hannah. I don't know whether she hasn't heard this whole conversation or is deliberately ignoring it. She finally addresses me directly though, for Mark's sake I suspect.

"You have a dress?"

"Yes, I do, my auntie helped me find it."

"Very well then," she says, "I would have been glad to help you choose a dress, but since you already have one..." Her voice trails off. She looks relieved. No doubt she's just as happy not having to go shop-ping with me as I'm with her.

And in the end it is a happy wedding. Bittersweet. I miss the two people I have loved the most: my mother and Nanette. I have never heard from her again and even though I think she has betrayed me, I miss her, miss our friendship. I really have no family to speak of, other than Aunt Sissy of course, who never married and loves me like a daughter.

Since neither Mark nor I are religious, we have a simple ceremony. It is held in Mark's building, in the beautiful community room which looks more like a hotel suite, with dark hardwood floors, crystal chandeliers, and set up with white damask tablecloths.

One of Mark's golfing friends owns a catering company and he has arranged everything: crystal glasses, flowers, and candles everywhere. It is very small, very intimate, and very elegant. Mark wears a satiny black Hugo Boss tuxedo and my heart melts looking at him. I have on an ivory coloured dress, kind of old fashioned, like something out of the Great Gatsby. And I have my hair tied up with curls cascading down my back and fastened by a single yellow orchid. I actually do look beautiful, but then I guess every bride looks beautiful in her own way. Aunt Sissy has gone with me to find the dress; she has taken me to the hair salon, and now she helps me get ready.

Just before we enter the room where the ceremony is to take place, she hugs me tightly. She is being so brave, trying to hold back her tears.

"What I wouldn't give for your mother to see you today. But you know what? I think she can, from wherever she is. She can see you and her blessings are with you. She was my sister, and I loved her. And if you wish, I'll tell you about your father, though I promised that I would not."

"Then don't, Aunt Sissy. Please don't. It doesn't matter. Mom was all I ever had and all I ever needed and I've never been in the least bit curious about him. Well, maybe sometimes, but Mom didn't want to talk about him, so let's just not."

"Well, that's ok then", she seems a bit relieved, "You must know though that he was a great man. A very famous man and your mother loved him more than any woman should love a man. But he is dead, God bless him. And maybe they're together now. Who knows?"

Aunt Sissy hugs me again and fusses with the short veil that half covers my face.

"I'll always be here for you, Stephanie, you know that, right?"

"Yes I know, Auntie, and I love you for it."

So you see, there is a lot of pain mixed in with the happiness.

But I have found a new family, at least the father I never had. Max insists we must visit them in Virginia, just as soon as the baby is born and he says he will do everything he can to get a job for Mark down there, since Mark has always wanted to live in that part of the States.

Mark's parents stay for a couple of days and it's almost as if I've known them forever. Hannah actually mellowed a bit at the wedding and gave me a hug after the "I do's" were over. Or perhaps she just mellowed because Mark's told them about the baby and, against what I had suspected, she doesn't scrutinize me up and down to see just how pregnant I am. So she seems to be kind of happy about the whole idea of her son marrying me, the baby aspect at least.

I only wish Mom could have met them too because she'd like them, especially Max.

So here I am. Married - pregnant - and as happy as I can be, considering the circumstances.

Being pregnant is easy for me and I don't know what all the fuss is about. I never get morning sickness, I never have any problems. None. And, apart from getting bigger, I can do everything I have always done.

I continue with my golf lessons because Mark loves the game so much and now I know why. When we play, we usually tee off around seven or even earlier. Being out there on the course in the early hours of the morning, when the sun is glinting on the horizon and everything is covered in dew and as fresh and still as the dawn of time, is something else.

Mind you, my golf is still forgettable, but Mark is very patient. And so I'm able to play more or less respectably. I mean, if I shoot under a hundred and ten, I'm happy. Being pregnant does not help my game in the least though. The bigger I get, the shorter my swing and now I have to give up playing altogether until the baby comes. Other than that, nothing much changes in my life. Even tying my running shoes is not yet a problem.

Today I'm going for my ultrasound. Alone, because Mark has a meeting he can't get out of. The doctor looks at me with a smile.

"Everything's normal, Stephanie. Everything's fine. You're doing exceptionally well. But, you know what? You'd better start knitting some extra booties. You're having twins."

Twins! They say twins run in the family but to my knowledge there have never been any in mine. Unless my father...

Mark can't believe it. Twins. He is beside himself, literally. He hands out cigars at the golf club way before the kids are born, he is so proud. As if he has achieved something really special.

The babies are born prematurely. Born after only seven months. Totally out of the blue. Mark is out of town on a business trip, Edmonton, I think. I had taken him to the airport on a Tuesday afternoon and he is supposed to return next week. Some conference or other.

It is the first time we are apart since our marriage. I am just to drop him off at the departure door, but I can't bear leaving, knowing he is still here. So I park the car and go into the terminal to say goodbye one more time.

And I see him leaning against the counter, obviously saying something funny to the pretty ticket agent, because she throws back her head and laughs. And I think, he's not sad at all. Not sad to leave me for a whole week.

He turns around as if he has sensed me looking at him and comes over with big strides.

"I thought you'd gone home, Hon," he smiles. "What's wrong? Why the face? I'll be back in ten days, no time at all."

"Ten days? I thought you're coming back next Tuesday?"

"Yeah, sorry, that's been changed. I just had a call from the office and they want me to meet a big client while I'm out there and spend some time going over his account."

"When were you planning to tell me that?"

"I only just found out. They called me on my cell and I had to change the ticket. It's not a big deal, Hon. Well, it is a big deal for the firm, but I would have called you the minute I landed. Ok?"

He lifts my chin and kisses my nose just as the boarding call rings out.

"See you in ten days. I'll call you. I'll call you every night, ok? Be my good girl."

I can't help myself. I sit down on a bench in the middle of the terminal and I cry. I have the strange feeling that he is not at all unhappy about spending the extra few days. And then I think, how ridiculous. He loves me. And here I'm sitting in the terminal with my big belly, crying like an idiot.

It feels odd, being in the apartment by myself. It is the first time that I'm spending a night here without Mark. I busy myself putting baby clothes in order. I look at every tiny piece. How small they are. I can feel the baby move, one of them anyway. I make a cup of tea and stretch out on the couch. Sapphire is draped over the armrest and stares at me. Knowing something, I don't know what.

The phone rings around seven. It is Mark. Yes, he's arrived ok. It is cold. The hotel is very posh, right downtown, and he's meeting the client for dinner.

"I won't call you again tonight, ok Puss? It'll be too late by the time I come back from dinner. We're two hours behind Toronto time here. You get a good night's sleep, talk to you tomorrow. Love you."

He calls, every night after dinner, Edmonton time, which is early for him, but late for me. I'm lying alone in our king sized bed. Except for Sapphire, who curls up at the foot of the bed, missing nobody! It's hard to sleep without Mark here. And it seems the babies rest during the day and start moving about at night, which doesn't help.

It is evening. A week after Mark has left. I carry my cup of tea over to the small den from where you can see the entire city, or so it seems. And then I get the strangest feeling. Something isn't right.

I do not have to go to the bathroom, but I feel water running down my legs in a warm steady stream. Water everywhere. God, what a mess. I start to shake, don't know what to do. I try calling Mark on his cell but I don't get an answer. Besides, what could he possibly do?

"Aunt Sissy? Thank God you're home. I think my water broke and Mark is out of town and anyway, it's way too early. Can you come? Please?"

"I'll take a cab. Be there in fifteen minutes."

So it is Aunt Sissy who takes me to the hospital. Aunt Sissy who paces the waiting room floor. Aunt Sissy who manages to get a hold of Mark and tells me that he'll be on the next plane home.

I'm not in labour for very long. I don't know, maybe six or seven hours, something like that. The only thing that hurts like hell is my back. There's a monitor on the night table, connected to the night nurse's station, I think. And every so often she pops in to see how I'm doing and at one time she actually says: "Do you have to moan so much?" I guess I'm disturbing her evening read or whatever. Bitch.

The babies are so premature; I guess that makes it easier for me to bring them into the world.

And they are small. So very, very small. A boy and a girl. The girl comes first and she only weighs a little more than four pounds and the boy a pitiful three pounds. And though they are as tiny as little dolls, they are the most beautiful babies I have ever seen.

The doctor allows me to hold them for only a few minutes before the nurse puts hospital shirts and hats on them. The newborn clothes are way too big for both of them and the little sleeves hang past their tiny hands and the little hats slip down and almost cover their eyes.

They are shut tight, their eyes, as if they aren't quite ready to look at the world, or at me, for that matter. And they don't cry. Neither one cries. They just lie there. Still. Eyes closed. In my arms. And then they take them away from me, down the hall, into incubators. And the next time I see them, they have tubes sticking out all over to get nourishment into their small bodies.

But they are fighters. Real fighters. They accept the milk that I have to pump every few hours, and they are out of the incubators within a couple of weeks and put into oxygen tents and most of the tubes are removed.

Mark is beside himself, not having been home for the birth of his kids. He goes to see them every day after work. Sometimes he even goes over at lunchtime. He stands behind the glass and stares at their little bodies. And he makes funny faces as if they can see him. And he prays. Prays for them to pull through.

And they do. In no time at all they've gained enough weight for us to take them home. Home to the little nursery off the master bedroom. Two little cribs. A little boy and a little girl. That is my world now.

In the end, we don't name the boy after Mark's dad. We name them Adam and Bettina. I don't know why. The names just seem to fit.

Time is a strange thing, you know.

There are moments, days, months, when time stands still or so it seems, and then you turn 'round and it's your birthday, or Christmas, or whatever, once again. Wasn't it Christmas just yesterday?

I'm busy with the twins and Mark, as I knew he would, turns out to be the best dad and husband that I could possibly have imagined. And he takes care of everything, the bills, the mortgage on the condo, the investments; I don't have to think about any of it. He's not exactly giving me an allowance; I'm free to spend how much I want on whatever I want. I have my own credit cards and access to our bank account. So yes, he's very, very generous.

"It's your money too, Hon, not just mine. It's ours, your own savings, your mom's inheritance; it's all working for us."

Maybe that's why there isn't as much cash in the account as I think there should be at times. But Mark has an accountant and an investment advisor and together they decide what's the best way to 'spread the money around', as Mark likes to say.

"No sense having it sit in a bank account earning little or no interest," he explains. And he's right, of course. Only I don't really concern myself with the details. I've never really had a sense for math, finance, investments, that sort of thing. Mom looked after everything, paid for everything, and perhaps that was not such a good thing. I mean, if I hadn't married Mark, I would be totally at a loss as far as managing my finances goes. Then again, I probably would have learned soon enough. It's surprising what you can do when you have no choice.

Like raising children on my own. Well, not entirely on my own, Mark is a great help to be sure. But you know what I mean? There are times, many, many times when I wish I could pick up the phone and ask Mom how to do stuff, or share a new little thing that the twins are doing, or have her listen to their first little words.. Weird and funny as they are. Bettina is the first to speak. "Mommy", she'll say, only it sounds like "Noney", she can't get the m's right yet. Adam, on the other hand, says nothing. He's just watching and listening as if he's filing things away for future reference.

Oh Mom, why did you have to go? Why did you leave me alone? Why didn't you see the bus? Why?

I guess, I'll never come to grips with the hole she's left in my life. At times I feel like an orphan, which I am, actually. Aunt Sissy does her best, trying to be a pseudo grandma, as it were, but it's not the same, is it? She's never had any children of her own and sometimes she looks totally at a loss when stuff happens, you know, stuff like a dirty diaper or spitting up. But she constantly brings little things for the twins, toys, books, whatever, and she absolutely adores Mark and she shows it by cooking his favourite Polish dishes.

And he loves her too, actually flirts with her a little, you know.

Calls her "the most beautiful Polish girl" after a song he knows she likes. And she'll giggle and is altogether charmed, so yes, they really get on.

"You've hit the jackpot, Stephanie", she tells me over and over, "your mother, bless her, would be so very happy to know you're being taken care of."

I guess the only dark cloud is that Mark works ridiculous hours, he travels an awful lot and there are times when I don't see him for a couple of weeks. Those times are lonely, even though the days are filled with taking care of the babies, the evenings are when I miss Mark most. Miss him, want him to be around to talk to, have dinner together, watch a hockey game, make love, you know? Everyday things. But that's soon to change.

Change comes with a phone call one evening. Mark is sitting on the couch reading his golf magazine with Sapphire curled into a content little ball in his lap. I pour a glass of wine for us and sink onto the couch with my feet in Mark's lap, something Sapphire does not look upon too kindly. So, as I said, the phone rings and Mark absentmindedly picks up the receiver.

"Dad," he sits up. Cat jumps down, ticked off. "Good to hear from you, everything ok? How's Mother?"

He listens for what seems like a long time. Then, his face breaking into a huge grin, he hands me the receiver.

"Hi Max, good to hear your voice. Oh yes, the kids are fine, growing like the proverbial weeds and they're so, so good, wait 'til you see them. They're actually talking. What? Ok, yes, I'll let Mark tell me about your conversation. Hi to Hannah."

I hand the receiver back to Mark.

"Thanks Dad, thanks ever so much. I'll get things rolling here, Steph is going to be so happy, you'll see."

He hangs up the phone, grabs me by the waist and swings me high into the air as if I weighed nothing.

"Guess what? Oh sweetheart, I can't believe it. Max has managed to get me a job in Richmond, oh man, I'm so happy. You'll love it there, Hon, absolutely love it."

"But, I don't know, it's so far away... it's such a huge change."

Mark puts me down on the couch. It's been ages since I've seen him this excited and it's catching.

"It's not that far, and not all that different," he says, "other than living in the country, but not far from the city," he adds quickly.

I have never been to his parent's house in Virginia, only seen pictures. Nice. Bucolic. Peaceful. Boring!!

We'd planned to go when the twins were a little bigger, perhaps in a year or so, but now it looks as if I'll get to see it sooner than expected.

"You'll get used to Virginia in no time, Hon," Mark keeps assuring me, "and it's a perfect place to bring up children, teach them different values, you know? I can commute to Richmond in less than an hour and will be home every evening. We'll ski, play golf, oh man, I can't wait."

He runs his fingers through his hair and paces up and down the living room, making plans in his head; he looks like a little boy.

"It's a great job. Head of advertising in a huge firm. Dad must have pulled some strings, I don't know and I don't care how he did it. One of the owners is a close friend, something like that."

The thought of living that close to Mark's parents, especially Hannah, does not thrill me, but I can't tell him that, of course. He loves his mother and I'm sure I'll get to love her as well.

Mark walks over to the bar and comes back with two large brandies.

"To our future," he hands me the snifter, "to our future, yours and mine - and, of course... our children."

I take a small sip and smile at him. It's good to see him this excited, this happy, this hopeful. And who knows? It might turn out better than I think it will.

Maybe Hannah will get to like me once she gets to know me better, and if not, well you can't please everybody. I take another sip of the brandy and stroke Sapphire who's parked himself on my lap.

"Yes, Mark, to our future, it will be wonderful, I'm sure."

We make love half the night; Mark is tender, sweet, mindful. He holds me tight and assures me over and over how much he loves me, how happy he is now and how much happier we will be, and how grand and glorious our future together is going to be.

I really want to believe him. I snuggle close and feel safe and warm, wanted and loved, and I fall asleep in his arms.

I wake with a start. The bedroom is dimly lit with the full moon throwing shadowy silhouettes against the curtains. It is eerily quiet. I have a strange sense of foreboding. I am afraid and I don't know why.

Mark is fast asleep.

BOOK II

Chapter 5

Coming to Virginia

It is a warm and sunny late afternoon in rural Virginia. Unusually so, seeing that it is just a few days short of November. The sun slants in great big glittering swaths through the trees and lights up everything in its path. The lawn is littered with fallen leaves, so dry and brittle they turn to dust when you step on them.

The sun's rays reflect off the little glass pots of herbs that sit on the windowsill above the sink and bounce off the crystals that hang on transparent strings above them. I lean against the sink and stare outside at the magic of it all. It will be over all too soon and it will be November, my least favourite month. But winter in Virginia has its own special charms with crisp air and virgin snow, such as you never see in the city. Everything is cleaner here in wintertime. Children's voices carry high and far in the thin air and the old man who lives alone at the end of the lane has an ancient sleigh, left over from his grandparents, complete with bells. Just before Christmas he'll take it out of the barn, polish it to a brilliant shine, and load up all the kids for sleigh rides round the block.

I push myself away from the sink. Too soon to think about winter, especially on such a glorious day, piercingly painful in its beauty.

I turn around and open the fridge. I love my kitchen more than any other room in the house. This is the room where my little family gets together every day, and this is the room most filled with light. Bright sunlight streams through the windows above the sink and through the beveled glass doors that lead out onto the porch. Everybody is happy here. Even Mark forgets the pressures of his job and jokes with the kids and every so often shoots loving glances my way and appreciative nods when I have cooked something he particularly likes.

This is the room where I am happiest and my love for him is like a tight knot in my stomach. But then, these moments aren't as frequent as they used to be and, more often than not, Mark's face is dark and unhappy, lined and brooding.

I think back to the day when I first saw the house. Mark's firm had arranged for us to rent it, so he had not seen it either. We were free to move somewhere else, of course, if we didn't like it. But it would do in the meantime, wouldn't it?

Would it? I fell in love with it the moment I saw it.

We had been driving since five in the morning when we finally arrived in the small town. It was a warm summer evening, not a cloud in the sky. A light haze enveloped everything and the entire place looked otherworldly, unreal. Like something you see in a movie or in an old painting.

Friday. People milling about on the main street in front of quaint shops, chatting in little groups and looking forward to the weekend.

Strange thing that. Coming to a new place. Knowing that everything will soon be familiar. I will shop at that Piggly Wiggly, set back a bit from the main road. Do my banking at the corner Wells Fargo and get to know the tellers and the lady in the post office and visit the little shops to see what's new. That's how it will be, to be sure. But that first day it was like driving into a movie scene: strange, dreamlike, yet oddly familiar.

Mark started fishing in his coat pocket for the directions.

"Can't be that difficult to find," he muttered to himself. "I mean, heck, nothing can be difficult to find in this town, right Sweetie?"

He squeezed my shoulder and looked around happily. I knew he would love it here, absolutely love it. Even though he had a high-powered job in the city and was at home in boardrooms in the company of top executives, or perhaps because of it, he was cut out for country life; he loved golfing, fishing, even hunting, at least that's what he says.

And Mark was right. It was not difficult to find the street. It wound around in a large half moon circle, just north of the main street, which was called Elm Street - what else? Well, actually, there were a bunch of elm trees lining the street. At least, I think they were elms.

And then we pulled up to the house. Coriander Drive. I couldn't have thought of a more beautiful name myself. It sounded sweet and warm and inviting. Coriander Drive. Number 30. There were no sidewalks, no fences. The lots just sort of ran into each other and all were full of trees. Full of them. Tall, tall trees and lovely blooming bushes and flowers everywhere. Straight out of Peyton Place.

Number 30 was a beautiful old two storey, white, with black shutters and a circular driveway. Mark had stopped the car and we both sat there for a minute taking it all in. He grinned from ear to ear, pleased.

"What do you think, Steph? Looks pretty decent, doesn't it?"

I threw my arms around his neck. "Oh God, Mark, it's fantastic, just fantastic. Let's have a look inside. Oh God, I can't wait." I was in tears, I was so happy.

The twins were asleep in the back seat. Mark took the keys out of the glove compartment and arm in arm we walked up to the front door where he fumbled a bit until he found the right key.

Though the house was completely bare of furniture, it was sparkling clean. Shiny hardwood floors everywhere. No huge surprises in the layout. A small tiled foyer separated the living room to the left from the dining room to the right, closed off from the huge country kitchen by French doors. A long narrow staircase led to the bedrooms, three in all, with the master having a small sitting room attached to it. It had a bay window overlooking the treed backyard and a fireplace. Imagine, a real fireplace in the bedroom.

I could see myself sitting there in that little room. Reading. Fire crackling. Looking out at the snow-covered yard.

Mark came back from the garage where he'd been poking around. Well, I guess a garage is pretty important to a guy. Check out the space, where to put the tools, the golf bags, stuff like that.

He took my hand.

"Let's go. The kids are still asleep. Let's go to the hotel and have an early dinner. The furniture will be here tomorrow. It'll be a pretty busy day. So you like the house? I'm pleased. You'll be happy here. We will all be happy here."

And he smiled that warm, crooked smile that had made me fall in love with him and that made me want to hug him every time. Every single time.

"Yes," I sighed, "yes, we'll be happy here. We'll be very, very happy here."

I had no reason to think that it would turn out otherwise. No reason at all. And I remember that day, almost every single minute of that day, as if it had all happened yesterday. But here we are. Six years later. And where is the happiness?

The day after our arrival it rained. Teemed. The moving van had just pulled away; Mark had popped over to the hardware store to get nails or something. I heard a knock on the back door. Curious as to who would be knocking at the back door and not the front, I stepped over boxes and made my way into the kitchen.

A small woman stood out there in the rain, clutching a dish in one hand and an umbrella in the other. I threw the door open.

"Come in, for heaven's sake, it's pouring."

"I'm Melanie," she said by way of introduction. "I live next door, over there." She pointed to the right. "I just want to welcome you to the neighborhood, that's all."

Melanie couldn't have been more than five feet tall. Cherubic face and the sweetest smile to match. She put down the dish on the kitchen counter. I shook her hand, surprised at the visit.

"I'm Stephanie. I didn't think people did that any more. You know, welcome someone new to the neighborhood."

It must be a country thing. I thought, and secretly hoped she hadn't brought a casserole. I hate casseroles.

"Well, we still do it here," Melanie replied and lifted the tea towel from the dish. "I hope you like cinnamon rolls. I made them this morning. I know you're busy and I won't keep you but let me just dash back and fetch a pot of coffee. We'll have a quick cup and get to know each other a little, ok? There's always time for that, don't you think?"

"Oh yes," I said, "there's always time for that. Always time to make new friends. You are very kind, and cinnamon rolls are my absolute favourite."

"Well, then you'll love these. I may not be the best cook in the world, but my cinnamon rolls, well…" she beamed and opened the door to run and get the coffee.

And that's how I meet Mel. Over a cup of steaming coffee, unpacked boxes all around us, and munching on hot moist rolls such as I had never tasted before.

Baking was not the only thing she was good at though. Melanie loved to talk. Not so much gossip mind you, just talk. She was perched on one of the stools, her legs reaching only half way to the floor, and before our little break was over, I had a good idea of who was who on our street and how happy she was that we had come to live here. She had a little boy, Justin, about the twin's age and there were no other kids on the street. Wouldn't it be great if they got along?

And they do get along. Get along very well indeed. Justin's a shy little guy with excellent manners, so it's no trouble at all to have him around. He especially loves to hang out with Bettina because he loves books just as much as she does.

My thoughts have come full circle, back to today, back to my kitchen and I start thinking about Mark. I don't know whether he's really happy. He always seems pressured by the demands of his job, so he says, but we have moved here to this small town to get away from the chaos of big city life. Sure, Mark has to commute but it doesn't take him more than an hour into Richmond, where he works in one of those tall faceless office buildings.

I push myself away from the sink. The kids will be home soon, time to make supper. I just wish I weren't so goddamned tired. I sit down and stare into space. I have no idea what's wrong with me. Must be that stupid flu again. I brush my hair out of my face and am surprised at how damp it is.

I don't remember when it started, really, this flu that never completely goes away. It can come on any time, summer or winter, it doesn't matter. Sometimes it lasts only a few days and sometimes it takes a couple of weeks. And I am coughing and hacking away and I think maybe I smoke too much, so I give up smoking for a while.

I talk to the local doctor, of course, but he doesn't have much of an explanation. He takes blood tests, other tests, 'well, physically you're fine, there's really nothing wrong, maybe you have allergies'.

Well, I've never had allergies in the whole of my life but it's possible, I mean, who knows? There are times when I can't walk more than five steps without having to double over and struggle for air and nothing seems to come into my lungs and I am terrified, absolutely terrified.

Slowly I get up and start toward the sink. And suddenly the floor gives way beneath me. My God, I'm going to faint. I've never fainted. Ever. I grope for the edge of the sink and see the floor come toward me and I feel myself drift into nothingness.

And everything turns black and silent.

Chapter 6

No matter how hard I try, I cannot open my eyes. It's like being trapped in one of those nightmares where you think you're wide awake but you can't move at all. Like you're paralyzed.

I hear voices but they are muffled and far away and I can't make out what they are saying or who is talking. And then I disappear again and I don't know for how long.

There is a sliver of light and with all the willpower I can muster, I open my eyes. I try to focus but there are only dim shapes. Everything is white. So very, very white. There's Dr. Miller. Why is he here? Where am I? I lift my head with some effort and recognize a hospital room.

Mark is standing with his back to the bed and whips around when he senses me stir. His dark eyes show more annoyance than compassion but he manages a little smile as he moves closer to the bed.

"My God, you gave me a fright, Hon, you honestly did! How are you feeling?" He strokes my damp forehead and bends down to kiss my cheek.

"I don't know.... why am I here? My head hurts so much and I can't breathe."

"You passed out in the kitchen. Luckily Melanie had tried to call you and she rushed over when you didn't answer the phone. She called 911 and they took you to emergency. They'll have to run some tests to find out what's wrong with you, ok?"

I nod. My head is pounding and I struggle for breath.

Dr. Miller steps in and quietly asks Mark to leave the room so they can start on the tests. They draw endless vials of blood. They wheel me into the x-ray room and take a ton of x-rays, and then back into the emergency room.

They hook me up to an oxygen tank and breathing becomes a little easier. It takes more than two hours to do all these tests and I lie there, waiting, wondering, and then Dr. Miller comes back and shrugs his shoulders.

"All we can determine at this point is that there is no oxygen in your blood and that you have pneumonia, Stephanie, but we don't know yet what type of pneumonia it is. We don't have the equipment that is necessary to run more sophisticated tests, so we'll have to send you to Richmond to an infectious disease specialist. Don't be frightened. They have very, very good people and state of the art equipment at Richmond General."

"Ok," I reply. I don't care one bit what they are going to do, where they are going to send me. All I want to do is sleep. Just sleep.

When I open my eyes again, Mark is standing beside the bed. I put my hand on his sleeve and he looks down at me.

"What is it, Hon?" he asks gently.

"How are the kids?" I whisper because my voice is gone.

"They're fine, don't worry about them. I took them to my mother's place".

"But they'd much rather stay at Melanie's. You know they don't like to stay at your mother's…"

"They'll be fine. After all, she is my mom. She'll look after them."

He looks hurt. "They are her grandchildren and she loves them."

"Yes, of course," I say weakly. "Of course she loves them. I'm sorry. Do they miss me? Are they scared?"

"They miss you a lot, darling, you know they do. I don't think they're scared as much as confused, but Max will cheer them up and keep them busy. Well, you know him; he's like a big kid himself."

Mark's smile is warm and loving, the way it always used to be.

"You just get better, ok Puss? All that matters is that you get better.

"Once you get into that hospital in Richmond, they'll find out what's wrong with you in no time. It's probably just some weird virus, but they'll figure out what it is, ok?

"And I'll be near you, I'll stay in the city for as long as it takes. I'll be with you all the way. I'll take some time off work; heaven knows, they owe me more than a few days anyway."

"Thanks, Mark, I'm not worried, I'm just tired. I'm so very, very tired. But I know I'll be ok."

I close my eyes and drift off, holding on to his hand. I don't know where I drift to. I just slip and slip and slip deeper and deeper, into no-where.

And when I wake up again, I'm in the ambulance. All by myself - in the ambulance.

"Where's Mark?"

Nobody hears me. There is an attendant but he has his back to me and he doesn't hear and I just lay there, my head pounding. In the ambu-lance. Alone. With a stranger.

And when we get to the new hospital they transfer me to a room all by myself. There is no one here. Just me. And they put this big screen around my bed. That's all I remember before everything goes dark again.

And then I wake up and there is a doctor I've never seen before and a nurse. She is wearing a mask but her eyes above the mask are kind, warm and smiling, the colour of black velvet

I have tubes sticking out all over my body, it seems, and I am hooked up to an oxygen tank, and she manages to put some liquid into my mouth because my mouth is so dry and I feel hot and I feel sick and ever so weak.

"You'll be just fine dear," she says in a low and lovely voice as she fluffs up the pillow. "You'll see, in a few weeks you'll be as right as rain."

But I feel strange. I can feel that something is wrong; something is not the way it is supposed to be. I am too tired to think … too, too tired and again I fall asleep.

This time when I wake up, I feel a little better, refreshed. Perhaps it is because of the drip that is stuck in my arm or perhaps it is all that oxygen. I don't know.

Then two doctors that I've not seen before start bombarding me with questions.

"How long ago did you get sick?"

"I don't know. I had the flu off and on, but it never lasted for more than a few days."

"When was the first time you had this flu, do you remember?"

"It was a few years ago, when I still lived in Canada. I had pneumonia then too but it didn't last very long. And I've been fine ever since, except for this flu."

"How many times during the last year have you had it?"

"Oh, maybe five or six times. I don't remember. I don't pay that much attention to it."

I can tell by the questions they are asking that they don't have a clue what is wrong. Do we have any animals? Cows? Horses? Pigs?

"No. We live in the country, but not on a farm. We had a bird once, a cockatoo type of thing. I didn't like it much because it would always try to land on my head and pick at my hair, so we gave it away."

"Aha, perhaps it was the bird. You could have picked up a virus from the bird."

I think about that for a minute.

"Maybe. Now that I think about it, we gave it to our neighbors who kept it for a couple of weeks, but they didn't like it either and brought it back and a few days later I had the flu again. I had to stop smoking because I couldn't move without doubling over to get air. It was pretty scary."

Both doctors seem baffled. They don't care about me having

been scared, but they seem to think that the bird thing is a distinct possibility.

But we got rid of the bird long ago so it really shouldn't have been the cause of me getting so sick.

And this time the pneumonia has come on so quickly and is so severe and the oxygen count in my blood is so low, they know it is not your typical pneumonia and they have to dig deeper to get to the bottom of it.

And again they hook me up to all kinds of equipment and take all kinds of blood and do all kinds of tests.

The blood tests aren't really too bad, you know. They stick a needle into your arm, it pricks a little, and that's that. But then they run the test to determine the type of pneumonia it could be, and it is awful. Gross in fact. Really, really gross. I don't know what the procedure is called and I don't want to know.

First they spray this stuff down your throat so that you can accept the tube and the spraying is disgusting. They spray it down your throat but it's all over your mouth too. It's like some type of gas, I think. I can't even explain it. All I know is that it is awful.

Then the doctor sticks a tube down my throat, which makes me gag, of course, and I panic and just want to rip it out. But they hold me down so I can't move. I start to cough and somebody yells, "don't cough!" but I can't help it and they get angry about that because all their work will be for nothing. But then the coughing stops.

So they stick this tube down and they puncture my lung and scrape out some kind of sample tissue, which will allow them to diagnose the type of pneumonia that has invaded my body. And I just want to die.

I pray that I will pass out and get away from this nightmare. But of course I don't. And then it is over and I weep and weep with relief and then I fall asleep again from sheer exhaustion.

This time when I wake up there is a big commotion. There are people everywhere it seems. There are doctors and nurses and interns and they are all wearing masks and staring at me as if I were some sort of exhibit in a zoo.

The tubes are still there, but I feel a little better. I guess they've given me something to soothe my throat and again I am on some sort of drip; I can see it dangling from the stand at the side of the bed. That's probably how they get nourishment into my body or whatever.

I am totally spaced out, as if I'm in a different and strange world where nothing is real. The head doctor, at least I think that's who he is because they all crowd around him and hang on his every word, the head doctor takes my pulse and clears his throat. He doesn't look at me. He kind of looks through me, past me, at the wall behind me or something, but not directly at me, as if I'm an object, not a person.

"Stephanie, we do have your test results. You do have pneumonia, in fact, you have a very rare type of pneumonia. It's called pneumocystic pneumonia."

Again he clears his throat and now he looks directly into my eyes.

"This particular type of pneumonia only occurs in people who are HIV positive. We'll have to do more tests, Stephanie. We will have to test you for HIV."

And if my throat weren't so sore, if my head wouldn't pound so much, I think I might laugh. And I do laugh, a hysterical little laugh. I mean, what kind of a stupid joke is that? I can only whisper.

"What do you mean? HIV?"

HIV. I don't even know what that is. Well, I kind of know what it is, but not really.

And I think, you are nuts, you know that? You are totally nuts. HIV? Me? Why? It's too ridiculous. This whole thing must be some gigantic sick joke.

But there is something in his face that I don't like. There is something in his eyes that tells me that he is serious. Whatever this pneumonia is…

"What kind of pneumonia is it? What's it called again?"

"It's called pneumo-cystic pneumonia."

"I've never heard of such a thing."

"Well, that's what it's called and it only appears in people who are HIV positive or have AIDS."

AIDS?...........AIDS?

The word hangs heavy in the room. AIDS? AIDS? I can't breathe any more. I look at him with my eyes as big as... I don't know what. I don't respond, I can't respond. I feel like screaming, crying, kicking someone, but I can't move, can't talk,

I just stare at him.

And he looks down at me and he kind of smoothes the blanket with one finger. And I look at his finger, smoothing down the blanket.

"That's what we fear, Stephanie, we'll do the tests in the morning for that. And I hope, I really, really hope that we're wrong, but..."

He stops in mid sentence and he turns around quickly and leaves the room, coat tails aflutter, and all the others trail behind him.

Gone. All of them. Gone. Except for the nurse.

All the terror that has ever been felt by humankind grips my heart at that moment. Everything in my body screams against the possibility.

No way! AIDS? Me? It's a joke! It has to be!

I can feel hysteria bubbling up in my stomach and racing toward my throat and the nurse approaches my bed and says softly, "Come baby, I'll give you something that'll make you sleep. You'll be fine... You'll be as right as rain."

Her name is Phyllis. I can see her nametag. It is gold and shiny. She must be the head nurse or something. She empties a vial into the IV and adjusts the little wheel.

And I look at her and she has the face of an angel... And I slip away into darkness.

Darkness. No Dreams. Nothing.

Chapter 7

Morning is slowly creeping into the room, spreading an eerie twilight. The blinds are still drawn, with just a sliver of daylight shining through and throwing strange patterns onto the walls.

Mark is sitting on a chair next to my bed.

I feel a little better but I am thirsty. Very, very thirsty.

I know that everything that happened yesterday was just a dream, a weird kind of nightmare. I look at Mark and he smiles back at me. He looks almost happy. And I think, yeah, it was a dream, of course, what else would it be.

And then I see tears in his eyes and my heart goes cold and I manage a whisper: "Do you know what they told me yesterday? Do you know what they're going to do? They're going to test me for HIV. Can you believe it? Can you believe anything so freaking ridiculous?"

But instead of saying yes, yes of course, that's ridiculous, he stares into a corner of the room and mumbles: "Well, I don't really know how to tell you this, but they want to run tests on me too."

I feel as if I have ice in my veins. I have ice water running through me and I shiver and I open my mouth and nothing comes out.

"But why?" I finally whisper, "Why?"

"Well," he hesitates and still doesn't look at me, "It's just a precaution; they have to do it. The more tests the better. The more tests they do, the more money they make, right?" And then he laughs, an odd, hollow kind of laugh.

The doctor comes in and nods in Mark's direction. Mark gets up to follow him, but before he reaches the door he turns 'round and gives me the strangest look, the strangest look ever. There's pity in this look, there's pity and pain and hurt and agony. I've never seen that look in his eyes, never.

And then he's gone. The door bangs shut behind them and the sound reverberates in the room. Really, really loud. And he doesn't return. Mark does not return and I am lying here alone. Alone and weak and scared.

Phyllis wheels in a tray with all kinds of stuff on it for more blood tests and the doctor follows her into the room. Again they draw a number of vials of my blood and I wonder just how much blood is in me to give. I look at all the vials that hold the answer to my future. I wonder what is in those warm little bottles. What is in there? Life? Or death?

"Stephanie", the doctor's voice, "I want you to know that I'm sorry. I'm so very sorry and I hope and pray that our assumptions are wrong. I have never wished more to be wrong than on this day. But it does not look good, Stephanie, so I don't want you to get your hopes up too much either. We will know for sure in a couple of days when the results come back from the lab and we'll take it from there. So in the meantime…" he lets out a deep sigh, tiny bubbles of spittle form in the corner of his mouth. "I don't know what else to tell you."

His voice is aquiver and he swallows hard and motions for Phyllis to come over and she strokes my hand.

"You'll be alright, baby, you'll be alright."

I look into her face, her kind face with eyes that are warm with emotion.

"I wish I could believe you. I wish so much that I could believe you."

And then she quickly leaves the room and I am alone again.

The next two days drag on. I'm waiting for the test results to come back. All that is spinning round and round in my head is the thought that perhaps they are right. Maybe I really am HIV positive? I know nothing about that. Nothing. Of course, I've seen movies, I've heard people talk about it, but I have never paid any attention. It didn't concern me and there was no way in God's creation why it should.

I mean, think about it. I live in the middle of nowhere, in a quiet little town where the raciest entertainment is at the bowling alley and at the local pub where everyone gathers most Saturday nights to have a few beers and socialize.

And we go too. Go to the pub and bowling. Sometimes Mark makes fun of the locals and mimics the way they talk, but he likes them well enough. And everybody likes him. He is a good bowler, that's for sure, and everyone wants him on their team. It's not like city life, but it is nice. More quiet, more real.

I spend my days cleaning, cooking, playing with the children and I love every minute of it, well, not every minute but you know what I mean. Mark's suggested that we hire a young girl to help out but I won't have it. I love being a housewife, love going shopping with the children, love keeping the house immaculate. We don't entertain that much, Mark's usually too exhausted when he comes home. But on weekends we sometimes have Mel and Peter over for dinner and a game of cards, or we just sit on the porch on hazy summer nights, talking. We'll have barbeques where everyone brings something and half the neighborhood shows up. We celebrate all the American holidays; Thanksgiving, the fourth of July, you know?

It's a really tight-knit little town and everyone looks out for everyone else. I never thought I'd like this kind of lifestyle but I've gotten used to it, I'm actually loving it, not missing the city at all.

And of course, there's the country club. The big attraction in an otherwise sleepy little place. The golf course is as good or better than many of the famous courses on the PGA tour, in fact, it's consistently rated in the top one hundred in Golf Magazines but it's a little too out of the way for tourists, so it doesn't ever get too crowded. We have a membership, but the club is semi private, so anyone can play. Since

Antonia and I have become friends, we golf regularly. Mark encourages me constantly, probably because he's happy about my friendship with Toni, but he's also proud that my golf is really getting quite good.

Sometimes I fear that this idyllic lifestyle can't last, it's too perfect, but then I don't think about that too often, I'm just grateful, grateful, content and very, very happy.

So how something as foreign and frightening as AIDS could possibly creep into our lives, I don't know. It fans terror in my heart; all I can think is that I'm going to die. I'm only twenty nine and I'm going to die! It seems to be the most ridiculous notion in the universe. But the fear doesn't go away.

Dying. Dead! At twenty nine... Dead!

And I keep thinking about the twins, Adam and Bettina, my children. All I can see in front of my eyes are their smiling little faces, their innocent eyes, their utter love for me. Sitting in the bathtub, heads full of shampoo, skin rosy and gleaming.

And again I think I'm going to die. I'm going to die and I won't see them grow up. I will not see their beaming faces when they bring home good marks from school, I will not see how ecstatic they are when their team wins a hockey or baseball game. I will have no part in all their childhood ups and downs, their hurts and joys. I will not be there for their prom or first date. I won't see them graduate from college. Nothing! And they won't remember me when they are adults. They'll look at pictures and they'll know that I was their mom. But they won't remember. They will grow up with strangers who will be close to them and love them instead of me, their mom.

I cannot bear it. A scream rises up in my body bursting to be released. That's all I want to do. Scream and scream and scream until this whole freaking nightmare is over. I sharply check my hysteria. Don't be crazy. Nothing's been determined yet. The tests will be negative. They have to be. I mean, where in hell would I have picked up something like that? I will just have to wait, that's all. Wait.

And so I wait. For the longest two days in my life, I wait.

Sunlight streams into the room on the morning on the third day and everything looks so much more cheerful – happy almost. I feel better. Way, way better and confident that everything is going to turn out all right. I take the compact out of my makeup case and study my face. I look fine, a little pale perhaps, but not bad. Not bad at all. This is the first time since I got sick that I care about how I look and I think, that's a good sign too, isn't it? I even reach for my lipstick and the creamy smoothness feels good on my chapped lips. I smile at myself in the tiny mirror. You'll be ok, kid. This is nothing but a really, really bad dream.

I hear music coming from the hallway. Some kind of country and western song. A happy song. And again I think that's a good sign and I smile a little to myself.

Dr. Miller comes into the room. He looks nervously at a piece of paper and takes my hand. And before he even opens his mouth, I know. I know what he's going to say.

"Stephanie, I'm sorry to have to tell you this," he puffs up his cheeks and lets out a big breath of air and he looks rather like a blowfish.

I don't want him to continue. Don't say anything. Get lost. Piss off and leave me alone. Don't talk. Don't say another fucking word.

But he does continue. "The tests have come back..... and .."

He looks so helpless. I want to tell him, it's alright; it's not your fault. But I can't. I cannot speak. I just lie on my back and stare at him. I can tell it is really hard for him and he closes his eyes for a second and then he stares out the window and continues. "Actually, it's worse than we had expected. You're not simply HIV positive.. You have full blown AIDS."

I'm holding my breath; I'm waiting for more, because this is ridiculous, absolutely and totally ridiculous. I stare at his face and wait for the next sentence to come out of his mouth. Like, oh, sorry, we've made a mistake, you're ok, nothing wrong with you, we got the charts mixed up .. But I hear nothing of the sort.

His mouth is clamped shut in a straight line, he keeps staring out the window as if not sure what to do next. He's like, frozen in time, you know? Waiting for me to react. Say something. Maybe something polite, like oh, don't worry, it's not your fault. And I finally manage to speak. Terrified, I still manage to speak and I don't recognize my own voice. It sounds like it's coming up from deep within a well. Deep, deep down, far, far away, not real.

"But, that's not possible! That's totally impossible! There must be some kind of a mistake. I don't even know anybody who has AIDS. Where the hell would I get it from?"

By now he has collected himself and stands straight up, ramrod straight. And I'm thinking he must have been in the military to stand so ramrod straight and to have this steely gaze and to show no emotion whatsoever. That's what they're being taught in the army. Ramrod straight. No emotion, soldier!! My mind is dancing around this imaginary army. Let's see. Who else is in there that I know? Ramrod straight. Not feeling.. Oh God!

"There's no mistake. We've done every test possible and the results are conclusive. You do have AIDS!"

If a bomb had gone off in that hospital room, it couldn't be more devastating. It couldn't be more destructive, more shocking. It takes my breath away. I am gasping for air. I'm trying to get air into my lungs, I'm trying to breathe and I can't.

And the nurse comes rushing over. Dear, dear Phyllis, comes rushing over and puts the oxygen mask over my face and my breath comes back in short, funny, rapid bursts and she cradles me like you would a little child and her face is wet with tears.

I push the oxygen mask aside.

"What does that mean? Am I going to die? Please, doctor, tell me the truth. You've got to tell me the goddamn truth."

"There is no cure for the disease," he replies, now without a hint of emotion and still looking straight out the window. It is as if he has detached himself totally; put his emotions on hold as it were. Well done soldier!

"You have maybe one year, two years tops, if you get treatments right away. We are waiting for your husband's test results; he too needs to get help if he carries the disease. In the meantime, we'll have to let him know".

I have trouble controlling my voice. "I'll tell him myself if you don't mind. He will be here soon and it's better if he hears it from me."

"As you wish, but ask him to come and see me straight away."

He turns on his heel and marches out the door, leaving me with my head splitting and my thoughts going round and round. There is no way out. There is no escaping this nightmare. I am not dreaming. This is real.

How could this have happened? Happened to me? I'm too young... Too young to die...

Mark is nowhere to be reached. I try at home, I try his cell phone, I try his parent's place. No answer, anywhere. I'm freaking, I need to talk to him, need for him to be near me to hold me to let me know that I'll be ok.. Oh Mark, where the hell are you?

It is late in the afternoon when he finally comes through the door. His face is the face of a ghost. Drawn, white, his eyes red rimmed and dead. And then I know that he knows. There's no need to say anything. He's had the tests. He knows.

He falls heavily onto the chair next to my bed and just stares at me. No words come out of his mouth. Nothing.

"You too?" I whisper the question that I already know the answer to. I have it, then of course, he will have it too. Where else would I get it from?

He nods, still not speaking, just nodding his head. I turn my head toward the window, I cannot speak, cannot accuse, cannot get angry. There's no use in any of that now. I feel warm tears streaming down my cheeks, flowing and flowing and flowing. There's no stopping these tears that bring no comfort, no relief.

Mark takes my hand but I cannot bear it, cannot bear him touching me, being near me. I turn my back to him and feel more than I can hear that he's sobbing, sobbing quietly to himself.

"Stephanie, I'm sorry, I'm so sorry," his voice is barely audible, "sorry, sorry, sorry" he repeats over and over again. I don't move, don't turn around, and he gets up and leaves the room, dragging his feet like an old man.

I am alone. And now, for the first time in my life, I really know what that word means, what it feels like. To be alone. Alone. No one to turn to, no one to talk to, no one who can help. Alone, now and always and forever. Trapped in an ice cold nightmare. In a nightmare that has a name… AIDS. Me, I have AIDS. Round and round in my head… AIDS! AIDS! I have AIDS! I will die!

I know I'm in shock. Shock is a strange thing.

I see my children's faces dance in front of my eyes. Wide eyed. Not understanding. Motherless. I cannot bear the pain. I feel panic rising up and ring the bell for the nurse; ring and ring and ring until a young day nurse rushes in, worried looking, with her hair flying all over the place.

"My kids," I sob. "I want to see my kids, now! Please help me see my kids."

"Calm down, Stephanie, please calm down. I'll give you something to help you sleep."

"I don't want to sleep, for God's sake, I'll be dead soon enough. I want to see my kids!" I scream out of control and my chest hurts from sobbing so hard.

The nurse is just a little unnerved. She reaches over and adds something to the intravenous, and calm washes over me. Sleep. Yes, sleep; maybe that's what I need. Not thinking. Not feeling. Not worrying. Just sleeping.

I wake up in the middle of the night and hear voices and I think, maybe I'm already dead. I hear voices in the corridor. I hear screaming, footsteps running up and down, but it's the middle of the night. Maybe there's an emergency. I am thirsty, so, so thirsty. My eyes are on fire and my head hurts and now my ears hurt too and I think, I don't want to go through this, I really don't. Not alone. I need someone to be with me and I fumble for the bell and I cannot reach it. It is just outside my grasp. I can see the little red light blinking, looking at me, as if mocking me and I cannot reach it. It is too far away.

Then the night nurse sticks her head in the door. She must sense me staring at her because she comes right over and whispers, "Is everything ok?"

"I'm very thirsty. I'm very, very thirsty. Could I have some water please?"

And she comes back with ice water. I have never tasted anything so delicious, ever. And I drink and drink and drink and the water runs down the corners of my mouth and onto my nightgown and I don't care. I just want this coolness to get rid of the fire in my body.

And then I fall asleep again and this time I don't remember anything.

Chapter 8

Today, I'm being released from the hospital. There's nothing more that they can do. No medication, no pills, no hope. I'm on my own.

Mark has come to pick me up. The drive home seems endless. Mark has a tight grip on the steering wheel and doesn't say a word. Not a word all the way home. Over an hour's drive and not a word.

A few times he glances at me sideways with an expression I cannot interpret. As if he's puzzled or something. As if he's wondering where this AIDS thing has come from and he's looking for something or someone to blame.

I feel weak and tired and terrified. The Beemer hums along, mile after mile after mile and not a word out of Mark. My thoughts go round and round and I can feel anger rising up in me.

"What's the matter, cat got your tongue?" I say in my most sarcastic tone, "Don't you want to discuss what happened? Don't you want to tell me where the hell this AIDS thing that we both have has come from? Say something! Anything!"

And again he looks at me sideways as if everything that's happened is my fault.

"I don't know, I don't know where it has come from. I don't even know if it's not all a big mistake."

And that's all he will say. Ridiculous. He grips the steering wheel even tighter until his knuckles are white. His mouth is set in a grim line and he stares straight ahead. And we drive on and on and the silence is like poison between us.

But he doesn't really have to say anything because deep in the back of my mind I know. I know where it has come from. I have AIDS, he has AIDS. I have never slept with anyone else so I got it from him because he's had sex with someone who was infected and passed it on. To Mark. The AIDS infected bitch has passed it on to Mark. Mark who claims, no swears, he's never ever had sex with anyone else since he's met me.

I stare out the car window and watch the countryside slip by. Trees and bushes and meadows are shrouded in rain and fog. Heavy raindrops are running down the passenger window like gigantic tears.

And in the silence between us and over the steady hum of the car's engine, my thoughts go back to that time when everything changed between Mark and me.

I remember it as if it had happened yesterday, that incident a couple of years ago. I had picked him up at the airport, coming back from one of his trips to heaven knows where.

And I could see in his face that something was wrong, the way his eyes shifted back and forth, not looking directly at me. Smiling but not really meaning it. A crooked, forced smile, as if he had something to hide, and a look, as if he'd rather be somewhere else.

I will never forget that look, ever.

And when we got home that night I kept asking, "What's wrong? I know something is wrong and you better tell me what it is."

But he kept saying over and over "No, no, everything is fine, you're imagining things. I'm just tired, ok? It was a stressful week.. " blah, blah, blah .. On and on and on.

But I knew that was a lie. I knew it was a goddamn lie and it was probably worse than I thought.

And in bed that night he didn't touch me. He didn't even want to cuddle or for me to hold him, which he used to love whenever he had problems or worries. He just lay there, staring at the ceiling. And finally he pretended to be asleep, with his back to me and his legs pulled up, curled into a ball.

And then the next evening during supper it all came out. The children were eating quietly, their eyes shifting from their dad to me and back as if they felt that something wasn't right. Mark was poking listlessly at the food and then he pushed his plate away.

I knew that something was coming, my stomach was in knots.

"I've met someone," he mumbled, not looking at me.

"What?"

"I said I've met someone, are you deaf?" he suddenly shouted and he pushed back his chair and it crashed to the floor. The kids sat there with their eyes ripped wide open, not making a sound.

Mark picked up the chair and sat down again. And then he kept eating like nothing had happened.

I don't know how I felt. Yes I do. I felt like someone had punched me in the stomach and I felt like throwing up, but I couldn't move. So I just stood there by the sink, holding a tea towel. Adam started to sob. Quiet little sobs, and his face was all scrunched up. I pulled myself together and took the children upstairs.

"Is Daddy mad at us?"

"No, no," I stroked their heads and sat them on the bed. "No, he's not mad at you guys.. It's just, well.. Mommy and Daddy have to talk about some stuff. It has nothing to do with you, ok?"

And Bettina had what I call her 'old' look, as if she knew more that she ought to. And I knew she understood. And we just looked at each other. The little girl and the grown woman, her mom, both hurting.

On my way downstairs I had felt dizzy and had to hold onto the banister so I wouldn't fall. And I walked back into the kitchen to find him still sitting at the table. But he had finished his dinner. How the hell could someone eat at a time like this? I picked up his plate and tossed it into the sink.

"Well, who is she?"

"What do you mean?"

"It's a simple question. You've met somebody, who is she? Who the hell is she?"

He stared at me, silently, with his eyebrows pulled tightly together, which gave him a bit of a demonic look.

"Where did you meet her? Some bar?"

"No," he answered brusquely, as if offended by my question. "We met at our branch office in Connecticut."

"So what kind of a tramp is she? Going out with a married man?"

"Don't call the lady names," he bristled.

"Oh please! Don't tell me she's a lady! What do you mean she's a fucking lady? She's a woman who slept with my husband! Did you tell her you're married? Did you?"

I knew my face was ugly. Totally ugly. I could tell by the way he looked at me, with distaste, real distaste. I bet she didn't look like that, but then she had no bloody reason to.

"Did you tell her you're married or didn't you?"

"Not in so many words," he shrugged.

"Yes or no, did you? Tell her you're married, you have two children?"

"Not in so many words," he said again.

"What kind of an asshole expression is that? How many words does it take?"

He gave me one of those looks, a look that says 'I wish you were dead', and spun around and slammed the back door behind him.

That night my trust in him vanished. My trust in my husband was gone, and I knew it would never fully return. And I thought, 'this is the beginning of the end'.

And then I thought, what end? What beginning? I have no money, no job skills. I have two children, what am I thinking?

Mark slept on the couch that night and I tried my best to irritate him in the morning. I banged pots and pans and generally let him know just how angry and hurt I was.

"So you picked up some ditzy young chick somewhere?" I couldn't help letting the sarcasm drip from my words. I wished they were knives to stab him with, to hurt him physically as much as he was hurting me.

"Young chick? She's not young. Actually, she's a little older than you."

"But why? Why? How could you do this? Don't you love me anymore? What's the problem?"

I tried hard not to slip back into my ugly face.

"You wouldn't understand, you would never understand," was his pat answer. "She understands me. She actually listens to me and thinks that my thoughts and ideas are important."

Oh God, not that! Not that 'she understands me like you never have' bullshit. God, how stupid can guys be? What a crock!

"You know something? That's the most overused and banal line I have ever heard. Actually, no, I've heard that line a thousand times, in every movie, in every cheap novel, in every freaking whatever. Don't feed me those lines, ok? Tell me the truth. Don't think I'm an idiot and don't treat me like one."

He looked at me and bit his lip, but nothing came out of his mouth. I guess it was the only line he could think of. He didn't know how to weasel himself out of this and he didn't want to.

"I'm late for the office," was all he said.

He walked into the hallway and put on his coat. I didn't turn around but I could hear him come back into the kitchen and he tried to kiss my cheek, but I moved my head aside. So he left. He left me alone to face a long, long day and I had to wait until evening to pick up where we had left off.

I didn't want to fight, I really didn't want to. I wanted things to stay the way they were. I wanted us to be happy, the way we used to be.

The kids sat at the breakfast table and looked forlorn. They were quiet and sad and I didn't want them to look like that. But they knew something was wrong, they knew that I wasn't happy. My eyes were red with unshed tears and they looked at me with big eyes and Bettina said, "Mommy, don't cry please, don't cry, Mom."

"No Sweetie, I won't, don't worry, it's alright. Everything will be ok. Mom and Dad just had a little fight," and I saw in her eyes that she didn't believe me, but she pretended to, to make me happy.

I bundled them up and we went into the backyard to rake leaves.

Thoughts went round and round in my head. Round and round. The kids were running up and down the yard, screeching and screaming with joy, jumping into the leaves. I made a little pile and they jumped into it and scattered the leaves all over the place. And I looked at their shiny little faces and I wished, how I wished, I could be as carefree as that.

Mine is an ordinary life. It is not exciting; it's not the life of a socialite or a world traveler, like Antonia.

It's the life of a housewife. I stay at home and I love it. I love going shopping and I love cooking stuff. But at times I feel lonely; at times I think, is that it? Is there anything else? Is this all I was meant to do in this life? Is this everything I need? Everything I want? Everything I've dreamed of? And I know it is not!

Deep down, I really want to be that other woman, want to be the exciting one; with fiery eyes and sexual prowess. I want to be that one.

But I'm not that woman. I wake up every morning and have little kids to look after. They hop into bed with me and they bring the cat. So no, I'm not that woman. As much as I would love to wake up with sleepy eyes and tousled hair and sweet baby's breath. A gypsy. Just like in the movies.

And over time, many months in fact, the hurt got less and the pain was not so sharp anymore. Mark never mentioned the incident again and everything seemed to have returned to normal.

He had begged me to forgive him, promised that it would never ever happen again, that he loved me and me alone and that he had made a huge mistake and that the children deserved that their parents be happy and loved one another.

And I believed him. I truly believed that he was sorry and regretted having hurt me that much. I believed him because I wanted to believe him.

But I never forgot that incident. It's like when you cut yourself and you keep touching the open wound. Gently touching it, blowing on it to soothe the pain. And then there's a scar, but the wound is still underneath and every so often you touch the scar and know that the wound is there and that it will never go away and that it will never heal.

All these thoughts go through my head during that long drive home from the hospital, that long silent drive.

Mark pulls into our driveway and the sharp jerk of the BMW cuts into my memories and brings me back into the present. I look over at Mark.

"Something wrong with the car?"

"It needs freaking service," he mutters, more to himself, "I should have taken it in, but with everything happening"... His voice trails off. He looks at me as if it is my fault. My fault that he didn't have time to take the car in for service.

Mark comes around and opens the car door; his face is dark and brooding. And he pulls me up by the hand and I nearly fall over because I suddenly feel faint. Faint and weak and very, very scared.

I look at the house as if I've never seen it before and I don't want to go inside because I don't know what is going to happen in that house in the months to come. It's not going to be years. I know that.

The house looks strange to me. It is quiet. It is quiet when he unlocks the front door and it is quiet when we walk in.

I usually leave some lights on and the radio, so when I get home it feels as if there's some life in the house. But not today. Just dead quiet today. I look at Mark.

"Are the kids at Melanie's?"

"No, they're still at my mother's. I thought you might want to have the night to yourself, to rest up."

"But I miss them, I want them home."

"Max is bringing them back tomorrow, ok?" He turns 'round and takes the overnight case upstairs.

I walk through the living room. It's the only room that I'm not fond of. It is too formal. Too cold. Too unused. I just want to be in my kitchen and make a nice fresh cup of coffee.

And this time, when I walk into the kitchen there is no sunlight. It is dark. A dark, dark, day. As dark as my soul, I think and then I think, don't be so bloody melodramatic. Your soul isn't dark, only what's happening to you is dark. We will deal with it. We'll deal with it because we have no choice.

I put on the kettle and my knees go weak and I sit down and wipe my forehead with the back of my hand. And I just sit here in the semi darkness, waiting for my coffee. Sitting... waiting... trying to figure out what to do next.

Before we left the hospital this morning, the doctors had questioned us. Both of us separately, like criminals who have to come up with an alibi. I guess they need to find out where the disease has come from, where we have picked it up.

They went down a long list of questions like: Are you a drug addict? Have you ever used needles? How many people have you had sex with in the last few years? Are you homosexual? On and on. Of course, I had to say no to all of these questions, but what about Mark?

He came out of the doctor's office looking pale; his lips pressed together in a grim line.

"Did you tell them?"

"Tell them what?"

"About the affair, the woman you met on the trip, way back when."

"No."

"No? Why not? That's probably where you picked it up. You've got to tell them, they have to know."

"There's nothing to tell. I told you over and over, I did not have intercourse with that woman. She was just..."

"Don't start with that 'she understood me like no one else' bullshit again, just don't, or I'm going to throw up. You're not really protecting her by not saying anything, you know. But be it on your conscience, I really don't give a shit anymore."

He didn't reply but we both knew that that's where it must have come from. We both knew that. Unless of course there have been others. Different trips, different women. Or men? What if he'd been with some homosexual guy? You know, to experiment? Oh God, I must kill that thought, kill it immediately. I mean, there is no way. Never. Not Mark. He's way too homophobic.

Phyllis had come to say goodbye before I left the hospital. I knew she had made a special trip because her shift didn't start until the evening and here she showed up at ten in the morning.

"I don't know what to say to you, Stephanie. I had hoped and prayed that you would be ok and I don't know enough about the illness to give you any kind of advice but here," she said, forcing back tears and handing me a folded piece of paper, "you may want to call this number; it's a hotline for people with AIDS. Somebody there may be able to help you."

I took the paper from her hand and stuck it into my purse.

"Thanks for everything, Phyllis," I mumbled and tried not to cry.

She turned 'round quickly and walked down the hallway and I knew I would never see her again. She was the only person at the hospital who had cared, the only one who had tried to help me in any way she could.

Not the doctor. Oh no, not him. He was of no help whatsoever. There was no mention of any treatment. He didn't tell me what to do or where to go. Just looked straight at me and said, "You have two years to live."

Not maybe. No. That's it. Two years. Find a support group, was the only advice he could come up with. A support group. Yeah, right! Here, in the middle of freaking nowhere, a support group?

All these thoughts go dancing round and round in my head as I sit in the dark kitchen, sipping my coffee.

Mark comes downstairs, pours himself a cup and sits down opposite me. His face is lined and drawn, old looking. Desperate, you might say.

"What are we going to do?" I whisper, "we have to find help… we…"

"Now, you listen to me. No one must ever find out about this AIDS thing, ok Babe? No one. Not Antonia, not Ken, not Melanie or Peter or my parents. No one, you understand? We'll deal with this in private, by ourselves".

"But how can we? We know nothing about AIDS, nothing! We'll have to find a doctor or a clinic or whatever who specialize in infectious diseases, or…" I pause and weigh my words, "I should rephrase that… sexually transmitted diseases!!" I spit out.

"Are you crazy? I forbid you to talk about this to anyone, you hear? Anyone! You know how people would talk? What the hell do you think they'll say if they find out? I'll have to leave the firm. We'll lose our friends. We'll be outcasts. Pariahs. And we'll have to go back to Canada, is that what you want?"

"No, of course not, but we have to do something! We have to find someone. We can't just pretend that nothing is wrong."

"Why the hell not?" His voice rises to a high pitch and his face turns red with anger. He slaps the table with his flat hand; the coffee cup takes a little jump.

"Why the hell not? This is probably all a big mistake and we'll deal with it in private. Never in the whole of my life have I asked strangers for help and I'll not start now. I can take care of us, believe me."

"But what about the children? We have to have the children tested too. You know that we have to do that, Mark."

"No. I won't have it. Don't you see, Hon, we can't do it here. This is a small town. Everybody knows everybody's business. You can't just pop in at your doctor's office and ask for an HIV test. No one must know. Understand?"

"I guess we can wait. The kids seem fine. I mean they don't ever get sick except for the odd cold, which is normal. But we have to be careful around them; I mean I would never forgive myself if they catch the disease from us." I'm trying to pacify him, cool his anger, make him think that I agree with him.

"They won't catch it. How could they catch it?"

"Well, we have to be extra careful with cuts and open wounds and things like that. That's how it is transmitted, I believe. Not the way a lot of people think, from utensils or toilet seats and things like that, but through saliva, blood, sex..."

Mark gets up and strokes my hair.

"I know you're worried about the children, Hon, and so am I. You must know that. And you're right, we'll be careful. We'll be super careful around them."

And that's as far as he will go in acknowledging that, yes indeed, we have a problem. A huge, insurmountable problem.

But I know in my heart that I will call the number Phyllis has given me. I will make that call. And I also know that I'll take the children to have them tested. Even if I have to do it behind Mark's back. I'll drive to the hospital in Richmond, I'll go and see Doctor Miller; he already knows anyway. Sitting here at the kitchen table and sipping my coffee, I make a promise to myself that I will do that!

But not just yet. Not now when everything is so fresh and unspeakable and enormous. I need a few days to rest. A few days to get my strength back, to think about everything, to sort things out in my head.

I hear Mark rummaging around upstairs, unpacking my suitcase, I guess. and I know that he doesn't want to talk anymore. And if I can't talk to him, then to whom? I wish Antonia were here. But perhaps it's just as well that she's not around during this nightmare. No one must know, that's what Mark had said - no one!

So even if Antonia were here, I would not be able to tell her anything. She's in Europe, has been for the last six weeks. Italy - Switzerland - France. The usual jet set hangouts. She's not really the jet set type but I guess Ken likes to make the rounds of all the famous places and expects her to be there with him.

"Not too crazy about such a long trip," Antonia had said on that morning so long ago. So very, very long ago. That morning before her departure. That morning when the world was whole, when everything was normal, that morning before...

"We'll be gone almost two months, but I'll back in plenty of time to play lots more golf. I'll miss you, Steph, but the time will pass quickly. I'll call you from wherever we are, ok?"

We had hugged and kissed and then she was gone. And that morning there was no way for me to know just how different everything would be when she returned.

But even though Antonia is supposed to return any day now, I know that I won't be able to confide in her. I cannot speak of the unspeakable, and so I'm facing the darkness that is all around me alone.

I pour myself another coffee and drink the hot liquid in small sips. It makes me feel better, makes the dizziness go away. I stare out the window into the still, grey afternoon. Nothing is stirring; a light fog hangs over the trees and bushes, everything is quiet. Still and quiet.

And suddenly I feel a presence, there with me, in the twilight.
Something intangible.
Something ominous, like a silent companion.
I don't know what it is and it scares me.

Chapter 9

Months have passed since our diagnosis. Thanksgiving has come and gone and it's almost Christmas.

Christmas. Mark loves Christmas more than any other holiday, even more than New Year's with endless football and all. We will not let this illness rob us of our Christmas. We have decided that. The kids will have their Christmas and we will have ours.

Bettina and Adam have made their lists, as they do every year. It's never a long list. Nothing extravagant. Just things they really, really want. Special things. The kind of wishes you save up for Christmas.

"Go get them anything they ask for," Mark says one Saturday morning, "anything at all. Who knows…" his voice trails off and his eyes are full of pain.

"Who knows what?"

"Well, next year, who knows…"

"Don't talk like that, don't even think like that. You'll be ok. We both will."

"Yeah, sure, I guess you're right."

He gets up from the breakfast table and stretches.

"I think I'll go and get the tree today. It's only a couple of weeks 'til Christmas Eve so the tree will be nice and fresh."

It is a brilliant winter morning, the kind where the air is so cold it looks like a zillion diamonds are dancing in the sunlight and it almost hurts to take deep breaths. And you feel fresh and clean and healthy.

"Don't get such a big tree," I remind him, because last year the tree barely fit through the front door and it had taken Mark forever to trim it down to size.

"Ok, I won't," he laughs, and calls the kids.

They love going with him and picking their own tree, cut right there in the woods.

A couple of days earlier, Antonia had picked me up in her Jag and once we were at the mall, I felt happy and more carefree than I had felt in months. I was going to buy something special, really, really special for the children and for Mark.

It didn't take me long to find everything on their list so I went in search of that something extra. I looked around in an electronics store but I didn't have a clue what I was looking for. I knew less than nothing about computers and I felt like an idiot having to ask for help. But the sales guy was friendly and understanding.

His name was Tom. It said so on his nametag. I swear he was about fifteen years old. His spiky red hair stood up in all directions and he was just a sneaker away from looking nerdy.

"Ok, lady, here's the basic stuff you need. This is a nice little package and will get your kids started."

He rattled off all kinds of foreign sounding specs that meant nothing to me. But he obviously knew what he was talking about and so I bought the computer and the monitor and the mouse and the keyboard and all the other things that he said I needed and that I knew nothing about.

"I know it's a little extravagant," I said to Toni who was standing beside me, looking bored, "but the kids want so little. And this will help them with their homework and keep them entertained at the same time. So it's a good investment, right?"

"Yeah, I suppose that's true. I have no use for computers myself; give me a good book instead. But I guess that's the direction the world is going in," Antonia laughed.

I gasped a little when the salesman rang up the total. But then I imagined about how surprised the kids would be and how thrilled, and suddenly the money meant nothing, absolutely nothing.

For Mark I managed to find an authentic Toronto Maple Leaf hockey jersey, autographed by the goalie. The Leafs are his favourite team of all time and I knew he would be thrilled with that. The jerseys only came in one size and I thought it would be awfully big on Mark, which gave me a little stab. But I bought it just the same and I was hiding all my treasures when I got home.

I am washing the vegetables for our supper when I see Mark and the children coming through the backyard, dragging a tree behind them. It is such a perfect picture. The children red-nosed and laughing, Mark looking healthier than he has in a long time, what with the winter air making his face glow, and he laughs along with the kids as they drag the tree through the back door. And a perfect tree it is. Not too tall. Nice and straight with full bushy twigs, still encrusted with rime.

"Isn't this the best tree you've ever seen, Mom?" Adam asks, proud, as if he'd grown it himself.

"It sure is, probably the most beautiful one we've ever had." I stroke his hair and they all take off their coats and sit down for a cup of hot chocolate.

Mark likes to celebrate Christmas the way his parents had done back in Germany. On Christmas Eve, we lock the living room doors so the kids can't come in and we trim the tree and put real candles on it.

There's nothing quite as festive and magical as the soft glow of the candles, the smell of the pine needles and the wonder in the children's eyes when they first see the tree.

Under the tree will be plates with gingerbread cookies and marzipan and nuts and all kinds of goodies and everybody gets their own plate. Even Sapphire.

This year we're doing everything the same way as any other year.

As if we want to stretch time and pretend that all is well. The presents are wrapped in shiny paper, waiting under the tree.

I put on Christmas music and Mark lights the candles and we open the door and the children stand in front of the tree in wonder. Both Bettina and Adam recite a little Christmas poem before they are allowed to open their presents. That too is part of the tradition.

The computer is a huge, huge hit. And so is the hockey jersey. Mark grins from ear to ear like a little boy as he puts it on. It hurts my heart to see how loosely it hangs on him. But he doesn't seem to notice and won't take it off all evening and even when we go to midnight mass, he is wearing it under his coat.

The twins have given me a little ashtray and a little creamer they've made in pottery class at school and Mark has bought my favourite perfume and hands me a small box with a stunning heart-shaped diamond pendant that has our names engraved at the back. He puts it round my neck and there is so much love in his eyes that I haven't seen in a long, long time. Love. And deep, deep sorrow.

On Christmas morning, we're sitting down for breakfast when there's a knock on the front door. Antonia and Ken burst into the hallway, loaded with presents for the children. Nothing too fancy, mind you. Little thoughtful things. Programs and games for the new computer, movies, books, a cute outfit for Bettina that Antonia has bought in Italy and a hockey stick for Adam.

Toni admires the tree.

"It's so romantic, real candles; I don't think I've ever seen that before. Isn't it dangerous though?"

"Not at all. You have to be careful how you place them, of course, and you don't go out shopping when the candles are burning," Mark laughs. "In Europe they've been using candles on their Christmas trees forever. It's just really festive and we like it."

And altogether, it is a happy Christmas. Mark's parents come over on Christmas Day and there are more presents and turkey and much eating and drinking and Mark eats a whole drumstick and stuffing and he looks healthier and better than I've seen him in a long time.

I feel happy and safe.

And the *companion* is far, far away.

Chapter 10

It's hard to remember when I first noticed the changes in Mark. They are ever so gradual, these changes. Little things, like his hair. He's always had really thick black hair and he is proud of it.

"It's the Italian blood in me, from my mother's side", he says and he is only half joking because he knows I like the dark haired, brooding, Latin type of guy.

Over the last few weeks though, his hair has thinned and a few strands of grey are showing up at his temples. Mark brushes it off, of course.

"My Dad got grey hair when he was just forty five or so. It runs in the family, and anyway, grey temples make a man look distinguished, right?"

"Sure, of course," I reply and I don't mention the fact that Mark is much younger because I know he knows and there is no sense in talking about that.

I watch him while he studies his reflection in the mirror. Intent. He takes a step back and moves forward again, scrutinizing his hair. Tries to fluff it up a little, or brush it down and a deep crease appears between his eyes.

He catches me looking at him.

"I think I'll grow a beard; what do you think?"

Trying to make light of the situation, as if he's only looking into the mirror to see whether a beard would be an ok thing to have.

"I don't know," I reply, "With your job, I mean a beard wouldn't look that professional, would it?"

And I too pretend that that is an important decision to make. Not the fact that his hair is getting thinner and peppered with grey. Not that. Oh no.

But like I said, these changes are gradual. And then I get paranoid and start to look for symptoms within myself. My body. My face. My hair. But there aren't any. None that I can see. Except, wait a minute, except I get these annoying little cold sores on my lower lip. Not that often mind you, and maybe it doesn't mean anything.

But, like everything else these days, it makes me paranoid and I look it up and I find out they are caused by the herpes simplex virus, and anything to do with viruses freaks me out.

You could say that the microscopic image in the encyclopedia is almost pretty. Like a snowflake, or some tiny alien galaxy. I just don't want it in my face, thank you very much. So yes, maybe it doesn't mean anything. But then, I've never had anything like that, never. My skin has always been flawless, just like my mom's. Even as a teenager, I never had a pimple, or acne, and my friends envied my perfect skin.

So this is something new. It starts with one. One lousy little blister that actually makes my lips look plump and sexy, except it is itchy and hurts when I touch it. And then they keep coming. One… two… little clusters… and eventually they take over my entire mouth and it hurts like hell if I try to open it.

I look disgusting and I feel ugly and Mark thinks so too. I can tell by the way he looks at me. Trying not to look at my mouth, shifting his glance higher, to the top of my head. If he looks at me at all.

"Can't you do something about that?" he snaps one morning at breakfast. "I'm losing my appetite looking at you."

And he pushes back his plate and stomps outside. Meanwhile, I'm trying to sip a smoothie through a straw, because I can't open my goddamn mouth and he's being an insensitive asshole. I mean, whose fucking fault is it anyway?

I don't want to admit it, but I know this is happening because of the AIDS. The AIDS that's killing my immune system so it can't even fight a lousy little virus that gives you cold sores that make you so ugly, your husband can't bear to look at you. Tears are stinging my eyes and I feel like kicking him and I watch him pacing up and down the porch, dragging deeply on a cigarette, his face like thunder.

The sweet guy in the drugstore at K-Mart gives me some lotion to dry up the sores and now my mouth is all white from that stuff.

"You look like a clown, Mom," Bettina says. "I mean happy, like a clown."

I know she's trying to comfort me and she looks at me with eyes that are too old for her age. And then, slowly, the sores disappear and I look my old self again. Flawless skin and all.

It has been a big scare though, a big scare for me. I become paranoid. Every night I examine every inch of my body, look inside my mouth, even check my vagina with a mirror. No. No herpes simplex. Nowhere on my body. Just tanned, healthy skin, shiny hair, moist pink lips. Nothing wrong!

And I check my weight too. Every day. Oh, yes. But, if anything, I've gained a pound or two since my appetite has returned. So no wasting. Not yet.

Even though my cold sores are gone and I'm back to normal, Mark doesn't touch me, hold me, kiss me. Nothing. We don't talk much anymore. Not like we used to. Maybe a vacation, a change of scenery, will bring us close again? I don't know. But that's all I long for, to be close again, we're in this together, we have to hold each other up, comfort each other, you know?

It's early evening. Mark is sitting in front of the television, staring mindlessly at some game or other. Then, without a word, he goes upstairs to bed. And I think about him lying upstairs and I think about how much I still love him and how I cannot bear seeing him like this and knowing that I am losing him.

Alone, I sit outside on the porch and I light a cigarette and feel rage rising in my gut. The kind of rage you cannot control. The kind of rage that makes you lose your mind and I feel like screaming. I take a big sip of my drink and the anger gets worse. I feel like lashing out at something. Anything. I want to grab a kitchen knife and run upstairs and kill him. Kill him for doing this to me, to us. Kill him for betraying me, for shacking up with some goddamn whore who's given him AIDS.

Or was it a whore? Was it even a woman? Could it be that...? No! Impossible! No way in God's creation. Not Mark. Not Mark, he is too goddamn homophobic. I mean, he hates homosexuals. Hates them. Or so he says.

They say though that some men only find out, or will admit to, having these feelings later in life. Many marry and have kids and are seemingly content in their marriage, and then, bingo! They suddenly meet some stud, young or old, it doesn't matter, and they fall in love. And they up and leave their families, give up their careers, and start a new life as a gay guy. But Mark? No fucking way. Then, I guess that's what those other women thought too. No fucking way, right?

I try to stop my mind from going there, but you know how it is. The more you try not to think about something, the more your mind latches on to it. Like a dog that won't let go of a bone, until I can almost picture it in all it's disgusting detail. And it is real, so real in my mind, and I feel bile coming up my throat and I feel sick and run inside and throw up. And I throw up again and again until there is nothing left inside me to be sick with.

And I rinse my mouth and walk back outside. Drained of everything.

So the summer months drift along and there are times when I forget about the whole thing. Times when everything is so normal, it seems ludicrous that AIDS is now part of our lives.

August is particularly hot and dry and we take the kids to the seaside for a couple of weeks. Mark's idea. He bounces into the kitchen one morning, happier than I've seen him in a long time.

"Let's pack up and go to Cape Cod," he says, totally out of the blue.

"When?"

"Tomorrow morning."

"That's way too soon; I have to prepare for it."

"What's to prepare? Throw a few things into a suitcase and we're off. The firm is closed for a couple of weeks anyway. Ken and Antonia are off to Italy, vacationing on somebody's private yacht no doubt," he adds with a touch of sarcasm. "So let's you and me and the kids take off too. Mom will look in on the house, ok?"

So seldom is he spontaneous these days that I agree. He doesn't say 'perhaps it's the last time'. He doesn't say that. And I don't even know whether he thinks it. Things have been going so well for quite a while now; perhaps he honestly thinks that it's all a big mistake, some kind of misdiagnosis. At least he pretends to think that. But then, I don't know what he thinks any longer.

His good mood is infectious. But all the while, I feel the *companion* nearby. Watching. Waiting.

I let the kids pack their own little suitcases and I'm amazed at how little they forget. I mean, even toothbrushes, for heaven's sake, and underwear and beach stuff, lots of beach stuff.

It turns out to be one of the happiest vacations ever. The drive is long but the kids are great. Adam plays video games and Bettina, as usual, has her nose in a book. I am happy and content. Every so often Mark looks into the rearview mirror and glances at the children and then he looks at me with a warm smile and love in his eyes. Yes, I am happy alright.

All of my life I have loved the ocean. Never can I get enough of the constant rhythms, the ebb and flow of the water, and I can sit for hours on end just watching, listening, thinking. No matter the weather.

We rent a small cottage right by the ocean, but off the beaten track, and we cook our own meals and Mark takes Adam out in a fishing boat and my daughter and I just sit and read, or we gather seashells and strange looking rocks to take home. In the evenings, we take long walks on the hard wet sand and life is good. The *companion* is far, far from my mind. Except for that one time, when something odd happens.

Bettina and I are strolling along the beach, wading knee deep in the waves. Mark and Adam are way ahead of us when suddenly I see Mark collapse. By the time I rush to his side he has already gotten up, soaking wet.

"What happened?"

"Oh, nothing, nothing at all, I stepped into some kind of a hole in the sand and lost my balance."

But he is pale and looks a little shaken and his eyes are vacant.

"Are you ok?"

"Sure, sure, don't worry."

The colour has come back into his face and he smiles at us. He is fine. Of course he is.

"Come on, I'll race you," he laughs and takes off. Weeks later, I would remember that incident.

Tanned, with suitcases full of sand and rocks and shells, we return home two long, lovely weeks later. Among the usual collection of bills and such, there is a letter from Antonia. She misses me, she misses America.

'Our friends here are lovely and it's quite a challenge to speak nothing but Italian,' she writes. 'The food is fabulous and the shopping out of this world. But I'm longing to come back; we still have a lot of golf ahead of us this season'.

I smile to myself. I miss her too. I miss playing golf with her and I miss our talks.

Looking out the window the next morning, I see her Jag pull into the drive.

"I've come for coffee," she laughs and hugs the hell out of me.

"You're back already? I guess I didn't check the date on your letter. I'm so glad to see you."

She kicks off her shoes.

"Oh, it's good to be back. I mean, it was a great vacation but still.."

"Hey, Antonia, back so soon? You look great," Mark gives her a quick kiss on the cheek on his way out the door. "Sorry, first day back at the office, must rush." He waves good-bye with a piece of toast he's grabbed from the table.

"Mark looks good," Antonia smiles. "Tanned, healthy.. a little thinner perhaps than I remember him."

"He's been working out, and he got a lot of exercise on our holiday," I reply.

I do not mention that he is actually eating less, way less, than he used to. I guess I've never really thought about that until now.

Mark has always been a good eater. He attacks food with gusto and enjoys a big meal, always followed by dessert. And he never really gains weight. He is solid, to be sure, but not fat.

But lately he's not having his usual second helpings, and there are times when he pushes his food 'round the plate and leaves the table before he's finished his meal. It all happened so gradually, I hardly noticed it at first. But now that Antonia mentions it..

The doctors have forewarned me. They have told me of what is called the 'wasting', the gradual loss of weight when the body doesn't get any nourishment and that is so typical in AIDS patients. Usually it's because of the medication that makes people nauseous, but Mark is not on medication; he doesn't even want to discuss the possibility of getting any. I think he is hoping it will just go away and he will miraculously recover.

But he won't eat. All he wants to do is sleep, and it gets worse. At first he just has long lie-ins, especially on weekends. But then he has a hard time getting up at all, even to go to the office. And in the evenings he comes home and goes straight upstairs. Without supper. Sometimes he just has a drink, but no food.

So I think, perhaps he's just sleeping so much because he wants to shut out the reality of what is happening. An escape sort of thing. But you can't make yourself sleep if you're not tired, can you? This has been going on for a few weeks now, not very long, and then he starts losing his balance.

The day at the beach comes back into my head, the way he had stumbled and dismissed it as nothing.

And then one evening, I am putting dinner on the table and he pulls out his chair and collapses. Falls down. Crashes to the floor. The kids stare at him, scared, and I rush over and try to help him. He pulls himself up and sits on the chair and looks at me with faraway eyes, as if he doesn't even know what has happened or where he is and all he says is:

"I feel a little tired, must be some sort of flu. Will you help me upstairs?"

"But you haven't touched your supper."

"I don't feel like it. Maybe later."

And I know that later will not come. Not tonight, anyway.

Upstairs he is lying in bed looking helpless and worn out with big beads of sweat on his forehead. I stroke his hair and tuck the blanket around him because he starts shivering, and almost immediately he falls asleep.

The kids are still eating their supper when I come back downstairs. They are being so good, so quiet, as if they know that something is terribly wrong.

"Is daddy going to be ok?" Bettina asks.

"I don't know." I can't lie to them, not now. "I don't know, love; I really don't know what's wrong with daddy. We will just have to wait, ok?"

"Ok," they both nod. "We'll wait."

After I tuck the twins into their beds, I pour myself a large Scotch, and sit on the porch. I actually hate Scotch; I only keep it in the house because Antonia loves it.

"Nothing like a decent shot of Scotch," she often says which is funny, coming from an Italian.

No, I don't like Scotch one bit, but it's the only thing I can find and so I water it down and sip it slowly, and I feel the warmth of the alcohol creep down to my toes.

I think about Mark upstairs. I think about the wasting. And I think what a terrible, terrible thing that is. I know his body is slowly dying; his body is eating itself up because it isn't given anything to fight with. No nourishment. No medication. Nothing.

I don't know when I'll start getting symptoms like that, or will I? I don't care about myself, just the children. And I don't want to go upstairs and lie next to that body that is fighting for its life. Or perhaps it has already given up?

It is late, very, very late when I finally go upstairs. Mark is breathing evenly; shallow, as if in a coma.

And I sense that presence but I am too weary to think about it. And I fall asleep from sheer exhaustion.

And in the middle of the night I open my eyes and I'm wide awake. And I look around the room which is bathed in pale moonlight and suddenly I know. I know what it is.

The presence.

It is the foreshadow of things to come, of tremendous aloneness, of death! My death!

And I'm lying in my bed, wide awake, and a paralyzing fear takes hold of my thoughts.

And then I know that that presence will forever be my *companion*.

Tonight and for the rest of my days.

Chapter 11

I don't think I've seen Antonia cry. Ever. I mean, she has tears in her eyes every once in a while, when she talks about home, her family, whatever. But not cry. She always says, that's what happens when you immigrate. You leave something behind. You leave some of yourself behind. And then, it's like you always remember the good times, all the good stuff you left behind, not the bad stuff. Not the reasons why you left in the first place.

Of course, it's not always bad stuff that makes you leave and go to a new country, oceans away. Sometimes I guess you just go because of the adventure, to see what it's like to live on another continent. I don't know whether I could ever do that and I admire people who can.

Anyway, that's why I think Antonia left Italy and came to the States. Adventure. And she goes home quite often; she has enough money to take these trips, heaven knows.

But today she cries, sitting in my kitchen.

"I don't know how to tell you this, Steph. I don't know where to start, but I'm leaving."

It is a dull kind of day. There's a greenish hue to the morning light, like being at the bottom of the sea. A sad day, pensive and sad at the same time.

"You're leaving? Where are you going? You can't leave. You only moved here a couple of years ago."

"Well, here's what's happened. Ken is opening a new branch up in Canada and we're going to move there, and eventually he'll have all his business up there. And I am going with him, what else?"

I start crying right along with her and we hold each other and we cry on each other's shoulder. Finally, she sits back and wipes her eyes. She wipes her eyes with the back of her hand, like a kid, and I swear her mascara doesn't even smudge. Or maybe she isn't wearing any, who knows? I look like a raccoon when I finally fish for a Kleenex, but who cares about that?

Toni reaches for a tissue and blows her nose like a trucker.

"It's not all that bad," she finally says. "I mean, it's not that far. You know by plane it only takes about an hour and by car, what, five hours tops? So we'll see each other often. And I'll call you, of course, every day until you're sick of me."

"Ok, where in Canada will you live? I mean, it's a huge country."

"Well, that's the good part."

Her cheeks are still wet with tears but she smiles that beautiful smile that lights up her face. And again, I think how much like a child she really is.

"We're going to live just outside of Toronto, in a small town. I don't know what it's called… Oakville, I think. I bet it's really cold though. Up there."

I have to smile. With all her worldliness and sophistication, she doesn't have a clue when it comes to Canada. Like most Americans, she thinks that just as soon as you cross the border you have to strap on your skis.

"The temperature is pretty much the same as here," I tell her, "here in Virginia, I mean. The winters can be hard, but not so much in Toronto because you have the big lake, so it doesn't get that cold. Not like, say, in Northern Canada. And it's beautiful there. Who knows? Maybe we'll end up there too."

"That would be the best thing that could ever happen. You're like a sister, more than a sister to me. I love you, you know that, don't you?"

And we look at each other and we know we will be friends for life.

So this is a sad day. A really, really, sad day.

But now she's already been gone for more than three months and summer is coming. And I know that summers will never be the same again. Never, ever, be the same.

Never mind summers, day to day life is never the same, and I know that before I see Antonia again, things will have gone from bad to worse.

Antonia calls at least once a week, so it's like I am still a part of her life. She tells me about her new house and friends she's made, about the golf club they have joined, and how much she likes living there.

"Oh, and I found a great stable where I'm boarding Magnolia and Ophelia, just north of the city, place called Ballinafad. Isn't that a lovely name? It's only a thirty minute drive for me to go see them. I would have preferred to have them with me but then we would have had to buy a farm or something like that and that's just not practical with Ken's work and all. Still, I miss seeing them every day, but they're happy were they are."

She talks about her horses as if they were her children, well, I guess they are, in a way.

The only thing I really miss is you, Steph," she sighs. "It would be brilliant if you moved up here too."

And then, one a warm summer evening, the phone rings.

"Guess what? I'm coming to see you. Ken had to go to Vancouver for something or other and I thought, well, I'll just zip down and visit Stephanie - and Mark, of course. How about this weekend? I can be there on Friday night if I leave here at noon, then we'll have three days to ourselves!"

I am thrilled. Absolutely thrilled. Things have been so depressing lately, what with Mark never wanting to do anything anymore, just sitting around, watching television, sleeping, not eating.

"Oh, Antonia, how lovely! We'll go shopping, we'll play golf. I'm so glad you're coming, I can't begin to tell you." I almost burst into tears, I am so happy.

"Great! I'll see you Friday night, and I'll throw my clubs into the car. Oh Steph, we'll have a blast!"

Her car pulls into the driveway late Friday afternoon, not the Jag but a new BMW. Antonia jumps out and hugs me. We're laughing and crying all at once.

"Oh my God, it's been so long, it seems like years."

She looks marvelous.

"Look at your hair, it looks great."

"Yeah, I had it cut short; it's more practical this way."

"But you had such beautiful long curls."

"It's only hair, it'll grow back," she laughs and hugs me again.

The two of us sit on the porch with a cup of coffee and a brandy, catching up. It's as if she has left only yesterday and then again, it seems it was a million years ago.

We have a super weekend. A super, super weekend. The kids are at their Grandparent's, so we have two glorious days to ourselves. Antonia invites Mark to play golf with us, but he declines.

"Thanks a lot, Toni," he smiles at her, "but I'm going hunting with a friend. We've planned this for a while, and anyway, you two girls will have lots to talk about, including me, no doubt."

So we play a round of golf by ourselves and it is wonderful. I even play a decent game, scoring 92, I am so relaxed. But mostly we talk. Talk about Toni's new life, about Ken, about everything under the sun except the really dark things that are going on in my life.

I don't even want to think about that. Not now. Not on this glorious weekend. The two days fly by. Totally fly by. And I feel a heaviness in my heart at the thought of Antonia leaving on Monday morning.

She comes down the stairs carrying her overnight bag. She's got a funny way of walking down stairs. She swings her arms, even with the bag in her hand. It looks precarious, as if she's going to come tumbling down any minute. But of course, she makes it and plunks the bag on the floor.

"I had a super time, Steph. When are you guys going to come up to Canada? You know it's just as far for me as it is for you."

She kisses my forehead.

"You'll absolutely love the golf club we belong to. It's not one of those posh ones that Ken wanted to join. I nixed that idea. It's about a half hour north of the city and it's beautiful. A little wild, like some of the courses in Scotland, and quite tough to play. I can't wait until you guys come to visit. But I must be off. It's been great; I'll miss you so much."

"You have time for a coffee, don't you?" I pull up a chair.

"Oh, sure," she sits down and blows a strand of hair out of her face. Sighing deeply, she takes a sip of coffee. Her face becomes serious.

"Steph, before I go, I just have to ask…" she pauses and bites her lip, "be honest with me, is it cancer?"

"Is what cancer?"

"You know, Mark. He has cancer, doesn't he?"

"Why would you think that? He's lost a little weight, but he's been working really hard in the last few months and…" I can't continue and just stare into space, avoiding her eyes.

"Steph, please, you can tell me. He doesn't look at all well and he's been perfectly morose during the last couple of days. I mean, he didn't even want to play golf. What's with that? He loves golf and I know for a fact he doesn't prefer hunting to playing golf. That was just an excuse, wasn't it?"

I swallow hard. My thoughts are racing all over the place. I take one long look into Antonia's eyes and I see nothing there but love. Love and compassion.

"No, Antonia. No. Mark does not have cancer. I wish it were that simple."

My voice trails off. My mouth is dry. I don't know just how far I can go. How much to tell her. I don't know how she'll react and I know Mark will be furious.

"What is it then? It can't be much worse than that. Please, Steph, you can tell me. Maybe I can help."

I take a big swig of coffee and sit up straight in my chair.

"Antonia," I hold on to my cup for dear life. "Antonia, nobody can help. Mark does not have cancer... Mark has AIDS. We both do. Both Mark and I have AIDS."

My words explode into the air like a bomb. I expect Antonia to shrink back. Be horrified. Be totally shocked. And she is, I guess, shocked. Her eyes open wide and her lips part, as if to say something, but she only makes a strange gurgling kind of sound and her hand flies to her throat.

And then she jumps up so fast that the chair crashes to the floor and she rushes over and hugs me so hard, I can barely breathe.

"Oh God. Oh my God. Oh Steph, what can I do? I love you so much."

That I had not expected. Not that. Not the hug. Not the total love I feel coming from her and suddenly it is all too much. I feel tears coming up from I don't know where, deep inside, unshed tears screaming to come out and despite all my efforts, I start to cry and cry and cry and I think, I will never stop.

And all the agony and all the fear and all the terror of the last few months come flooding out of me with those tears. Antonia holds me close and she too cries, until we are both exhausted and sink back on our chairs with nothing to say to each other. Looking at each other, with a deep knowing. Knowing that our friendship goes deeper than anything this life can possibly throw at us.

"I'm not going to ask you how it happened," Antonia finally says, "and it doesn't matter. The only thing that matters is that we deal with it. What are you doing about it? What kind of medication are you on? I have to admit, I don't know much about AIDS, but I know there are treatments of sorts."

"We're not doing anything at all," I admit. "Mark doesn't want anyone to know. He's in total denial and afraid of losing his position in the firm and of people in the community finding out. He won't even admit to himself that something is wrong. But, Antonia, something is wrong. Terribly, terribly wrong. And I'm scared; I'm scared for my kids, for myself, for Mark. But for now we have to deal with it the way he sees fit."

"Let me see what, if anything, I can do when I get back home," she replies and takes my hand in hers. "I will do whatever is in my power to help you. You know that, Steph, don't you?"

"Yes, of course, of course I know," I squeeze her hand, "but you have to go now. You have a long drive ahead of you."

"Yes," she picks up her bag and arm in arm we walk out to her car.

"Call me the minute you need anything, anything at all, you hear?"

"Sure, of course, you know I will."

Antonia puts on her sunglasses and backs out of the driveway, waving. I don't know how long I stand here, staring down the road where her car has disappeared.

Chapter 12

I had expected Mark to be angry when I told him that Antonia knew everything. Angry, furious even, but I guess you should never assume anything.

I had kept it to myself for a few days, but then we hardly talk about anything anymore, other than the everyday stuff. We are strangers. Strangers living in the same house, sharing the same table, sleeping in the same bed, but strangers nonetheless. And all we have in common is this thing. This thing we don't talk about, this thing we pretend isn't there.

It has been months since we have made love. Months, literally. Ever since we were diagnosed. And to be honest, I don't want him to touch me, not even kiss me, nothing.

Just thinking about these other women, maybe even men? I want to throw up, the images are too disgusting.

And then I think about the consequences of what he did, what it did to my body, this thing that is now a part of my life, this thing that has invaded my body and robbed it of all its defenses. Like some kind of monster living inside of me.

And the closeness is gone, the trust is gone and there is nothing left to share, other than the fear. And we lie next to each other at night and we both know that we cannot talk about that.

"I told Antonia," I tell him at the breakfast table on the Thursday after she has left.

"Told her what?"

"I told her about us, the AIDS. I told her about the AIDS."

Like I said, I had expected him to be angry, but he is not. He just looks at me. Eyes dark. No expression in them.

"What did she say?"

"She was shocked at first. Of course she was shocked, who wouldn't be? But she is ok with it. I mean, not ok, but she understands. All she wants to do is help; it's been a relief talking about it and seeing that she isn't horrified and disgusted. Don't worry, she won't tell anyone, not even Ken. She promised and I trust her."

Mark is strangely quiet. "I see," is all he says and stands up. "I see. I have to go. I'll be late for the office."

And he leaves, just like that. He hasn't even touched his toast, just had a cup of coffee, that's it.

And a few days after that, Andrew, Mark's partner calls. It's in the middle of the afternoon so I am scared. Afraid something has happened to Mark at work. I don't know Andrew all that well. I've only met him a couple of times at some corporate function or other; we don't socialize at all. So I wonder what he's calling about.

"Hi, Stephanie, do you have a minute?"

"Is Mark ok?" I ask.

"Yeah, yeah, he's ok. But, well, actually that's why I'm calling. I think there's something wrong with Mark, physically wrong I mean. He's not been himself for quite some time now and, to be honest, it's affecting the company and our clients. He can't concentrate, he's abrupt with people and today he walked out of a meeting. I had a lot of explaining to do to our client. Is there something I should know?"

"I don't think so, he's just been very tired and he isn't eating well. Perhaps he's anemic or something. I've told him to see a doctor but he's a little stubborn that way. He thinks it's going to pass."

I know I'm babbling and I hope he can't hear the desperation in my voice.

"Well it looks to me as if it's a little more serious than anemia.

I'll talk to him. Thanks Stephanie, sorry to bother you with that, I'm just concerned."

My heart is pounding when I hang up the phone. They know; they must know. What does that mean? Don't be silly, nobody would ever suspect what's really going on, why would they?

I hear the car door slamming shut in the garage and it startles me. Mark never slams the doors of the Beemer. "Don't slam the door, It's not a Chevy," he jokes when I do it, but I know he's not kidding. He walks into the kitchen, looking drawn and tired. I don't tell him about the phone call.

"I've been asked, no told, to stay home for a few days," he says at suppertime, poking round on his plate. "They think I need a rest. I haven't really taken time off in a while, so that's a good thing. Maybe they're right, I could use a rest."

"But that's all you do, rest. Rest and sleep. Mark, you have to tell Andrew. He has a right to know."

"Tell him what? That I have a goddamn homo disease? Tell him that? You must be out of your mind! He'll kick me out of the firm…they'll cut me off Medicare without a job… we'd have to go back to Canada! What do you think we're going to live on? You know there's no way I can tell him anything, and you're to keep your mouth shut too, do you understand?"

His face has turned bright red and his eyes are bulging but all I see is desperation. Fear and desperation. He drops his fork. His hands are trembling.

"Of course, Hon, I won't tell anyone, but you must see a doctor. We'll go into Richmond where no one knows us. We'll go back to the hospital; they'll be able to do something, anything. We can't go on pretending that everything's ok."

Tears well up in his eyes. He doesn't want me to see him like this. He doesn't want me to see the pain, the fear, the utter hopelessness that has taken hold of him.

He looks at his trembling hands and he gets up and viciously swipes the plate off the table and it shatters into a hundred pieces and there's food everywhere.

The kids had begged me to let them go over to Melanie's in the afternoon and now I am glad, glad they aren't here to see their dad losing it.

Mark falls heavily onto his chair.

"Maybe next week," he agrees. "Maybe next week I'll see someone."

He says that without a hint of sincerity and I know he just wants me to shut up and continue the charade we've been living for so many months.

I feel like hitting him. I feel like throwing something at him, anything. Anything to shake him out of his denial. It's just not fair. Not fair to me, not fair to the kids. Not fair that I have to carry the burden of everything. The cleaning, the cooking, looking after the children and pretending that everything is normal.

Just because I don't have any symptoms...yet doesn't mean that I'm not frightened, that I'm not scared, that I don't need a shoulder to lean on!

He looks so small, so frightened, his eyes are far away. So instead of hitting him, I get the broom and start cleaning up the mess and the food is all yucky and sticky and it makes me sick and I run into the bathroom and throw up.

Mark does not move in his chair, he doesn't even look up when I come back and finish wiping the floor.

Strange thing though, neither Bettina nor Adam have ever commented on their dad's changed behavior. Sure, they are still young, but they must notice that he doesn't want to do anything anymore? Not even with them? Sometimes they look at me as if they want to ask questions, but then they never do.

And oftentimes I see Adam take his sister's hand and they go out into the backyard or upstairs to play and they never say a word and that is worse, worse than a thousand questions. Because they know something is not right and they don't know what it is and they don't want to ask because they know it will hurt me.

So I watch them silently, taking care of each other as it were. And it breaks my heart.

"Sorry about the mess, Hon," Mark mumbles, more to himself. "I just, I don't feel.." he gets up. "I'm going to lie down for a bit."

"Yeah, what else? You're lying down for a bit and then you'll go to bed. Nothing will change, will it? Nothing! You have absolutely no intention of doing something, anything, to maybe get better. If not for yourself then for us."

And suddenly, he disappears. Just like that. He has crashed to the floor as if his legs have been kicked out from under him.

I try to help him up; I put his arm 'round my neck and pull as hard as I can. Strange thing that. Even with all the weight he's lost, he is still heavy and I have a really hard time getting him to his feet. And all the while he stares at me with an odd, accusing look, as if it is all my fault and here I'm just trying to get him onto the couch or something.

"I'm calling 911," I say. "You have to get to a hospital."

"Forget it, Babe," he replies and now he is quite calm. "I just lost my balance. I've had a bad headache all day and I guess not eating doesn't help. I'll get better, I promise. All I need is a good night's sleep. Help me up to bed and we'll talk about it in the morning, ok?"

He smiles. The colour has returned to his face. And I believe him. God knows I want to believe him and so I try to help him up the stairs. And half way up he slips out of my arm and falls over backwards. His head bumps against each step with a sickening, thudding sound and then he's sprawled on the bottom steps. Eyes wide open, not seeing.

And I panic and run to the phone and call 911 and I think about the kids and how scared they'll be when they see an ambulance pull up and I call Mel.

"Mel, there's something wrong with Mark," I manage to stay pretty calm. "I've called for an ambulance but I don't want the kids to be scared. Can you look after them until I call you back?"

"Of course, honey, but what's wrong? Do you want Peter to come over and help?"

"Oh yes please, yes please! Oh Mel, I can't talk right now, I'll call you later."

I rush back to where Mark is lying and put a cold, wet tea towel on his forehead. His eyes are closed and his breathing is labored and raspy. His skin has turned bright red. There are big drops of sweat on his forehead and I've never been so scared in my life.

Peter comes running through the door without knocking.

"Let's get him off the floor," he says in a matter of fact voice. I am glad he is so calm, glad he is here with me. He lifts Mark off the floor as if he weighs nothing and puts him down on the couch.

We hear the siren of the ambulance long before it comes to a stop in the driveway and I am thinking they should turn those sirens off so as not to scare people and at the same time I realize what a ridiculous thought that is.

"Do you want me to come with you to the hospital?" Peter asks.

"Would you? I'd feel a lot better if I'm not alone."

"Of course, just let me call Mel so she'll know."

I climb into the back of the ambulance. Just before the doors close I catch a glimpse of Melanie's living room window and I see Adam and Bettina standing there with Mel's arms around their shoulders, their scared little faces light up.. Red, white, red, white, red, white.. and fade away as the ambulance takes off.

I don't remember much of the ride to the hospital. It doesn't take very long anyway; nothing takes very long to get to in this town. Mark comes to and looks around, scowling. He is wheeled into emergency just as Peter comes running through the door.

A bored looking nurse starts asking questions and I try to answer as calmly as I can, but Mark is getting annoyed.

"There's nothing wrong with me," he pipes up. "I have some kind of flu. I slipped and fell. That's all."

Even now he won't say anything. Even now he will not tell them what the real problem is. My God, what the hell does it take? If I am scared out of my mind, surely he must be too?

"We'll have a doctor check you out, he'll be here in a minute," the nurse says.

"But why? I feel all right now. I just want to go home."

"It's procedure. You can't leave without having seen a doctor."

To say that she is abrupt would be the understatement of the year but then you can't blame her, being faced with such an asshole attitude.

Mark looks at me balefully. It's all my fault. I know, I know, blame everybody but yourself.

The doctor, looking just as bored as the nurse, takes Mark's pulse. He peers into his eyes, and he too starts asking questions.

"How long have you had this?"

"Had what?"

"Falling down, losing your balance."

"Once or twice, I don't know," Mark's expression is sullen. He barely opens his lips as if he doesn't want to let anything slip out.

"He has AIDS," I say.

And I can see myself standing there, as if from the outside in. I'm very calm, very quiet.

"He has AIDS. It will cut down on the tests you have to take, if you know that."

If I had pulled down my pants and peed on the floor, no one could have been more shocked. The room is dead silent.

I turn round to find a seat and look briefly over at Peter. His mouth hangs open. He looks as if someone has deflated him. Without a word, he stands up and leaves the emergency room. That hurts. It really hurts. But what can you expect? He's Mark's best friend. They do everything together. I can't even imagine what is going through his head. Still.

"Could I please have a cup of coffee?" I ask the nurse. "I'll wait here. Do your tests."

They've whisked Mark into the next room and I sip the coffee she gets for me from a machine. It is horrible, truly horrible, but it is hot. It burns my tongue. It makes me focus on something other than the stares that are sent my way.

I have to call Melanie. By now, Peter will be home with the devastating news and she must be freaking. Mel must have been waiting by the phone because she answers at the very first ring.

"How is Mark?" by way of being polite.

"They don't know what's wrong; they are still doing their tests.."

Pause --

"Mel, I guess Peter told you.."

"Yes, yes he did and I'm shattered, Stephanie, absolutely shattered. What about the kids, do they.."

"No, they're fine," I say with as much conviction as I can muster. "You don't have to be afraid to be catching anything from them."

"And you?"

Pause --

"I see," her voice is small and far away. "I see. Oh Stephanie, what can I say?"

"Nothing right now. I'll stay here until I know more. If you could keep the kids overnight, I don't know how long this will take."

"Sure they can stay, just keep me posted."

"I'll do that. Thanks Mel, thanks a whole lot."

It takes hours for the doctor to return. He is wearing rubber gloves and pulls the mask off his face as he comes down the corridor, in slow motion it seems.

"The news isn't good, Stephanie, not good at all. It looks as if..." he pauses and removes his gloves, "No, it is almost certain that Mark has Cryptococcal Meningitis. It's serious. Very serious. We don't know how long he's had it and with his condition..."

"You mean the AIDS."

"Yeah, sure, the AIDS. Well, with the AIDS.. anything can happen. He's very dehydrated and we've hooked him up to an IV."

"Will he get better?"

"No," he replies bluntly. "No, he won't get better. It could take days, it could take weeks, but from here on in it's just a waiting game. You might as well go home now. Nothing is going to happen overnight. I'm pretty sure of that."

"Can I see him?"

"He's sleeping, but if you wish.."

"I wish."

God he must think I'm a bitch, but who cares what he thinks? So what if I'm a bitch? Deal with it.

Mark looks small in his bed with all that hardware he is hooked up to. Small and ever so thin. I touch his hand.. it is cold and dry. I brush away my tears and leave the room without looking back. All I want to do is go home.

It is just past midnight when the taxi stops in front of our house. Funny, it seems a lot later than that. I pay the driver and let myself in. No sense in getting the children now, it's way too late.

I pour myself a drink. Heaven knows I need it and I light a cigarette. I walk out onto the porch and look up at Melanie's house where my children are sleeping. And their dad lying in a hospital room, fighting for his life, and they may never see him alive again.

Tears stream down my face. Stinging tears. The kind of tears that go on and on and won't stop. The kind of tears that bring no relief, no comfort.

And I can sense the *companion* sitting silently beside me.

Chapter 13

I wake up with a start, knowing something terrible has happened, knowing that this day is going to be one of the hardest days I have to live through and that the days and weeks ahead will be harder still.

For a few minutes I lie on my back and listen to the silence. The cat is lying curled up beside me; the only other living, breathing thing in the house. I do not want to get up. I do not want to face this day. But I know what I must do.

I pour a cup of coffee and take the phone out to the porch. It is a cool morning, cool and damp. The fog has not yet lifted and silvery dew is clinging heavily to the grass.

Max answers the phone after the second ring.

"How's my favourite girl?"

"Max..." I don't know where to start, "Max, something terrible has happened. Mark... well, Mark is in the hospital and... And..." I'm stammering, searching for words.

"Ok, slow down, Stephanie."

Max's voice is calm, reassuring, not at all alarmed.

"Tell me slowly. What's wrong with my son? Has he been in an accident?"

"No, no, not an accident. Max, you and Hannah have noticed it too, haven't you? In the last few months Mark's gotten, well, very thin, tired, listless..."

"Yes, of course we've noticed. Hannah thinks he's working too hard... So what are you telling me? What's wrong with my son?"

I take a deep breath; a deep, deep breath...

"Max", I whisper "Mark is very, very sick. He has AIDS, Max, my husband has AIDS. He didn't want me to tell you, you or anyone else, and now... He's dying Max... dying!"

There's dead silence at the other end. I hear Max breathing, he can't speak, I guess.

I cradle the receiver and wait.

"How long?" Max clears his throat... "How long has he had this AIDS? How did he get it? Sorry, stupid question. Stephanie, it breaks my heart... I don't know what to say, it's too sudden... it's too crazy... it's..."

I hear him breathing into the receiver and I can see his kind face in front of me. I hate to hurt him like this, hate it, hate it!

"What about you, Steph? I'm worried sick about you..."

"I'm ok for the time being. Mark caught an infection that has caused meningitis and with his immune system not functioning..."

"I understand. I must go now and tell his mother!"

"Thank you, Max."

"I will come and get you later; you and the children must stay with us. In the meantime Hannah and I will go to the hospital."

"We would rather stay at home, Max. I don't want the children's routine to get too disrupted, they're better off in their own environment and feel safe for now... It's going to be rough enough as it is."

"I understand. I'll come by later and see you," he gently puts down the receiver and I sink onto a chair, thinking of him having to tell Hannah that her son, her one and only son whom she adores, has a dreadful disease and is going to die! Oh God, Max, why did this happen? Why?

There's no sense in freaking out now. I must pull myself together and be strong for the children. I wash my face with cold water and walk over to Melanie's to fetch them.

Mel only half opens the door. Her eyes are red as if she'd been crying. She doesn't ask me to come in but calls for Adam and Bettina to come downstairs.

"Melanie…"

"Please don't say anything, Steph. I'm in total shock as you can imagine and I don't want to hear anything about this AIDS thing. I'm very, very disappointed that you wouldn't confide in me but I probably wouldn't have handled it very well either."

"I understand, Mel. Thanks for looking after the kids, I'll call you later."

"Is daddy ok, Mom? Is daddy still at the hospital?"

"I'll tell you all about it when we get home, ok?"

Adam and Bettina give me a quick hug and run across the lawn into our house.

"Stephanie," Melanie is looking down at her feet, avoiding my eyes. "Peter, well, Peter has asked that you don't come over here anymore. He, well, we both think, it's best, considering…"

"I see, Mel. You're right, it's probably best… considering…"

I am shocked. Mel is my friend, I'm shocked at her words and at the same time I think I understand. I don't know how I would react if the situation were reversed. But it hurts. It hurts like hell.

I walk back to my house and can feel her eyes following me. I sit down on the front step and try to collect my thoughts.

So this is how it's going to be. People will react in different ways; most of them will shrink back, keep their distance like you're a leper. In a way, I guess, it's understandable. AIDS is not the kind of thing that people have to deal with on a daily basis. It's not like cancer, say, which is terrible enough but people are not afraid of it because it's not contagious. But AIDS? You could catch it, you could die and still, to this day, for many, many people there's the stigma associated with homosexuality.

I must get used to this reaction if I want to survive, I cannot take anything personally. Not everyone is like Antonia and for a moment I wish with all my heart that she didn't live so far away.

I walk through the front door and smell fresh coffee. Bettina is busy in the kitchen making toast.

"Here Mom," she sets a mug in front of me, "I've made coffee for you. You look tired,"

I wrap my left arm around her and hold her tight, and I grab Adam with my right hand and pull him close too.

"We three must stick together now," I whisper, "Daddy is very, very ill and will be in the hospital for a while. So you'll be my big girl and my big boy and help me, ok?"

They both look at me with big knowing eyes and nod their heads and this very minute I swear to myself that I will do everything in my power, everything, to make sure that they have a mother to look after them for as long as possible.

I slowly drink the coffee Bettina has made and even though I don't feel like it, I butter toast and manage to eat a couple of slices. If I want to fight this disease, I must put nourishment into my body; I'll not act like Mark who refused to eat and simply gave up with no consideration for me, or for the children. I will not do that, I will not give up and I will not give in. As long as there is a breath in my body, I will fight, no matter what it takes.

My thoughts go back to Max; I wonder how Hannah has taken the devastating news. She must have sensed that something wasn't right. Mark's been wasting away for months and there were times when I saw her looking at him with concern in her eyes but she wouldn't ask questions because the one time she did, Mark almost bit her head off.

"I'm alright, mother," he had snapped, "I'm not your little boy any longer, so stop pestering me with questions. If something were wrong, you'd be the first to know."

His voice was dripping with sarcasm and Hannah's mouth had set in a straight line. She had pushed back her chair and left the room. Ever since that day she hasn't asked any questions but I can see in her eyes that she is worried sick.

As if on cue, the phone in the hallway starts ringing. Adam runs out to answer it.

"Mom, it's for you…. It's grandpa," he yells.

I pick up the extension in the kitchen and tell the kids to go up-stairs and play in their rooms.

"Stephanie?" his voice is small and sounds far away.

"Hi Max… how is Hannah?"

"She's beside herself, as you can imagine. She refuses to believe just how sick Mark is and she doesn't want to hear anything about AIDS. She thinks it's the most ridiculous notion that her son would have such a disease, insisting it must be a mistake, a misdiagnosis. We're driving to the hospital in a few minutes and then…." he heaves a deep sigh.

"The doctor said that Mark isn't going to get any better, Max, he's going to get worse and worse. His body has nothing left to fight with and he will die, Max, he will die."

I have to check myself sharply to keep my voice under control. There's no sense in getting hysterical, it's not going to help and again, I remind myself that I must stay calm and control my emotions for the sake of my children.

I think I can hear Max sobbing at the other end of the line then his voice comes back, barely audible now.

"I'll see you at the hospital, Stephanie, we must stick together now…. We're family." And he softly puts down the receiver.

Chapter 14

The doctor is right, Mark isn't getting better. His body can't fight the meningitis because of the AIDS.

At noon I am back at the hospital and sit with my husband. He deteriorates minute-by-minute, right in front of my eyes.

And all day long I stay with him and I watch the invisible bacteria take over and turn him into a hideous non-human. And I recall how I once read about this flesh eating bacteria that you can't see and that eats you up alive, limb by limb. And it makes my skin crawl.

I mean, cryptococcal meningitis, who would ever think of getting it? And how the hell do you get it?

Cryptococcal meningitis is a common
opportunistic infection in AIDS patients,

That's all I know about meningitis, looked it up in the dictionary. I mean, opportunistic infection, what the hell does that mean? Sounds obscene if you ask me, and indeed, it is obscene. Obscene what it does to you once it has crept into your body and is sucking the life out of you.

Mark is hallucinating. He looks at me with eyes large and glassy from the fever. He looks at me, but he doesn't see me, not me, not his wife.

"Look," he whispers, his lips cracked and dry. "See? She's here, my grandma is here."

And he points to a corner at the ceiling, grinning idiotically.

"Don't you see?" he says again, impatient, crazy-like. "She's there, right there."

And then he starts singing a lullaby, but his voice is blurry and you can't understand a word. Only the melody. Sort of. And all the while tears trickle down his cheeks, which are blotchy and swollen with tightly stretched skin.

He tries to rip out the IV and sit up. The strain of it makes him froth at the mouth, and the veins at his temples pop out with the sheer effort. There is no way I can hold down Mark's body, weak as it is, and I ring and ring and ring for the nurse and then I run into the hallway and scream for someone, anyone, to help.

An orderly in hospital greens rushes in with a nurse and together they restrain him, practically lying on top of his flailing body and tying his wrists and ankles to the bed. And they are both wet with perspiration and they look mad, as if this is something they shouldn't have to do, something that is not part of their job description. And they leave, muttering to themselves. Not looking at me.

By the time the doctor comes in to give Mark an injection, he has calmed down and just lies there, shaking, sobbing like an infant and every bit as messy.

He is not aware of any of it, I know. It's his body reacting to the insidious bacteria that is feeding on him, devouring him. Mark isn't here. But I am. I'm here all this time, disgusted, nauseous, and wracked with pain at seeing him like this. It is wrong; it's just so fucking wrong and unfair. Unfair to him, to me, to the kids.

I can't take it anymore. It is too much. I can't be in that room with that thing that is my husband, but really isn't any more, not like this. And I leave. Turn around and leave without looking back.

The house looks cold and deserted when the taxi pulls up in the driveway. Of course, it looks deserted; no one is home, the children being at their grandparent's and all. It is late afternoon, a drizzly fall day with fog hanging heavy in the trees and bushes. I feel the damp chill air on my face, salty, mixed with tears.

I know now that I have no options left. I have to tell everybody the God-awful truth.

I feel hurt, alone, abandoned.

I sit down at the kitchen table with a large, steaming mug of coffee and light a cigarette. The coffee burns my lips. I welcome the pain. Then I call everyone in my little address book. Everyone.

But first I call Mark's parents. And again, Max answers the phone; I guess Hannah doesn't want to talk to me. I mean, she hasn't even made an attempt to call me. I don't understand why but whatever her reason, I really don't give a damn, not today.

"How is Mark? Any changes?" I can hear in his voice that he already knows that there are no changes, at least not for the better.

"No, Max, nothing's changed. I had to leave the hospital; he didn't even know I was there and…"

"Why don't you stay with us tonight? I'll come over and get you," Max's voice is cracked and raw with emotion. "You shouldn't be alone in the house and the children are asking…"

"Thank you, Max," I drag deeply on my cigarette and try to make my voice sound as calm as possible. "I don't want to upset the kids too much. Seeing me like this, you understand?"

"Sure, sure I understand." He clears his throat. "Listen, if you need anything, anything at all, call me, any time. And if it's in the middle of the night, it doesn't matter. Promise?"

"Promise. Give the kids a hug from me. I'll see them tomorrow, depending on …"

I cannot finish that sentence. I cannot tell him that I too have AIDS. Not tonight. It would be too much. Softly I put down the receiver and reach for another smoke. I've just put one out, but what does that matter now?

I call my Aunt Sissy and tell her what has happened. And I'm surprised, surprised at how well she takes it; not condemning, not judging, even though she knows less than nothing about AIDS, I'm sure. But maybe that's the reason why. Not knowing too much about it is probably a good thing.

The last person I call is Antonia. I know I don't have to be brave with her, don't have to pretend. She picks up the phone on the third ring, out of breath.

"Hey, Steph, good to hear from you. I was just outside running after the stupid cat who was trying to make a getaway. What's up?"

"Toni... Mark is, well, Mark is..."

"What?"

"Mark is sick. Very, very sick. He's in the hospital... Toni.. I think he's dying."

"Oh God, oh my God .." I hear her gasping for air. "I'll come down to see you. I'll stay with you. I don't want you to be alone now."

"Don't Toni. Let's wait. Maybe Ken wouldn't understand. I'll keep you posted. I'll call every day, ok?"

"To hell with Ken. If he doesn't understand, he can go to fucking hell. I'll be there, I promise."

And she comes. The next morning she rings the doorbell. I know she's been driving through the night, but she looks great, the way only Antonia can pull it off. Her hair is tied back in a ponytail and though she's only wearing a black sweat suit, she could have stepped out of the pages of Vogue.

"Oh, Toni, I can't tell you what it means to me that you have come," I cry as she hugs the hell out of me. "You must be dead tired. Please lie down for a while, will you?"

"Not a bit," she assures me and I believe her. Her eyes are bright and clear and her skin has its usual rosy glow. "Just give me a good cup of coffee, and make it strong. Since you don't have an espresso machine, regular coffee will have to do."

I butter toast and make soft-boiled eggs and I sit down and actually have breakfast with her, which surprises me because I'm not one bit hungry.

Mark is heavily sedated when we arrive at the hospital, and if Antonia is shocked at seeing his distorted, motionless body, she doesn't let on. She pulls up a chair and sits next to me, not looking at the bed, just holding my hand and talking about nothing in particular. Just talking, filling the air between us with noise so we won't have to think.

Mark's parents come. I am aching to see the twins but I had asked for them to stay at home with a sitter. No way do I want them to see their dad like this; they wouldn't understand. They'd be too upset. So Max and Hannah come alone.

I can see that they are shocked at Mark's appearance. They haven't seen him in a couple of days and he hadn't looked quite so bad then. I mean he was feverish and incoherent, but he still looked like himself. Now his body is bloated, his head swollen to almost twice its size. It doesn't look like Mark at all, that sick, grotesque lump of a person, hooked up to God knows what and barely breathing.

They don't stay for very long in that hospital room. Not long at all. They stare at what is left of their son and I have a sharp pain in my side, looking at Mark's mom, her face white and without makeup, and with lines I have never seen before. She does not cry, but her eyes are rimmed with red circles as if she has done all her crying the whole night long. And she holds onto Max's hand until her knuckles are white. And him with a face like stone.

Max comes over and hugs me and I can feel him trembling when he kisses the top of my head. Hannah does not come over to hug me. She's standing by the bed, holding on to Mark's hand, and tears shoot up in her eyes and her nose starts to drip and she wipes it with the back of her hand.

And then they leave, suddenly and abruptly they leave, and I am alone with Antonia.

LORENE ALBERS

"I'll stay here with you, Stephanie," she says. "I'll stay for as long as you like, though, to tell the truth, hospitals give me the creeps."

"It's best if you go, Toni. It would actually help me more if you'll pick up the children and take them to the movies, or the mall, or something like that, you know? Heaven knows, they have a hard enough time ahead of them, and they don't know it yet."

"Sure, you're right, anything you like. I'll come back later, ok?"

I sit at Mark's bedside until darkness falls and the room is bathed in a ghostly, pallid light.

I wipe the drool off his mouth, and I hate myself for feeling sick and disgusted. I listen to his breath that is coming in short gasps; laboured and raspy. I wipe the sweat off his forehead and call the nurse when he soils himself because he cannot control his bodily functions.

Again, I hate myself for feeling sick from the smell and wanting to be somewhere else, anywhere, not here.

On the fourth day of this freaking nightmare the doctor comes into the room.

"I'm sorry to have to tell you this, Stephanie, but you have to know. The meningitis is so advanced that Mark's brain has swollen to twice its size. He is brain dead. There is no hope, none whatsoever," and he says all that without any emotion. "You'll now have to make a decision either to wait it out or take him off life support."

"Why me?"

"You're his wife; only you can decide what to do. That's the law."

He leaves the room and leaves me with yet another burden to shoulder. I call Antonia who picks me up in her Beemer and takes me home.

"I took the twins to the mall for a bit of shopping and then dropped them off at your in-laws," she explains. "They've been asking to come home but you know your kids are quite amazing. They are still so young but you can talk to them like adults. They totally understood that you miss them but can't come and see them for a couple of days, because you have to be at the hospital with their father. I think you need time to rest up. Things are not going to get any easier."

"Thanks, Toni. I'm dying to see the children but I don't want them to be burdened like this. Kids should not have to be part of this nightmare. It'll be bad enough for them as it is."

Antonia has made spaghetti sauce and bought fresh pasta.

"Let me just heat up the sauce. The pasta will be ready in no time," she says. She actually looks funny, rummaging around in the kitchen, out of place. Far too glamourous to be domestic.

"I don't think I can eat, Toni. Thanks so much, but.."

I sit down at the kitchen table and put my head on my forearms. The tears come even though I try hard to hold them back. They keep coming and coming; tears that drain your soul but bring no comfort. Toni wraps her arms round my shoulder and says nothing. For the longest time she holds me, her chin on my hair, her own tears dripping down my neck.

"Ok, enough of that," she finally says. "You must eat, you simply must and you know it."

"I can't. I don't even want to smell food."

Toni sets a plate with pasta and sauce in front of me. She puts freshly grated Parmesan into a glass bowl and gives a final toss to a colourful salad. She pours a ruby red burgundy into my best crystal glasses and sits down herself.

"Go ahead, eat. Mangia!"

And you know what? I eat. I actually eat. Slowly at first, mind you, but the pasta is so good, the sauce so delicious, the salad fresh and crispy with just a hint of garlic, I finish the whole plate and ask for seconds.

"There's my girl," Toni smiles, "and, if I say so myself, the sauce turned out great, even though I didn't have home-grown toma- toes."

After dinner, we sit out on the porch. It is chilly and Toni has brought sweaters and a blanket. I have a smoke and we sit silently, looking up at the sky, ablaze with glittering, cold, uncaring stars.

This is what I like best about Antonia; we can be together for hours without having to talk. Now she sits quietly, wrapped in a blanket, sipping wine, her beautiful face luminous in the starlight.

A slight wind has come up and it's getting a little too chilly to stay outside. I walk back into the house. I call Mark's parents and tell them what the doctor has said and the decision I have to make.

"Whatever you decide, Stephanie, we'll understand," Max assures me, his voice seems far away. "This is not the life we wish for our son. This is a living hell."

Max and Hannah bring the children to the hospital the next afternoon so that they can see their dad for the last time. They stare at the lifeless form of their father, not understanding, not recognizing him, and not crying. I wonder what they're thinking. I cannot talk to them, not now. I will not be of any comfort to them because my own heart is ripped to shreds.

I want to shield them from the enormity of this thing, want to assure them that their dad is going to be ok. Yes, he'll play with you again. Yes, he'll go into the woods with you and chop down the Christmas tree. Yes, he'll see you grow up and get married. Yes, yes, yes! I bite my lips so hard, they start to bleed. I can't break down. Not now. Not in front of them.

Their eyes are big and serious, old beyond their age. They come over and cling to me until Antonia pries open their little hands and gently leads them out of the room.

Hannah steps over to the bed and looks down at her son, lying there, motionless, eyes closed, not seeing, not hearing. It's like a scene out of a movie. You can hear nothing, just the hissing of the machine that keeps pumping air into Mark's lungs, preventing him from choking altogether. She strokes his hair and a terrible, terrible sound comes from deep inside her. It is a sound I'll never forget as long as I live. It is the wail of the banshee, the sound only a mother can make when her young is taken from her. The most grievous, agonizing sound in the world and Max takes her arm and she slowly leaves the room, dragging her feet, her eyes blind with tears.

Now everyone has gone. Everyone has left, gone wherever they have to go. So it's just me here in this hospital room. Me and Mark. Alone. I'm so, so tired, but it's only my body that's tired, not my mind.

My mind is in a very still, very calm, very cold place. I know I cannot leave, I know I cannot sleep. This is our time, Mark's and mine. I should like to think that he'd stay with me, or what's left of me, if it were the other way around.

It's very quiet, awfully quiet in this hospital room. There is no sound apart from the slight hissing coming from the oxygen tank or whatever it is that Mark's hooked up to. The nurse comes in, silently. She adjusts something or other and looks over at me sitting there in this functional hospital armchair.

"Do you need anything?" she whispers. And I think, why is she whispering? Mark doesn't hear anything. But she's trying to be mindful. I know that. It can't be easy, her job.

"Actually," I say, "it would be very nice if you could turn down the light, or turn it off altogether if that's possible."

"Are you sure?"

"Yes, I'm sure."

So she turns off the bright neon lights above the bed. And now there's only a soft glow emanating from a small nightlight.

"Thank you," I say.

"Be sure to call if there's anything you need," she replies and quietly closes the door behind her.

And now I hear nothing. I look over at Mark, his breathing is barely audible. He's hooked up to some kind of monitoring device that measures his heartbeat and other vital signs. A small green light shows me that there's still life in him. But I know it's only his body not willing to give up, not his soul. Not my Mark, not the father of my children, not the love of my life.

I move my chair closer to the bed and take his hand in mine and I'm praying with all my heart that he'll know that I'm with him. The words the doctor had said earlier keep drumming round in my head "brain dead, brain dead, brain dead". But what does that mean?

I know I cannot leave, I know I will not leave. His hand feels waxen and his fingernails are without colour. I keep stroking his palm the way he used to like it and I'm saying my long goodbye, because I know in my heart that's what this is.

I also know that I've made my peace with him, as much as I'm able to. I know he's hurt me beyond hurt, but many men have affairs. Many men, and lots of women too stray once or more in their lifetimes, and it's a hard thing to forgive and even harder to forget. In fact, I don't think you ever forget it altogether. But no one deserves this; no one deserves this ultimate punishment.... And for what? A night of passion? A chance encounter? A hop in the sack? Call it what you want. No one should have to pay with his life and the life of his wife and sometimes even his children's lives for that.

All of these things go through my head as I caress his hand, fully aware that it doesn't matter to him, that he doesn't even know I'm here. But it matters to me. To be here matters to me. And I spend the longest night of my life knowing I have to make a decision in the morning, the most agonizing decision that anyone can be asked to make.

So here I sit. I'm stroking the hand that doesn't feel anything anymore and here, right here and now, I swear to God that I will fight as hard as I can. I will not give in to this disease. I'll see my kids grow up. They will not see me like this, a bloated, useless piece of humanity; unrecognizable, ugly, helpless like a beached whale. No, they will not see me like this. Whatever way I can find, whatever it takes, I'll do it and I will let nothing and no one stand in my way.

You gave up too soon, Mark. You didn't even fucking try and all because of what? What you thought others might think. What the fuck does that matter? You'd rather be dead?

I mustn't get angry. That's the easy way out, and anyway, it doesn't change anything. If only he'd confided in me, if only he'd... whatever.... But he didn't and so here we are, or rather here I am, trying to figure out what the hell happened to my life, his life, our life together.

Even the longest night comes to an end and I can't be sure that I didn't fall asleep for a bit. Eventually greyish light filters into the room. The doctor comes in to check on Mark which, in essence, is just a formality because nothing has changed and he just lies there like a lump, without any sign of life, bar some laboured breathing, thanks to the machine he is hooked up to.

"Have you made your decision, Stephanie?" he asks, after shooting a few furtive glances my way.

"What kind of decision do you think I could possibly make? What kind of fucking choice do you think I have?"

I know I am getting hysterical and I know he knows why. And he doesn't even try to say something asinine like, calm down or something to that effect and I am thankful to him for that.

"Is there somewhere I can freshen up a bit?" I ask by way of apology.

"Sure," he puts his hand on mine and squeezes it slightly. "Go down to the end of the hall and make a right. There's the nurse's private bathroom. You'll find everything you need."

I look at him questioningly.

"Don't worry," he says, as if reading my mind. "I'll stay with him until you're back. And get a cup of coffee while you're at it, ok?"

I nod and stumble out the door and walk along the corridor. I find the nurse's bathroom. It is empty.

I run hot water over my hands and wash my face. My skin feels dry and tense. My eyes look back at me, the eyes of a stranger. Huge, tired, frightened, exhausted. The hot water helps a bit. I fish in my purse for a brush and run it through my hair. My head is pounding. Slowly I make my way to the cafeteria and sit down with a cup of coffee and a muffin.

I don't feel like eating, but I know that I have to. The muffin is hot and steamy, buttery, the way Mark likes to eat them. With tears running down my face, I bite into it and, to my surprise, I finish the whole thing and I actually feel a bit calmer.

I know what I have to do. I know what is facing me and I don't want to go back into that room, not yet, not right away, not ever. I get myself a second cup of coffee, light a cigarette, and inhale deeply. It feels good; it feels damned good to be honest. It feels so good, I have another. But I know what I'm doing; I am stalling. It's almost as if I can see myself from the outside in, sitting there, smoking, stalling for time.

I look up at the clock on the wall and wonder why hospital clocks are so damned ugly; white, with great big black numerals on them and a second hand that jumps in tiny little increments that suck the life out of you. You find such clocks anywhere people are facing some sort of deadline, at airports or bus stations. Functional, nothing else. Telling you what to do. Do this - not that. Go - don't stay. Die - don't live. It is one of the ugliest things I have ever seen and I want to smash it so that I'll never have to look at it again.

I stub out my cigarette, fish for some gum, and go back to the room. The room. The room with death in it. The room where I will be the one to pronounce the death sentence.

Dr. Moore has left. I have probably taken too long to return, but a nurse is standing at the window and turns round when she hears the door open.

"Dr. Moore had to see to a patient but he'll be back in a minute," she assures me. And, as if on cue, he walks through the door.

"What do I do?" I ask, wishing with all my heart that I could have a cigarette, a drink, anything to get me through this.

"You'll have to sign these forms authorizing us to turn off the life support," he replies, in a matter of fact voice.

"By law, only a wife or other close family member is authorized to do this. But, as you know, Stephanie, there is no hope. Absolutely and positively none. Mark could remain in this condition for an hour, a day, or even weeks. No one knows for sure. The only thing we're certain of is that he won't ever get better."

"Ok, ok, I understand. I'll do it. I'll do it for him."

Dr. Moore hands me the form, which is attached to a clipboard such as you get at a garage when you take in your car. Yes, fix my brakes, change the oil, whatever. Call me and let me know when it's ready.

I feel dizzy and grope for a chair. The nurse hands me a pen and my hand shakes so bad, I have to take a few deep breaths before I hastily scribble my name. It is the hardest, physically the hardest thing I have ever done in my life. Putting my name to that form is killing me inside, but I do it. I do it. I have officially ended a life. Mark's life. My husband's life. I feel terror bubbling up inside and have to bite my lip hard to keep from screaming.

Then, suddenly, I feel a deep calm, warmth, almost like a presence in the room. And it's not coming from the bed where Mark's body lies motionless. It feels as if he is here. Here with me in this room, telling me it is ok, everything is ok. I don't know what happens next. Someone gives me coffee and I can smell the brandy in it and I take a great big gulp and it explodes in my head.

I don't remember how I get home. I fall onto my bed and I pass out with all my clothes on and someone is covering me with a blanket and I welcome the blackness and silence that follows.

Chapter 15

Almost every time you see a funeral in the movies, it's a grey, rainy day, with lots of people carrying huge black umbrellas, as if to punctuate the sadness of it all.

Mark's funeral is not like that. It's a brilliant fall day with the red and yellow leaves dancing in the bright sunlight and the air so crisp and clean it makes you dizzy when you take a deep breath. It's the kind of day that he had loved so much. A day for golf or fishing. Coming home with his catch, all proud. Cheeks rosy from the cold. Eyes sparkling with the joy of life. That's the kind of day it is.

Mark would have liked this day, better than any other. He would not have liked rain and dark and grey. It's almost a happy day. A happy day filled with terrible, gnawing pain.

There are hundreds of people here, it seems. I don't even know where they all have come from. Most of them I know, some I don't. Mark's parents stand next to me and have the children between them and hold on to their hands. And Antonia is still here with me. Without Ken, who is overseas. She stands really close and holds my hand and I squeeze hers so hard it hurts my ring finger. The ring cuts into my flesh. The ring I have never, ever taken off, not since the day we married.

And I stand here in that blinding sunlight and watch this horrible ceremony. A ceremony that doesn't give you any comfort, or faith, or anything at all. And I watch them lower the coffin into the big, gaping hole in the ground.

And I think what a barbaric ritual this is, this funeral, and I cannot figure out how people can take comfort in seeing someone being buried. Buried deep in the ground. And I think of Mark lying down there. By himself. And I totally lose it and cling to Antonia. And I feel a scream rise up inside of me but I cannot let that happen. I have to keep it together, I have to.

Adam and Bettina are huddling between their grandparents. And they have big, big eyes with no tears in them and they can't understand where their father has gone. And they look so empty. And my heart rips wide open when I look at them. I reach out and hold them, one in each arm.

"It's going to be ok, everything is going to be ok, you hear?"

"Yes, Mom, sure. Don't cry and if Dad is with the angels, we'll take care of you. Ok?" says Bettina in a voice so low, only I can hear her.

The wake is held in the best hotel in town, well, the only hotel in town, you can't count motels. Antonia has arranged it all. The best caterer, the best florist. So everything is perfect. There are lots and lots of candles and sweet smelling gardenias. And pictures of Mark, everywhere. Mark on the golf course; Mark sailing; Mark holding up a huge trout; Mark lying in a big pile of autumn leaves with the kids on top of him, Mark, Mark, Mark..

It's almost like a typical Irish wake kind of thing, you know? Even though none of us are Irish. Lots of drink, lots of tears, lots of laughter, lots of food and everybody gives a little speech. And everybody says what a great guy he was and how much they loved him and how they will miss him. And nobody once, not once, alludes to why he has died and what he has died of.

And I am glad about that I guess. And nobody shies away from me either, having the same disease and all. They don't shy away. They don't do that. People come over and hug and kiss me and try to comfort me with words, as much as they know how.

John is here too; our lawyer. He comes over to where I am standing in a corner of the room. He's holding a glass in his hand.

"We have to talk, Stephanie, we have to discuss certain things, important things."

"Not today," I said, "not today, please. No."

He looks at me with an odd expression, an expression that I don't really like. Not with compassion or understanding, not comforting. He just looks at me strangely.

"Stephanie, the sooner the better, come to my office tomorrow morning, no wait, I'll come to your house. Try to get some rest and I'll see you around eleven, ok? Is that good for you?"

"Eleven is good, see you then."

John arrives at the house at eleven sharp; he carries a big briefcase and sets it heavily on the floor. I pour a cup of coffee and he bends down and pulls out a file. He puts his hands on the file folder; fingers spread apart and looks at me over the top of his glasses.

"Stephanie", he takes a sip of coffee, as if to buy time. "Steph, I don't quite know how to start, I mean, what are you going to do now? You cannot work, you have the children."

I have to laugh.

"Work? Work? Why on earth would I work? We have a lot of.. I mean we're not rich by any stretch. But we're comfortable. I'm well looked after. Mark has told me that many times. If anything ever happens to me, he used to say, you and the kids will be ok, for the rest of your lives."

John shifts uneasily in his chair and takes off his glasses.

"Stephanie, Mark has made some very, very bad investments. Somebody must have told him about some surefire stocks and they bottomed out, totally. I tried to warn him, I told him not to put all his eggs into one basket. But he wouldn't listen. You know how he could get when he had made up his mind about something."

I nod and bite my lip.

"How bad is it?"

"There's nothing, Stephanie. Nothing. Pension funds, RSP's, shares, all gone and the house is rented, as you know. There's nothing for you to live on. Maybe a few thousand dollars in his savings account and whatever you have in your joint account. That's all."

If he had hit me in the stomach, it would probably feel about the same. I feel sick, I feel like throwing up. I take a big sip of coffee and keep the hot liquid in my mouth as long as I can. I need to feel pain. Sharp pain. Anything to take my mind off what I have just heard.

John still has his hands on the unopened folder. I guess it's just a prop for him, the folder is. He has tiny little beads of perspiration on his forehead and he looks out into the backyard. Doesn't want to look at me, I guess lawyers too have feelings. This is not the kind of news you want to give to anyone.

"I'll waive my fees, of course, but that won't make much of a difference."

I swallow.

"Thank you John, I'm grateful for that. I guess it's just another thing I have to deal with now. I want to be alone, if you don't mind. I have to think, right now I'm just stunned, totally stunned."

"Sure, I understand. I'll call you tomorrow. There are a few formalities we have to take care of and then I can give you a clear picture of what we're looking at, the bottom line. And we'll see what we can do, for you and for the children. You have no money of your own?"

"Money of my own? Well yes, my mother had life insurance and left me her savings. But Mark took care of all that; he said he had a financial advisor and that the money would work for us. I have never worked. Well, I worked for a while, part time, after school, before I got married. But in any event, I could not have worked in the States; I would have had to get a green card or whatever. And there was no need to. I mean Mark had a fabulous job, he was partner in the firm, and I was content to stay at home. Loved it, in fact. And I can't work now, I can't. I have to spend time with my children. I don't know how long I'll be well enough to do that."

John nods. He removes his glasses and polishes them with a crisp white handkerchief he's pulled out of the pocket of his blazer. He pushes the file folder across the table.

"Well, all the documents you need are in here, Stephanie, you can look them over but, as I said, there's no money left. This will just give you a paper trail of where it went. I'm sorry, Steph, I truly am."

And with that he gets up and heads out the door.

The children are out with Max. He's picked them up in the morning; they're going into Richmond to spend the day at the zoo.

"Hannah has locked herself in her bedroom," Max had explained. "She won't come out; she won't talk to me or anyone else. I'll just have to leave her to deal with her grief. I had to get out of the house, see my grandkids and take them into the city for the day."

Which is good, because right now I have to figure out.. I don't know what I have to figure out. I still have bills to pay. The caterer alone is a couple of thousand dollars.

I have my own little bank account, of course. Mark has given me money for this and that and I've spent some and put some away and never given it a second thought. So yeah, I have some money there, but it isn't much.

There's only one thing to do. I am Canadian; I have to go back to Canada. I have to go back to the only family I have, Aunt Sissy, and perhaps I can get some assistance there with medical bills, whatever.

That's what I'll have to do. It is ironic that the thing Mark feared most, to have to leave the United States, is now a thing I have to consider. It's the only way out for me. And in my mind and in my heart I am angry. I am fucking furious at him for not telling me, for not letting me in on such important matters.

Mark has always been prudent with money, at least so far as I knew. Somebody he trusted must have told him about this surefire thing and it must have happened way before all this drama started in our lives. Maybe that's why he was so unhappy, maybe he knew I would be destitute when he was gone and he couldn't handle that. Couldn't talk about it or make some sort of plans. He chose to ignore it but it must have weighed on him just the same. And it probably speeded up the course of the illness.

The next few days are a blur. I talk to my in-laws. They, of course, want me to move in with them. But even though their house is big, it could never be big enough for me to live with them.

Not with Hannah's accusing looks all the time as if I had killed her son. As if it is my fault that he has gone elsewhere, slept with another woman. Because he was not happy at home.

Max will never think that. He understands why. He knows that men stray and that they don't necessarily love the woman, or women, they have affairs with. Hannah does not understand that. All she knows is that Mark wasn't happy at home so he went elsewhere and got AIDS and now he is dead. Her son is dead. I know that will haunt me. If I stay in their house, I will have to live with that every single day.

In the afternoon, Max brings Adam and Bettina home and I take them out into the backyard.

"You know, your Dad is gone and you mustn't be unhappy about that because he will be in your heart. Always and forever. And we'll always think about the good things he did. Remember when we were on vacation? We went to the beach and he took you fishing and he helped you look for beautiful shells and stones. He was a good, good dad. But he got really, really sick and now he's gone and we have to see how we can deal with that."

Neither of them says anything. Just look up at me as if I have all the answers.

"You two and I, we will go on a trip. We'll go up to Canada and visit my Aunt Sissy. And maybe we'll live there, won't that be nice?'"

"Can our friends come?" Bettina asks.

"Nobody can come, only the cat. But we will come back to visit. We'll come back and visit Grandma and Grandpa lots of times and then you'll see your friends again. And you'll make lots of friends up there too, you'll see. And you know the best part?"

They look at me. Their faces red; their eyes big and innocent.

"There's a best part?"

"Yes there is, Antonia lives up there, really close to where we're going."

Their eyes light up. "Oh yes, Antonia, we love her."

I take their little hands in mine and we go for a walk down the lane. And I feel shattered inside; shattered and empty. But I have them. And for them I have to be strong, as strong as I can be; and do the best I can possibly do.

And I swear to myself. I will not let these little children grow up as orphans. I will fight with whatever it takes and whatever I have to do, I will do. To be with them. To watch over them. To see them grow up.

I will not let the companion triumph.

Not yet. Not for a long, long time.

Chapter 16

And again, it is morning. A cold, damp morning. Not a ray of sunshine. There is no cheer in this morning only a sense of dread and hopelessness.

I am drained of energy but ready to do something. Max has picked up the children and taken them to school. He's going to pick them up again later and take them to the park or a movie.

Max has taken a few days off work to help me out. He is shocked when I tell him about my situation and I can see in his eyes that it pains him that he cannot help me, financially that is. But he is helping in every other way he knows how, with his love and support. With his love for his grandchildren and his love for me. And I am grateful for that.

I sit at the kitchen table, light a cigarette and sip my coffee. I have a big block of paper in front of me and I start to evaluate my situation. And my situation does not look good. Not good at all. A couple of thousand in my own bank account. Mark has left a few thousand in our joint account, but there are bills to pay. Not many, mind you. The big one is going to be for the caterer. If I had only known. Never mind. What's done is done. Deal with it. I will simply have to sell everything we don't absolutely need, load up the rest, and go home.

Last night I was on the phone with Aunt Sissy for what felt like forever.

"You know you can stay with me until you find your own place," she suggested. "It will have to do for a while; I'll help as much as I can. You know, I'm happy you're coming home but I didn't want for you to come home under these circumstances. You know that, don't you? And you know that I love you and the kids and I'll be here for you. I wish I could do more, I wish I could.." She stops and I know she's crying.

"Please Aunt Sissy, don't. Don't cry. I have done all the crying for all of us together."

So here I sit with my block of paper trying to map out my life. What it will be like. Without Mark. Without my house that I love so much. Without money and without any kind of future.

And even though it's still early in the morning, I get up and pour a good shot of Cognac into my coffee. And I take a big sip and I feel the hot liquid burning down my throat and it makes me feel better.

And I think, never mind all that. I will simply have to find a way. And I will find a way. So I write down everything I have. All the assets. My jewelry, everything will have to go. It doesn't matter. The only thing I will keep, of course, is my wedding ring. But all the other stuff Mark has bought me over the years, I will simply sell it.

There is a knock on the door and Antonia comes in before I can get up. She takes one look at me.

"Let me have a cigarette too," she says.

"But you don't smoke."

"Yeah, I know, but I feel like trying one right now."

So she lights a cigarette and I can see she doesn't know what to do with it. But she puffs away bravely just the same. Just to keep me company.

"Ok, Steph. What are we going to do? How can I help?"

"Toni, it's worse than I could ever have imagined. Far worse. I have no money, I have nothing."

"But Mark had such a great job. I mean surely you must have.."

"Look, I don't want to go into details, but apparently he's made some bad choices, some very bad choices and, of course, without telling me and.. Well, it is what it is and I have to do what I have to do. I'll sell what I don't need, starting with my jewelry. But one thing will make you happy, I'm moving back to Canada."

She lets out a little yelp like a puppy and jumps up to hug me.

"That makes me very, very, very happy. At least that way I can keep an eye on you. I can't think of what else I can do. I'd offer you money but I know you won't take it."

I take one long look at her and shake my head, but I have a lump in my throat. Antonia stubs out the cigarette she isn't smoking anyway.

"Ok, let's see what we can do. You need your car. You need your clothes, and you need your furniture. I'll arrange to have it shipped up to Canada through a friend. He has a moving company and he'll do it for peanuts, ok? That leaves your jewelry. I know a good jeweller over on Derry Road. He'll give you a fair price for it. I'll take you over there, ok? Let's do it straight away, I'll call ahead to make sure he's at the store."

"Yes, thanks, I know there's no other way and.. Well, they're only things, so.."

She walks into the hallway to make her call and I go upstairs and I bundle up my jewelry.

We don't talk on the drive to Derry Road, not a word. Antonia concentrates on the road and I clutch my little bundle of memories. And I try not to think about where each piece has come from when I finally empty the shimmering contents onto the jeweller's counter.

He is a short man. Well groomed, with a cosmopolitan air about him. He wears a black suit and tie, almost like an undertaker, and his hands are tiny with manicured nails.

He bends over the counter and scrutinizes each piece carefully. The emerald ring Mark gave me when the twins were born.. My grandmother's engagement ring that Mom had kept all those years.. I bite my lip hard and force back the tears. They are only things.. Only things.. Inanimate things. You can't buy groceries with things.. Don't be a sentimental idiot, I tell myself.

"I can offer you fifteen thousand dollars for everything," the little man finally says, straightening up and moving the pieces around the counter top with his little finger.

"Fifteen thousand? But surely, they're not worth that much."

I glance at Antonia who looks on impartially, bored even. When she catches my eye she bends down and studies a pearl necklace, shimmering softly in the showcase.

"Fifteen thousand even. I'm afraid that's all I can pay. I'll give you a cheque right now if you're in agreement."

I nod, dumbfounded. The little man goes to the back of his store and returns with a piece of paper and a cheque.

"Please sign here," he says. "That will make it legal."

I sign the bill of sale he has made up and put the cheque into my handbag.

"Oh, and I have no need for this."

He pushes Grandma's ring back across the glass topped counter.

"People aren't interested in old pieces like that. The diamond is of really good quality, but it would be a shame to take the ring apart for its stone."

I look at him, stunned.

"Thank you. Thank you very much."

"Not at all. And good luck."

"Why did you say that? Good luck?"

He hesitates for a moment and studies his manicured nails.

"Well, nobody sells their personal things, especially jewellery, unless they have a reason and most of the time the reasons are sad ones. So, I'm wishing you luck, with your life. With your future."

"Thank you, I appreciate that."

"You had something to do with this, didn't you?" I say to Antonia as she starts the car.

"To do with what?"

"You know perfectly well with what. The money, the money the guy gave me for my stuff. I know it's not worth that much."

"Stephanie, Marcel is an expert in his field. If he says it's worth that much, then it's worth that much, ok? I had absolutely nothing to do with that, believe me."

"Ok, I believe you but….."

"No buts, let's just say every little bit helps, ok?"

She turns her attention to the road and drives back to my house.

"You know Steph, I hate to leave you now, I really do. But Ken's due back from Europe this weekend and.."

"Of course you must go home, don't even think about it. Your coming down here and staying as long as you have, has helped me more than you'll ever imagine. Heaven knows, I needed a friend by my side to help me through this ordeal. And anyway, there are things I must do immediately and the first thing is to go back to the clinic and have a complete evaluation so I have an idea what I'm dealing with. And I'm having the children tested at the same time."

"Good girl," she hugs me, "perhaps if Mark had done that a long time ago, he might.." her voice trails off and she bites her lip as if she's said too much.

"I've thought the same thing myself," I assure her, "many times, but it doesn't change anything, but I won't give up; at least not without all the fight I have in me."

Antonia leaves at night and I feel utterly alone. The kids are still with their grandparents. The house is filled with an eerie stillness, as if no one is living in it any longer. Well, no sense in wallowing. I'll deal with it later. Later I will mourn my loss. Later I'll cry over my ruined life. Not now. Now there are things I have to do.

I light a cigarette; it's only my third one today. And I march upstairs, armed with a dozen or so big black garbage bags.

Without stopping to think, without looking at every item and reminiscing, I take all of Mark's clothes; suits, sweaters, underwear, socks, shoes, all of it, and stuff it into the bags. Someone will take it to the Salvation Army store later. At least that way it will come to good use.

The bags are lined up against the wall like so many dead bodies. Stop it! Forget it! Don't think in those terms! These are garbage bags, stuffed with clothes that are no longer needed. Nothing else. Just used clothes.

The bedroom looks barren. Totally barren. Open doors. Empty hangers like skeletons in the closet. Drawers pulled out. As if someone had left in a real hurry. And someone had. Left in a real hurry, not ever to come back. Stop it, just get on with it. Get on. Get on.

I drag the bags downstairs and line them up in the garage. Max will take them tomorrow.

It's almost eight o'clock when I'm finished. The phone rings shrilly through the house.

"Stephanie, why don't you come over for dinner?" Max's voice. "The children are asking for you. They are getting quite restless."

"Yes, of course, I'll come. Give me fifteen minutes, ok?"

Hannah has cooked chicken a la king, which she knows I like and I am touched by that. Imagine her cooking something just for me. I haven't eaten all day and suddenly realize how hungry I am. I finish a whole plate, more than I have eaten in days, and I have a glass of wine with it.

"I think you should stay here tonight, Stephanie," Max says. "The children are tired, being outside all day. I don't think you should stay in your house all alone and.." he doesn't quite know how to finish his sentence and drags on his pipe and stares at the ceiling.

"Sure. Ok. We can all sleep in the same bed, Bettina, Adam and I. Won't that be fun?"

Both kids have a big smile on their faces and rush upstairs to take their bath and get into their pyjamas. I tuck them into the queen-sized bed in the guest room and take one of the fairy tale books off the shelf.

"Read Hansel and Gretel," Bettina begs.

"No, something with dragons in it," comes Adam's voice. "Something scary."

"I don't want scary."

"Why don't we read a new story, one you've never heard before?" and they both nod in agreement. Their faces are shining, scrubbed clean, and their hair is damp from their bath. And it breaks my heart seeing them so eager to hear a story. With their dad all alone. Deep in the ground. Gone.

'Shut up,' I tell myself. 'Just get on with it.'

I open the book and start reading the story of Rumpelstiltskin who had magic powers and could spin straw into gold and in the end that didn't do him any good at all.

The kids only half listen. They start dozing off. I stroke their foreheads and kiss them softly on the cheek.

"Can you leave the light on 'til you come back, Mommy?" Bettina whispers as I am about to leave the room. And I turn on the nightlight and make my way downstairs.

Hannah is washing the dishes. I grab a towel.

"Never mind, Stephanie, I'll do it myself", she says without looking at me.

"But I don't mind, it keeps me from thinking".

"From thinking what?" she suddenly turns around, holding a wet plate in her hand.."From thinking what? From thinking that my son is dead, dead and buried in the ground?"

I'm so shocked, so startled by her outburst; I don't know what to say.

"Oh yes, you just keep yourself from thinking. You killed my son and you know it!" her voice has raised to a shrill pitch, to an uncontrolled screaming.

"Hannah!" Max calls out sharply, "stop that right now. You don't know what you're saying."

"Oh yes I do," her voice is calmer now, calm, icy and calculated. She's still holding the plate. "Oh yes I do. I know perfectly well what I'm saying. Without her my son would not have had the need to stray, look for companionship elsewhere. If he had been happy at home.."

"That's enough, Hannah, you take that back." Max's gets up from his chair, his mouth is set in a grim line, "you have no right to talk to Stephanie like that, no right whatsoever. It's not her fault. Mark was just that type of guy, I'm sorry to say."

"Then be sorry. I know my son. I know my son better than anyone else knows him. And I know he was a good man, who would never.." Her voice becomes a whisper as she stares at me malevolently ... "you and you alone are responsible for his death. And you and you alone must live with that."

Hannah turns around and throws the plate into the sink. It shatters into a thousand pieces. She stomps out of the room, banging the door behind her.

I am paralyzed.. I'm numb.. Cannot believe what she's said, what she's thinking.. Oh my God, how could she? Even if she hates me there's no reason to.. But all I can think is, I hope the kids didn't wake up, didn't hear the commotion, aren't scared..

I run upstairs and quietly open the door to the bedroom. They're fast asleep, both of them. Thank God for that.

For the longest time I sit on the floor outside their room, trying to digest what Hannah has said, trying to get over the shock of seeing that hatred in her eyes, of hearing those acid words dripping from her tongue.

I've always known that she was not overly fond of me, hell, I guess she wouldn't be fond of any female that took her place in her son's life, or so she imagined. But I tried to make the best of it, for Mark's and the children's sake. Well, I guess my best wasn't good enough and I'll just have to get over it. Heaven knows, I have more important things to deal with now and somewhere deep inside, I feel a little sorry for her. Just a little.

I get up and slowly make my way back downstairs. I find Max on the porch, sitting on the swing.

"Come sit with me.." he pats the seat beside him. "Hannah's locked herself in the bedroom. I'm so very sorry about her outburst but there's no talking to her right now. You know that she didn't mean what she said but that's not an excuse."

I lean my head against his shoulder and he puts his arm 'round mine.

Max is drawing on his pipe and staring up at the starlit sky as if looking for answers.

For the longest time we sit like that, neither of us saying anything. Just looking at the stars.

Both hurting and wondering about it all.

Chapter 17

The jarring ring of the phone wakes me at 9 a.m. I didn't think I'd be able to sleep but sometime during that long empty night, I must have drifted off.

"Stephanie? It's Andrew."

Mark's partner. What could he possible want from me?

"Hope I didn't wake you? You sound tired."

I swing my legs onto the floor and grope for my slippers.

"What can I do for you, Andrew?"

"Well, we need you to come into the city to clear out Mark's office, his desk, take home his personal belongings, his laptop, you know?"

"Yes, of course. I have an appointment at the hospital on Thursday, I can come by once I'm finished there, around noon, I think."

"Very good, Stephanie, and .. I'm so sorry about all that has happened."

"It's ok Andrew, thank you. See you Thursday."

I put down the phone and make my way downstairs. My God, is there no end to this? Do I really have to go and do that? Well, I guess I don't have an option. Someone has to get Mark's stuff, whatever that might be.

I call Max. He answers on the second ring.

"Hi Max, you know that I have that appointment at the clinic on Thursday to have the children tested for the HIV virus and Andrew just called, he wants me to stop by the office and clear out Mark's desk. I don't know why they can't do that themselves but perhaps it's procedure, in case he has some personal stuff, I don't know. And

I was hoping that you or Hannah can come with me and stay with the kids..."

"Hannah's gone, but of course I'll come with you honey, you don't have to ask..."

"Gone? Hannah? But where.."

"She's gone to stay with her sister in Texas for a while. I don't know for how long and to be honest with you, I'm not upset about it. Life with her has been unbearable since, well you know, since Mark.."

"Yes, Max, I understand. I'm so very sorry.."

"Don't be. I'm ok, it's best if I'm by myself and try to sort things out in my head. Hannah hadn't talked to me in days, didn't want me to help her, didn't even want me to be near her.. Well, everyone chooses how they want to grieve. I prefer to think of the good times and all the joy my son has brought me, but she.. Oh well, as I said, everyone makes their own decisions. I'll see you Thursday morning then, around nine, is that ok?"

"Yes, Max, that works just fine. Love you."

"Love you too, take care of yourself."

On our way to Richmond I tell the children that they need to have tests and maybe even a needle or so before we can go to Canada. I mumble something about immigration laws and that I too will have to have shots and maybe even the cat.

"Will it hurt?" asks Adam.

"Don't be a baby, Adam," Bettina looks at him sternly. "Needles don't hurt, it's only a little prick and over before you even feel it."

I know she's trying to be brave for both of them because she is just as afraid of needles as Adam is.

I wait until they're taken into the lab before I leave for Mark's office. Max will be there in case they're done before I return.

Luckily, the hospital is only a ten minute drive from the office building and I arrive at Mark's office just after noon.

"Park in Mark's spot", Andrew had said, "it's still vacant".

And I think how ironic that sounds. Yeah, vacant, as vacant as my life without him.. Shut up, Steph, just shut up. All this talk in your head doesn't do any good and will just make you crazy. But driving into the underground at the office tower gives me a creepy feeling. Mark has driven down this ramp countless times, countless! I find his spot which is close to the elevator and lock the car.

Twenty six floors up the door glides open silently and I enter the posh foyer of Mark's firm. The receptionist is new; I've never seen her before.

"Good afternoon, I'm Stephanie. Stephanie Saunders, Mark's wife. I've come .."

"Oh, good afternoon," she stretches out her hand, "I'm Pamela, Andrew told me to expect you. Please follow me."

She gets up and leads me down a long carpeted corridor. I swear she's wearing the shortest tightest skirt I've ever seen, barely covering her butt and she has legs up to there. But she's pleasant, sweet and pleasant.

"I never knew your husband," she volunteers as we're walking along, "but everyone speaks so highly of him. I'm so sorry.."

She doesn't know how to finish that sentence.

"It's ok. No need to say anything."

She pushes open the door to Mark's office; Andrew is sitting behind the desk, expecting me, I think.

He walks round the desk and gives me a quick hug.

"Thanks for coming, Stephanie; I'll leave you alone to go through Mark's things."

I fall into the huge leather chair and swivel around. What a grand office this is, I think, elegant yet masculine, all glass and leather and floor to ceiling windows with a view as far as forever. You can see the entire city from here.. All the landmarks.. The river.. The parks.. The office towers.. No wonder Mark loved it so much.

I turn 'round, and put my hands flat on the desk. I don't want to be here, I don't want to go through his stuff.. A picture of me and the twins is sitting next to the computer.. A happy picture, kids smiling, me smiling.. Nothing to smile about now.

I turn the picture upside down and slowly open the desk drawer. Papers, folders, all sorts of stuff that I don't really want to look at, stuff that has nothing to do with me.

There's a knock on the door. Irene walks in carrying a couple of banker's boxes. I know her of course, she was Mark's personal assistant .. executive assistant, that is. A pretty young thing, to be sure, pretty in an unusual way. Long wavy dark hair, greenish blue eyes that now have tears in them. She's upset.. Of course, why wouldn't she be? She's been with Mark from day one, from the first day he entered this building.

"Hi Irene," I greet her, "thanks for bringing the boxes, let's get this over with as quickly as possible. Perhaps you can help?"

She takes a couple of steps back. Hesitates.

"I was going to get a head start on it," she volunteers, "but Andrew wouldn't let me. Mark's office has been locked since.. since.. Well, you know."

"Since he died," I finish her sentence, "Yes, I expected that."

"I want you to know how very sorry I am," she says in a low voice, "Mark was very special, very, very special. And he loved you, you must know that."

What a strange thing to say, I think, strange and a bit cheeky coming from his assistant.

"Well, thank you Irene," my voice is clipped, I can hear it, but I don't feel like discussing the love or non-love of my husband with her. "Shall we get started?"

She opens the bottom left hand drawer, pulls out a couple of file folders and a day timer and sticks them into the box.

"Wait a minute," I stop her, "let's just have a look at these documents before we stow them away, shall we?"

Irene seems flustered. She quickly takes out the day timer. "This is last year's". She mutters, "There's nothing relevant in here that we should be keeping."

"Please, let me be the judge of that," I hold out my hand. She has no choice, she hands me the book and I leaf through it quickly. It is indeed last year's and the entries, so far as I can glean, are of meetings, appointments, client lunches.. Lunch with I? Lunch with I again? Meet I at 6 pm. Quite a few entries with "I".

I look up. Her face is ashen.

"Judging by your reaction, I assume that the "I" stands for Irene?" I ask calmly, very calmly.

"Yes," she whispers, "yes, Mark and I.. I and Mark.. Well we.. We had been seeing each other.. and.." She stops.

"Seeing each other? Is that what they call it now? Seeing each other?"

My voice turns to ice. I feel mean and vindictive. I want to hurt her, slap her, scream at her. Kill her!!

She's picked up the book that I had tossed onto the desk and is holding it to her chest as if for protection.

"I'm sorry," now she's shaking, "I'm so sorry but I thought you knew. Mark always told me that you have an open marriage. That you don't mind him seeing someone else.. That you were free to do what you wanted too.."

I'm speechless. All I can do is stare at her, but I don't feel sorry for her, not one little bit. Only rage, anger, hatred.. But why am I so surprised?

"It's ok, Irene," I say in the calmest tone I can muster. "It's ok. You're not the only one, believe me, there have been others. Many, many others. Probably at the same time he was, shall we say, .. seeing you?..... He was seeing other women as well, many other women."

Irene has regained her composure.

"I don't believe you."

She all but spits at me.

"I don't believe a single word. Mark loved me. It was not just the sex. He really loved me."

"Yeah, yeah, the way he loved anything in a skirt."

I can't help myself. I want to lash out, make her hurt as much as I'm hurting.

Andrew sticks his head through the door.

"Everything ok? I sent Irene because she knows where everything is, better than anyone else, I venture to say."

"Thanks, Andrew, I'm sure she does. Better than anyone."

He closes the door behind him and I throw a couple of things into the second box. Our picture, Mark's laptop, a little Lalique crystal kitten I had given him for good luck when he first got the position because it reminded me of Sapphire.

"You can go through the rest of the stuff," I say over my shoulder to Irene who stands frozen to the spot.

"I won't need any of it nor do I want to know about it."

She fills up another box with mostly file folders. I can see tears rolling down her cheeks but I don't feel pity. No pity at all.

"I guess I'm done here," I finally say when all the drawers are gaping open, emptied of their content.

"Oh, and by the way, during all the intimate conversations you and my husband had, did he also tell you that he had AIDS? That's what he died of, you know, complications from AIDS."

It's my turn to spit the words at her.

Irene drops a couple of file folders. The contents scatter all over the carpet. Her hand flies to her mouth, her eyes are ripped wide open in terror. No sound comes out of her only an uneven gasp like a deflating balloon. Then she starts shaking and fumbles for a chair to hold on to.

And still I feel no compassion. Still my anger and hatred are hot in my body. And I can't help but deliver the final blow. And I say to her, as slowly and as sweetly as I can:

"Don't worry, Irene.. You'll probably be ok. In any event, don't worry just yet. It takes about four years for the virus to incubate, sometimes longer."

She's put her head on the desk. Her shoulders are shaking with uncontrollable sobs. Little pools of tears appear on the mahogany desk top. I stand and watch without pity.

She lifts her head to look at me. She's no longer pretty. Her nose is running, her skin blotchy, her mascara all over the place.

I don't care. Sob all you like. Maybe next time you'll think twice before you screw around with somebody's husband.

I grab my box and leave the office without another look at Irene. Andrew meets me in the hallway and gives me a quick hug.

"Don't be a stranger," he says.

"No, I won't. Oh, and you better look in on Irene. I don't think she's feeling that great."

I step into the elevator and catch a last glimpse of his astonished face.

The doors slide shut.

I'm done here.

BOOK III

Chapter 18

It has been forever since we left Virginia. Forever since the moving van pulled away from the empty house. The house I had loved so much, the house in which we'd all been happy when life was good. How naïve I had been and how trusting. Believing that things would always stay the same, believing that Mark would love me as deeply as I loved him, always and forever.

And all the love and all the pain and all the betrayal that has happened in the past few years will be etched in my mind for the rest of my days.

So this day was just another piece in the mosaic of my life. The day I left Virginia. The day I left Coriander Drive.. The corner bank... The Piggly Wiggly... The bowling alley. The old pub where they'll all gather and wonder what has happened to the folks from Canada.

Surprisingly, Melanie had come over the night before we left, not quite knowing what to say, but not wanting me to leave without saying goodbye, I guess. She sat with me in the empty kitchen with only a couple of stools left at the counter.

And I thought back to the day when we had moved in... The rain... The umbrella... The cinnamon rolls... And Mel hoisting herself up on the stool, her legs reaching only half way to the floor.

"You know Stephanie, I'll miss you more than I can say," she said between sips of coffee, "and I'm so sorry I haven't been around to help you when Mark died, but with your ... sickness..."

"The AIDS, you mean the AIDS, Mel, don't you?"

"Yes, of course, the AIDS. I don't know anything about that,

Stephanie, and I was scared, and I think Peter was even more scared than I was and that's why he didn't want me to, you know..."

"It's ok, I understand, I would have been scared too before... "

I looked out the dark window and saw only our reflections in the glass and nothing but blackness beyond.

"If I ever come to Canada, I'll visit; you know that, don't you?"

"Yes, of course, I know that... If you ever come to Canada."

And that was the last time I saw Melanie.

By now it was late fall. All the leaves had turned crimson and gold and every shade in between; a riot of colour, they were dancing brightly in the sunlight. But there was already a hint of frost in the air. It was just the kind of day Mark had loved; we both had loved.

And when I started the car and slowly pulled away from the curb, I took one last look at the house. And a little piece of my heart stayed behind.

But I had the children. They looked up at me with serious faces. Their whole little world had collapsed and they had only me now. But for how long? There was no sense thinking about that.

So here we are. Back in Canada, staying at Aunt Sissy's small apartment, with my furniture in storage. The kids and I have to sleep in the living room on the pullout couch. But it's ok for now, cramped, but cozy.

The first thing I do, of course, is try to find a doctor. God knows, I need all the help I can get to fight this disease, to hold on as long as I possibly can.

It's strange, the one thing Mark had been so afraid of, the one thing he had dreaded more than the AIDS itself, was the fear that people would shun us. Treat us like lepers. And that one thing he feared the most has not happened.

The few friends we had before we moved to Virginia were shocked. Stunned in fact. But they didn't shy away from me.... I am amazed at that. Amazed and grateful for all the love I receive.

And it seems that people are a little more informed here. Or perhaps it just appears that way because I'm back in a big city now.

I call the AIDS helpline and they put me in touch with a doctor who, apparently, is a leading capacity in infectious diseases.

Dr. Sanford's office is all the way in downtown Toronto, so it's not that easy to get to. I have to take a bus and the subway. It takes over an hour to get there. It would have been easier if I still had the car but as soon as we got back to Canada, I had sold it. It was hard; I had really loved that car, almost as much as Mark had loved it. But I could not even afford to pay the insurance, never mind the regular upkeep. I did get a good price for it though and I've put the money straight into the bank. So, along with what I got for my jewelry, there's a tiny bit of a cushion for the children in case something happens to me.

I like Doctor Sanford the minute he opens the door and kind of flies into his office where I'm waiting. He doesn't wear a lab coat and his shirt is rumpled and unbuttoned and has a stain on it. His dark hair is all over the place because he has this habit of running his fingers through it. He has a nice smile, friendly and warm and he speaks with a faint Irish accent.

He leans over and shakes my hand. His hands are big and warm with short stubby fingers and his grip is firm.

"Stephanie, good to meet you, even if the circumstances are not. So you have AIDS... damn shame. Care to tell me how it happened? Not that it really matters, so you don't have to."

"No, it's ok. I got it from my husband... he died a couple of months ago. Where he picked it up I don't know."

"Right. Ok, let's take a look at you. Let's see what we can do. You're a fighter, I like that. It helps, believe me. We'll have to do a thorough assessment, all kinds of tests to see where you are, to see how far the AIDS has progressed. Some of these tests won't be too pleasant, I'll warn you now so there won't be any surprises, ok?"

He doesn't say: "You have two years to live". He doesn't say that.

And he says AIDS the same way one would say mumps or something. Not threatening, not pussyfooting around.

"The medication we have right now is a drug called azidothymidine, AZT for short. It doesn't cure or prevent AIDS, it's designed to slow down progress of the disease.

But there are new developments, very exciting developments. There is reason to hope, Stephanie, good reason. And I'll fight with you. So don't let me down. Ok?"

"Don't worry; I'll do whatever it takes. I don't want my kids to become orphans. Believe me, I don't want that."

And I leave his office with a glimmer of hope, a small glimmer mind you, but a glimmer nonetheless, and somehow the whole day looks brighter.

"I can't afford a goddamn thing in this city," I whine to Aunt Sissy when I get back from the doctor's office. "Look at the money they want for apartments, never mind houses. It's ridiculous."

I've scanned the newspaper ads for weeks now, trying to find a place to live with my children.

"You may have to ask for help," she answers in a low voice.

"Ask for help where? From whom?"

"You may have to go on welfare."

"What? Welfare? Me?" I yell at her.

It's not her fault but I yell at her anyway.

"Never! Never in my entire life will I go on welfare."

"Can you think of another option?" she continues quietly.

She is sitting on the couch, knitting something or other and does not look up from whatever she's doing.

"You can't work, not with your condition."

"It's called AIDS, Aunt Sissy, AIDS! It's not a condition."

I know I am hurting her but I can't help it. I am too scared. Scared shitless if you want to know. Then I feel like crying when I see her cringe at my words.

"Sorry Auntie, I'm sorry. Ok, if that's what it takes, I'll have to go and apply. I need treatments. My kids need a roof over their heads. I'll go on bloody fucking welfare."

She ignores the profanity.

"It's called social assistance now," she offers timidly. "It doesn't sound as bad, does it? And there's no shame in it. It's not your fault that this has happened to you. I wish there were something I could do but…"

"I know you would. It's ok, we'll find a way. Don't worry."

The woman at social services is anything but helpful. She is a mousy little thing, with a scrunched up face and a thin, reedy body. Her name is Muriel. Muriel Masterson. It says so on her name plate. A grand name for such a shriveled up slip of a woman.

"Don't you have any skills?" she asks. "You're young. You could work."

"No, I cannot. Listen, this is hard enough for me, don't make it any more difficult."

"I'm only doing my job". She bristles, "We have regulations, you know. And someone your age should be able to support themselves."

"I have AIDS."

"What?"

"I have AIDS. I cannot work. My husband died from complications due to AIDS and I don't know how long I'm going to be well enough to care for my children."

"But how did you get it?"

"I don't think that matters, does it? The fact is that I need assistance, for myself and for my children."

She looks as if she has shrunk even more into herself, shrunk into her tiny little body. She hands me a pen and a bunch of forms to fill out.

"We need documentation, of course. Doctors certificates, things like that."

"Of course."

I fill out the forms and hand back the pen. She looks at it as if it were poisoned.

"Don't worry; you can't catch it from a pen."

I am being sarcastic and at the same time I feel sorry for her. She can't help it. Being ignorant. I might have reacted the same way not so long ago.

"My immediate need is for shelter for myself and my children," I explain.

"There's a waiting list for assisted housing," she replies, "as long as a year or more."

"But I can't wait that long. I'm living at my aunt's apartment and it's awfully crowded. She is on a small pension and..."

"Sorry, we can only do what we can."

For the first time I feel that I am losing control. There is nothing I can do. Something else has taken over. Red tape. Bureaucracy. Government employees.

When I return home, Antonia is sitting in Aunt Sissy's kitchen having tea. Aunt Sissy loves Antonia, loved her from the minute they met.

"She's a wonderful person, a real Mensch," she said to me.

"Auntie, that's a Yiddish word, you're not Jewish, you're Polish..."

"I know, I know... But it's a good word, there really is no expression in English that says the same thing quite as well, is there?"

I laughed and had to agree.

As usual, Antonia looks like a million bucks. Pale blue cashmere sweater, navy pants, her titian hair pulled back with a few ringlets escaping 'round her beautiful face. She's munching on a huge Polish donut and has icing sugar on her chin.

"How did it go?" she asks with her mouth full.

"I don't know. I may have to wait up to a year to get a place."

"What?"

"That's what they told me. Up to a year. Maybe longer."

"But that's not acceptable. There are lots of people who actually could work, if they wanted to, people who are taking advantage of the system. And someone like you who is helpless, quite literally, is being treated the same as those people are?"

"Well, what can I do? Give me a cup of tea too, would you please, Aunt Sissy?"

"We will see what we can do. Let me make some calls. You know Steph, some of these cooperative apartments are actually quite nice. The newer ones, I mean. One of Ken's friends has a management company that looks after a couple of these buildings. If you could get into one of those, it may not be too bad."

"Yes, that would be nice Toni, but the way they talked to me today, I'm not overly optimistic."

I sip my tea… I am so tired… Tired and without hope.

"I think I'll lie down for a bit," I say to no one in particular.

But less than two weeks later the phone rings. It's social services.

"We think we've found a place for you," says a friendly voice at the other end. "We'd like you to come and take a look at it. There'll be more paperwork to fill out, of course, but nevertheless.."

I know, I just know, that Antonia has had something to do with this, even though she vehemently denies it.

"You were just lucky," she says when I call her with the news. "You were in the right place at the right time, that's all. I had nothing to do with that, how could I? Ok?"

"Yeah, whatever, but thanks all the same."

And that's how I ended up here. The building is clean and modern and without beauty. Strictly functional.

My apartment is also without beauty but I am allowed to paint it any way I like so long as I change it back to hospital white if and when I move out.

The first time I walk into the sterile hallway of the apartment, the house in Virginia pops into my mind. The dark oak floors, the tall trees all around, my kitchen. I check myself sharply. You're not in freaking Virginia, get over it. That was then, now is now. This will have to do. It's clean, it's affordable, and it's safe. And it's only a couple of blocks from Aunt Sissy's place so she can come over anytime and help with the children when I have to go for treatments.

"Wait until your stuff is in here," Antonia says. "It will look totally different and you'll feel more at home."

And she is right, of course. Newly painted and with my own furniture in it, the place doesn't look half bad. Antonia brings one huge plant and a few little ones as a housewarming present, which make the place look a lot friendlier.

"Why don't you and the children come to my house for dinner Friday," she says on the phone one night. "I'll pick you guys up around six o'clock. I want to talk to you about something."

"Something bad?"

"No, not something bad. Something that's been on my mind for a while."

"Can't you tell me on the phone?"

"I'd rather talk to you in person. Anyway, I want you to come and see what I've done with the place. Bring your pj's so you can stay over, ok?"

For the next couple of days I wonder what she wants to talk about but I am feeling increasingly weak and my cold sores have come back full force. They are so bad that I can't even open my mouth fully without being in pain. And I can only eat soup and drink through a straw. Not that I am feeling hungry anyway.

I think of Mark and how he'd gradually lost his appetite. And I think about the wasting that is so typical in people with AIDS and what it does to your body, causing it to rapidly lose weight and aid in the progression of the disease.

I don't want this to happen to me. And so I force myself to eat as much as I can. But it doesn't always work and there are times when I just stare at the food and move it 'round the plate and my stomach turns and I push the plate away. And now I know how Mark had felt and I fear that it's catching up with me too.

Then panic looms large in the room, especially at night when I'm alone and everything is silent.

And, for the first time since I've left Virginia, I can again sense the presence of my companion.

Chapter 19

Antonia buzzes my apartment at 6 o'clock on Friday night.

"The place looks nice," she looks around approvingly, "but you don't. You look thin, are you feeling ok? Did you eat?"

"Not much. I try. I just get nauseous; I mean just smelling food makes me sick. I have to cook for the kids, of course, but more often than not they eat at Aunt Sissy's."

"Well, let's go to my place. Are the kids ready? Have you packed your stuff?"

"Sure, what there is of it. Bettina and Adam are staying at Aunt Sissy's. They have a couple of friends that live in her building come over and they want to play video games or watch a movie, something like that."

"I guess there's not too much to do for them at my place; I must get a computer and some of these games so they'll be able to have some fun. Honestly though? I haven't the faintest where I would start; they'll just have to help me with that."

"I'm sure they'd be delighted," I laugh "but Aunt Sissy is happy to have them stay over, she misses the company."

"Right. Ok then, let's go."

Antonia doesn't live far from my apartment building, only about 15 minutes by car. But you might as well be on a different planet.

Her house is at the very bottom of a cul-de-sac and the property runs all the way down to the lake. It's almost like being at the ocean, the lake being so big and all. Here the streets are tree-lined and quiet and you hear no traffic noise. Ever. The house is a lot like the one she had in Virginia. Tall, tall trees and a garden brimming with wild flowers.

"Come in, take a load off," she shakes loose her hair and leads me into the kitchen that overlooks the lawns that stretch down to the water.

"Oh my God, I love what you've done to the kitchen," I look at the brightly coloured walls, painted in buttercup yellow. She's replaced the old brown cupboards with cream coloured ones that have glass doors and show off the china and crystal inside.

"It's gorgeous, Toni. I absolutely love it. And look at this cool sink."

"The faucets are imported from Italy," she says without a hint of pride. "I always think if you have to do dishes and shit like that, it might as well be in beautiful surroundings, don't you agree?"

"Sure, yeah, everybody should have imported faucets from Italy. I think I should run that by the co-op management. They might think it a good idea."

Antonia looks at me and bursts out laughing.

"You're an idiot, but I love you anyway. Let's go out on the deck and chat for a bit before dinner."

Antonia has whipped up an exotic looking concoction in the blender.

"What the hell is this?"

"I don't know. Try it, you might like it."

"Ok, I will. Just don't stick one of those ridiculous umbrellas into it."

"Yeah, right!" She gives me one of those Antonia "you're a nut" looks.

It is a really, really good drink though. You can barely taste the generous amount of vodka she's added and it has a hint of coconut and a slight taste of pineapple and a dash of cinnamon.

"This is great; I think I'll have another."

Antonia goes back into the kitchen through the French doors and returns with the entire pitcher and a bucket of ice cubes.

"Saves me running back and forth," she says, and pours us another drink.

We've gone quiet for a moment. That's another thing I love about Antonia. You can just sit with her, being quiet. And sometimes we sit like that for a long, long time. Quiet, not talking. Once in a while we look at each other and smile; there is no need for words, ever.

It is getting late and the sun is ready to dip out of sight at the brink of the horizon. There is a strange beauty and a kind of glassiness in the air and not a sound to be heard.

"This is wonderful, Toni. Thanks for asking me over. It is so calm here, so far removed from the city, it seems."

"Don't thank me. Don't ever thank me, Steph, for anything. You know I love your company, I love to talk to you and..."

"Speaking of which, you were going to tell me something."

"Oh yes, that. Let's have dinner first."

Those god-awful cold sores have dried up quite a bit in the past couple of days; I guess the new medication that Doctor Sanford had prescribed is really helping.

I still don't have an appetite, but maybe it's the drink or maybe it's the delicious gazpacho soup or the light shrimp dish and the salad with Stilton cheese that Antonia has prepared, but suddenly I am really hungry, and finish off just about everything on my plate.

Antonia watches me eat; I can tell she is pleased.

"You're a pig," she says. "I thought you weren't hungry?"

"Well, I wasn't, but you've gone through so much trouble. It would have been impolite...."

"Yeah, sure, whatever you say."

And we both burst out laughing.

By the time she brings out the coffee and brandy, it is almost completely dark and stars have popped up in the sky. One by one. And even though it's nothing like the starry sky in Virginia, you can still see a heck of a lot more of them hovering over the lake than just a few miles off in the city.

"Here's a sweater for you, Steph."

"I'm not cold"

"Take it just the same; it does get a bit nippy at night. Summer is almost over, I'm afraid. But I love the fall too, and the winter, even though there's no golf."

I take a small sip of cognac and light a cigarette.

"So what's up?"

Antonia has stretched out on a lounge chair; a light cashmere blanket is covering her legs. She looks beautiful in the candle light. Young and beautiful with her red hair softly framing her face and her dark eyes flashing.

"It's Ken," she says. "We're getting divorced. I know he's seeing someone and I know who it is. He denies everything, of course. But it doesn't really matter one way or the other."

I am dumbstruck.

"What? A divorce? You always seemed to be so happy. I mean…"

The words are stuck in my throat. I don't know what to say. Here, for all I've ever seen, is a perfect marriage. I won't admit to it but I've always been a little envious of their relationship. The houses, the boats, the trips overseas, the glamour and glitz. Ken adores Antonia. She is gorgeous, smart, cosmopolitan…

Antonia looks at me as if she can read my mind. Hell, she probably can.

"It's ok, Steph, really ok. It has been a long time coming. I know Ken loved me, probably still does in his own way, but I wasn't enough for him, do you understand?"

"I can honestly say that I do not," I manage to say. What is there to understand?

"It sounds utterly ridiculous and cliché, but Ken is married to his work, his company, his success. And with that success comes a little blonde secretary who adores him. I've never adored Ken. I loved him, I respected him, but I never adored him. And perhaps that's what he needs, adoration."

Antonia sounds so matter of fact, so totally unhurt, it's impossible to feel sorry for her. I look at her, sitting there in the candlelight. Calm. Sure of herself. In control.

"It's ok, Steph," she continues, knowing what I'm thinking. "It's actually very ok. I can now live the way I want to, without all the glitz and jet set bullshit that was never really me. And I'm well off, financially that is, so it's not a big hardship. And, actually, that's the main reason I wanted to talk to you."

"But why? What can I do?"

"Well, I'm keeping the house. It's a little on the big side but I love it too much. It would make more sense to move into a condo or something like that, but why should I if I don't have to?"

"Right, I understand," I mutter even though I understand nothing.

"Well, the house being so big and all, I thought..." she pauses and looks at me as if fishing for the right words.

"Thought what?"

"Well, why don't you move in with me? You and the kids. We'll have a great time."

"You're nuts," I laugh out loud. "Totally nuts. You don't know what you're dealing with, you know, the AIDS. And the kids can be a handful. So, no. Thanks for your offer, but it would never work."

"Adam and Bettina are teenagers. What could be so hard? They are great kids and most of the time they're in school anyway. That's not a reason, Stephanie. Why don't you tell me what you really object to?"

"I don't want to hurt your feelings, Toni, you know that. But somehow it smacks of charity. Even though you're my best friend, I would feel totally dependent. And there's another thing..."

"What?"

"If I move out of the subsidized apartment, social services will only give me a certain amount of money. Just enough to meet my needs, as they call it, and if things don't work out between us I'll have a hell of a time getting another place."

"Perhaps you have a point. I don't mean things not working out between us, because I know they would. But the responsibility with the AIDS. You're right, I'm no Florence Nightingale, that's for sure and I'd be totally useless in a crisis. I mean, I practically faint when I cut my own finger. But here's another idea and this time I won't take no for an answer."

She looks at me probingly and all my suspicion flags go up.

"Shoot!"

"Ok, I know how you are with your ideas about charity and all, but I want you to really, really think about this. Bettina and Adam. I want to become their guardian, in case something happens..."

"Happens? You mean when I die, right?"

"Yes, if you must put it that way, yes, when you die. It could happen ten years from now or twenty, or..."

"Or it could happen next week. I know Toni. If anyone is aware of that fact, I am. But I don't think about it, I can't afford to. I have to concentrate on taking one step at a time, one day at a time, hell, one hour at a time."

I stretch in my chair. I feel good. A little drunk perhaps, but good. And talking about dying doesn't bother me that much. Not any more. Strange thing that. I used to be so goddamned paranoid. I used to think it's bad luck to talk about it. I guess most people feel that way. So they use euphemisms: "Going to sleep", "Passing over", or even "Kicking the bucket". Pick one. But not dying, never dying. Even in funeral homes they have "slumber rooms". Well, I have news for you, people don't slumber in there, they're dead!

I look over at Antonia; she's biting her lip, an anxious look in her eyes.

"Well, Toni, why not. My children are the only reason I'm trying so hard. They are my main reason for fighting this thing, the reason I'm putting up with all the crap I have to put up with.

And if there's one person I know who will love them as much as I do, it is you. Aunt Sissy is getting on a bit and even though she's in good health, she wouldn't be able to cope. And I know that the kids would never want to live with Mark's parents, though they would probably be awarded custody, being the closest living relatives..."

I pause for a while and think of Max and Hannah. Max calls every so often and he's sent a little money here and there, for the kid's birthday and Christmas, you know, the usual. And every time he calls, I miss him and I miss Virginia and I miss Mark. But I've heard absolutely nothing from Hannah. Not a word. I know she never liked me, I know she's blamed me for her son's illness and his death, but you would think that she'd be interested in her son's children, wouldn't you? But for her, it's as if they're dead, as if everyone had died along with Mark.

I look over at Antonia and continue...

"So, yes, Toni, I'd be honoured if you'll be the children's guardian and no I don't think of it as charity."

Antonia jumps up so quickly she knocks over her glass and it shatters into a million pieces on the terrazzo tiles.

"I was hoping you would say that," she has tears in her eyes as she hugs the hell out of me.

"Yeah, yeah. Ok. But look at the mess you've made. Can't you have plastic glasses on the porch like everyone else? Does it have to be freaking crystal?"

"Plastic? Plastic? Surely you jest," she says with mock horror. "But never mind the glass. I'll sweep it up in a second. And anyway, in Europe they say that if you break a glass, it'll bring good luck. That's why they step on a glass at Jewish weddings, you know? To wish them luck. The newlyweds... wish them luck."

"Well, we're not Jewish and this is no wedding. So let's just clean up before we're too drunk to do it."

"Drunk? Who's drunk? I know what; let's have a little toke. You have some, don't you?"

"Yeah, I have some, but you don't smoke, ever. You don't even know how to..."

"I will tonight. At least I'll try, if I don't cough my brains out."

She goes into the kitchen and comes back with a broom to sweep up the broken glass while I roll a joint.

We smoke. She coughs and hands the joint back to me.

"I'll never get the hang of it, it's just too weird. Let's just sit and look at the stars."

The combination of the drinks and the joint has so relaxed me that I feel as if I'm on another planet. A different universe. A universe where nothing can touch you and everything is all right. Always.

But the *companion* is nearby.

Somewhere in the shadow of the bushes.

I can sense him hovering there, but I don't fear him.

I don't fear him tonight. Not tonight.

Chapter 20

I don't like the look on Dr. Sanford's face when I see him again. He looks serious, too serious, so that can't be good news.

"I got back some of your tests, Stephanie. I must say, I'm not happy. And you've lost weight."

"Yes, I know. I know that I've lost weight. I'm not an idiot." I am getting testy, accusing. Like it's his fault.

Just this morning I looked at myself in the full-length mirror after I got out of the shower. Most of the time I try to avoid looking at my body now. In the beginning, it wasn't so bad. I've always thought myself too chubby and suddenly I've become skinny. Well, that's one way of putting it; I know goddamn well it is the AIDS that causes the weight loss. Might as well call it what it is. Wasting!

So, like I said, this morning I took a good long look, from my toes up to my head. Yeah, I am thin alright. I can see my ribs when I lift my arms and my skin looks pasty and transparent. Bluish.. Luminescent.. Not healthy.

"Losing body weight is one of the side effects of the medication," Dr. Sanford continues, ignoring my remark. "I've told you that before. You must absolutely force yourself to eat. I know it's hard, but anything at all will do."

"I'm sorry doctor, sorry I snapped at you. It's not just having no appetite at all, it's getting exceedingly difficult to do even normal everyday things. I'm always tired and my body is weak. That's how it all started with Mark; all he wanted to do was sleep. It scares the hell out of me. And now I've developed this skin condition, like a rash. It itches like crazy, especially at night, and I have to scratch and scratch until I draw blood."

"That too could be a side effect of the drugs; I'll give you a prescription for a cream that will help.

But the fact remains that you don't eat, or cannot eat. We'll have to do something to get nourishment into your body."

"Like what?"

"We'll have to put you on intravenous."

"You mean I have to go to the hospital?"

"Initially yes, but then we'll have a nurse come to your house to monitor the IV."

"Will it hurt?"

He looks at me with his dark eyes and runs his fingers through his unkempt hair.

"Didn't I tell you it won't always be pleasant Stephanie? You're tough, you can handle it. It's the only option other than…" he bites his lip as if he's said something he didn't mean to slip out.

"Other than dying, you mean, don't you?"

"Yes, other than dying. Your body will waste away and no drug is going to help you if your system can't fight back because it's undernourished. We can't let that happen. You have your kids to think of and most of all yourself… you don't want…"

"No," I interrupt, "no, I know what you're going to say. No, I don't want to end up like my husband. I mean giving up without even trying. I will do what needs to be done."

"There's my girl. I'll make the appointment with the hospital as soon as possible."

It is the first of many, many hospital visits I will have to make. Looking back, I don't think I would have had the courage to go through it all, had I known what lay ahead. One step at a time, I think, just one little step at a time.

That first step isn't too bad, actually. Antonia has taken me to the hospital which is quite close; at least I don't have to go all the way downtown. I am nervous, to be sure, but I am also weak and tired so if this will make me feel better, then ok, let's do it.

Dr. Sanford had explained the procedure to me. He showed me a diagram that depicted exactly where the line will go in and what it's for.

"It's a peripherally inserted central catheter, Stephanie, or PICC line for short. You go in for day surgery and they feed a thin tube up your veins. It goes in right here," he points to a spot just below my elbow, "and then the line goes all the way up the arm and into your chest."

"And how does that help in getting nutrients into my body?"

"Well, without getting too technical about it, you'll be receiving what is called parenteral nutrition, meaning we're bypassing the normal eating and digestion process and feed vital nutrients such as glucose, vitamins, and dietary minerals directly into your body."

"Will it hurt?"

"The procedure? You'll be anaesthetized, you won't feel a thing."

"Will it hurt, once it's in, I mean?"

"No. You'll be able to feel it being there, but it won't hurt, I promise."

And he is right. It doesn't hurt.

When I wake up, Aunt Sissy and the kids are there at the hospital and I am so thrilled to see them. I look down at my arm. It is all bandaged up and nothing shows. And I get to go home the same day.

"We've arranged for a nurse to come to your house every day to administer the IV." The hospital doctor reiterates what Dr. Sanford has already told me. And the next day she shows up at our apartment.

I am actually feeling quite well and have some hot milk and a slice of buttered toast for breakfast. Ever since I was a little girl I've loved hot milk, it's my comfort food, like chocolate is for other people, I guess.

Nurse Helga is a big woman. Not fat, but solid in a Germanic kind of way. She is wearing big sensible shoes and a pale blue twin set. Her blonde hair is tied back in a bun and her face is glowing and healthy looking, as if she scrubs it clean with soap and water and that is all she ever needs to do.

She comes bouncing into the room carrying a shiny black bag and I know we'll become friends, she and I, and I am happy to meet her.

"So you're Stephanie," she smiles and reveals a row of small gleaming teeth. "We'll have you feeling better in no time. The IV really helps, believe me, I should know."

"You have other patients like me?" I ask.

"You mean patients who have AIDS? Yes, I visit a couple of them every day. They're both men; you're my first female."

It is Saturday and the children are at home. They are extremely interested in what is going on. They know the nurse is here to help me and they take an instant shine to her.

"Do you think the children should go into their room while we do this?" Helga asks and glances in their direction.

"No, it's ok, I want them to stay, so they know there are no secrets."

"Perhaps you're right. I'll explain the procedure to them."

The kids watch, fascinated, as Helga administers the IV through the little tube that sticks out of my vein and then cleans the small hole with a cotton swab and covers it with a Band-Aid.

"There, that's all there's to it. I'll be back tonight and we'll do it all over again."

"I think I can do that," says Adam.

"Maybe when you're a little older," Helga strokes his hair, "I'm sure you will be able to do it then."

And so we get to know Helga really well. Sometimes she stays for a cup of coffee and talks about her little dog, a Yorkie named Slick. She lives alone and the terrier is her only companion.

"What a cool name, Slick," Adam says. "If I had a dog, I'd call him Slick too."

"I named him that because that's exactly what he is, slick. Everywhere at once and into everything at the same time," Helga jokes, but you can tell she is very fond of the little guy.

You get to know someone when you see them twice a day. You get to know them when they see you at your worst and when they're happy because you're having a good day.

And I am having good days, though the bad days far outweigh the good ones. The IV is keeping me alive, that's about it. It does nothing for my appetite and I still have to force myself to eat. I can hardly get anything down without gagging. And I get thinner and thinner. My clothes are hanging on me like those on a scarecrow. My face too is thin, which makes my eyes look huge.

But all this doesn't happen overnight. It happens very gradually and most days I wear track pants and loose, comfy tops so the weight loss doesn't show so much. Except for that one night on my birthday, when Antonia takes me out to dinner. Dinner and a show, she'd said.

I haven't been out of the apartment in a long, long time. It's too bloody awkward, what with the IV and all. But tonight Helga comes a little earlier than her usual time, and I am all set to go.

When I put on my pantsuit, I am shocked. I have to really tighten the belt and the pants look more like a skirt, they are so loose. The jacket is ok. Even though it is big on me, it looks chic in a sophisticated, Parisian sort of way.

How I would have loved to have a figure like this ten years ago, when all I had was curves. I look like a model, only I don't feel like one. I am catwalk thin, like many of them are. Anorexic almost. But with a little makeup and my hair hanging loose and long, I feel almost beautiful.

We have a super evening, Antonia and I. The show itself is forgettable, but it is fun to be out among a bunch of happy people. I even manage to have a little roast beef for dinner and a couple of glasses of wine, which makes me laugh much more than the play merits.

"Maybe that's what you should do," Antonia says.

"What?"

"Have a little wine now and then. It seems to stimulate your appetite. You actually managed to eat three bites of meat and an entire potato."

She says that without a hint of sarcasm. Just concern.

"Yeah, and maybe I should start smoking pot, like we used to do when I was in high school. That always made us hungry, that's for sure," I laugh, and I think of the times when we all sat around and had a few joints and listened to music and loved each other so, so much.

Antonia looks at me with a serious expression.

"You know what? Maybe that's not a bad idea at all."

"In case you have forgotten, it's totally against the law."

"I know that, but in your case? They give it to people for medicinal purposes you know. It's something to look into, for sure."

When I ask Dr. Sanford about that, he's a little skeptical. But he also knows that I have to eat to be able to fight whatever the next unknown thing might be that is lurking in the background, ready to attack my body.

So now I can get the medical cannabis and it's perfectly legal.

I need something that will relax my body, something to help me sleep, and something to make me want to eat food again. And when I smoke pot, it helps a bit.

And it keeps the companion at bay. I know he is still here. I can feel him watching me, but only through a haze.

The edge is off and he is no longer a threat. Just a silent presence.

Chapter 21

"I'm seeing a lot of black dots," I tell Doctor Sanford during my regular checkup which is almost every week now. I might as well be living in his office.

"Dots? What kind of dots?"

"Little black dots, lots of them. Dots in front of my eyes."

"They're called floaters, everyone has them," he grins and blows a strand of hair out of his eyes. "You're not going hypochondriac on me now, are you?"

"I don't think so, and I know what floaters are," I am a little annoyed. Calling me a hypochondriac. I mean, me, of all people. "But there are so many of them and sometimes, when I open my eyes quickly, it looks like there are huge spiders crawling up the wall and along the ceiling. Real fast like, which is pretty creepy and disgusting. But when I start to focus, they disappear."

"Hmm, that is odd. We'll get you to see a specialist to check it out."

Oh, shit.., yeah.. Another specialist. Exactly what I need.

The first guy he sends me to sees nothing wrong, nothing. But, of course, Dr. Sanford won't take that for an answer and he sends me to another guy who says, "There's a problem here, definitely."

And then this guy sends me to an ophthalmologist, a woman.

In a way I'm lucky, in spite of all the shit that has happened. It seems that whenever I need one, an angel appears. I don't mean a winged heavenly creature, but an angel nonetheless. An angel in human form and sometimes they look far from angelic. And Doctor Martineau is such an angel, believe me.

The first time I visit her office, I'm a little intimidated. Her office is really posh, with soft leather furniture and mahogany paneled walls in the waiting room and good pictures. And plants everywhere. You immediately know that she is successful at what she does. I mean, who has an office like that? Not a guy in a walk-in clinic, that's for sure.

I expect to meet a snooty person with an impersonal attitude, as many are, but it just goes to show how wrong you can be. I am looking at the usual chart on the wall in her office, you know, the ABC one where the letters get progressively smaller to test your eyesight, when she comes galumphing through the door. I am a little shocked, shocked and surprised, when I first see her. She is big. A big, big woman with an enormous behind. She's not actually fat, but she has arms and legs like a wrestler and huge hands with a firm grip, as I soon find out when she shakes mine.

Her brown hair is pulled back into a bun and her blue eyes have a mischievous sparkle, as if she likes to laugh a lot.

"So you're Stephanie," her voice is surprisingly soft and sweet and doesn't go with her appearance at all. "Doctor Sanford told me all about you; he's a good friend. Nuts, like me. I know you have AIDS, so we can get straight to the point without any bullshit. I won't ask how you got it. I know you are a widow with two kids and you lived in no-where Virginia, right? I don't need to know anything else; all we have to do is address the problems you have right now, ok?"

I feel like hugging her and I know without a doubt, I've found another angel.

"Thanks, Doctor Martineau, I.."

"Call me Mary. Makes things less formal, don't you think?"

She heaves her big backside out of the chair and comes over to where I am sitting.

"I love Virginia," she says. "I go there almost every winter to ski. A friend of mine has a chalet, which is great. You wouldn't think I can ski with this big caboose, right?" She laughs as if reading my thoughts.

"Well, it makes for a softer landing when you fall on your ass, but I'm a pretty good skier, if I do say so myself. You don't have to be skinny and lithe to be good at sports, right? Ok, let's have a look at your eyes."

I am reclined in something like a dentist's chair.

"Is it going to hurt?"

"No, it won't hurt, but it'll be uncomfortable. I'm going to put some drops into your eyes that will dilate your pupils and that's not a lot of fun. No sense telling you that it will be."

She is right. The procedure is not painful but it's almost unbearable because the light is blinding me so much. It pierces my eyes and shoots straight into my brain. Like looking into the sun with your eyes unprotected, the way we used to do when we were kids and didn't know any better. But the whole thing doesn't last too long and Mary covers my eyes with gauze to take away the glare.

"There is a virus in your eyes that can cause you to go blind unless we do something about it. You have cytomegalovirus retinitis, CMV for short, Stephanie. I kind of suspected that. It is caused by the HIV and it destroys your retina. In fact, it's the leading cause of vision loss in AIDS patients."

CMV Retinitis? It means nothing to me. Well, here we go again. Another fucking thing to worry about.

"Can it be treated?"

"Sure. Right now we can give you the medication intravenously, I know you already have the line, or we can administer injections into your eye right away and that gets to the site a hell of lot faster than the IV."

"Injections? Into my eyes?"

I feel my lips draw back from my teeth. I'm going to throw up, I know I will. I don't think I've ever been so terrified of anything. Needles in my eyes? Oh my God.

Mary puts her hand on my forehead and brushes back my hair.

"It sounds worse than it is, Stephanie," she says in a soothing voice, "but I understand your panic. Most people freak when you tell them they have to have shots into their eyeball. It's a natural reaction. But it's not as bad as you think; fear of the unknown is the worst fear of all."

I take a deep breath and wait for the nausea to go away. What options do I have? What options do I really have? I sit up straight.

"Ok, I'll do it," I say and bite my lip. "When?"

"The sooner the better. How about next Friday? You need to have somebody drop you off and take you home again."

"Right, ok, next Friday."

"You're a brave girl, Stephanie, I've seen men break down and cry at the prospect, you have guts, I like that. I'll give you a couple of valium that you can take before your appointment, to take the edge off. You'll be fine, just fine, trust me, ok?"

I call Antonia as soon as I get home.

"What?" she almost screams. "What? Needles into your eye? Oh my God, Stephanie."

"Yeah, I know, Toni, I know. I'm pretty scared. Will you take me?"

"Of course, you don't have to ask. Of course I will, but needles in your eyes?"

"I'm trying not to think about it. I guess the alternative would be worse, I could lose my sight."

Sometimes it's a good thing that you don't know what's going to happen to you in life, otherwise you'd probably give up. When we arrive at the clinic I am petrified. I feel like throwing up, but I have nothing in my stomach, of course, because you can't eat or drink for several hours before the procedure and I didn't take the pills either.

Antonia looks awfully pale and she has tears in her eyes when she drops me off.

"I'll be here when you're done," she says. "God, I wish there were something I could do. I feel so bloody helpless."

"It's ok. It'll be ok," I take her hand. "I don't know what I would do without you Toni, thanks for being my friend, thanks for caring."

LORENE ALBERS

I am a basket case when Mary's assistant, Angela, leads me into the operating room. I don't know what to expect. The whole idea freaks me out and now I wish I had taken the valium.

I calm down a little when Mary comes into the room.

"It will be over soon," she says. Her assistant leans over and clamps my eye open with a metallic device, which is really uncomfortable. She pours in some kind of liquid and it doesn't take long before I stop feeling the clamp. I mean, my whole eye is frozen.

"Look over to your left as far as you can," says Mary. "Just look at Angela, ok?"

It is the oddest feeling. I mean I can move my eye but it doesn't feel as if I'm moving it. Like when your mouth is frozen when you come from the dentist and you can't feel your lips or anything. God, how I wish I could just pass out, but that doesn't happen.

I can see Mary bending over holding the needle. She had been right; it doesn't hurt, not one bit. But you can feel the needle go into your eyeball. It's like something out of a horror movie but it's over before I can think about it for too long. And I just space out and float away and I don't know how much time has passed.

"Done," Mary says. "You've been extremely brave kiddo. I've had one guy faint on me. Big strapping guy he was too."

She smiles and helps me sit up and I am so thankful that it's over, I could kiss her.

I am wheeled into the recovery room and I have no idea how long I'm in here. Hours, it seems. My eye is covered with a patch. The fear and nausea have subsided and I am so relieved that the tears are rolling down my cheeks. And I have no control over that, no control at all.

Antonia picks me up. Me and my patch.

"You look like a freaking pirate," she tries to joke but her voice is shaky, "How bad was it?"

"Well, not as bad as you imagine. It's just the whole idea..."

"Yeah, I know, don't talk about it. Let's just go home. I'll take you home with me. Your Aunt Sissy is with the children, ok?"

"Thanks, Toni. Thanks for everything."

"Don't thank me, I'm just being selfish. I need a good drink and you never have a decent bottle of Scotch at your house."

I know she tries to make light of the situation. A couple of times during the drive to her house I catch her looking at me with such pity and helplessness that I want to cry all over again. And I feel blessed, truly blessed to have a friend like Toni.

It is a dark, drizzly evening. We are sitting in Antonia's living room. Actually, I am sort of lying in a recliner and she's brought a soft cuddly blanket for me.

I'm always amazed at how she can make any room look bright and happy. Even on a grey evening like this.

There is a fire crackling in the fireplace and she has vases full of bright yellow chrysanthemums placed all over the room. And candles everywhere. Not only on the coffee table, but all 'round the room. Little candles in honey colored glass holders that throw pools of light everywhere.

"Now that I'm the kids' guardian.." she starts as she hands me a cup of tea..

"Whoa, wait a second; we haven't even done the paperwork yet. And in case you haven't noticed, I'm still very much alive. Patch and all."

"You're right, I'll call my lawyer in the morning and we'll get him to draw up everything. It shouldn't take more than a couple of days. Anyway, now that I'm the kids' guardian, I want you to listen to me, listen very carefully, Steph."

"Ok, I'm listening. Shoot." I take a sip of the soothing peppermint tea and I feel very relaxed, glad that ordeal is over, and glad that there isn't any pain, at least not yet.

"I want you to allow me to send Adam and Bettina to a private school."

"Are you nuts? I can't afford that, not in a million years."

"I know. But I'm their guardian, remember?" She goes on quickly before I can get a word in. "There's a college near Lausanne in Switzerland that is coed, so they can both go to the same school and stay in the same dorm. I actually know the headmistress. It was my alma mater, you see."

"Out of the question, Antonia. I know how much you love the kids. I know how much you want to help, always have helped, but this is too much, and anyway.." I stop in mid sentence.

As if reading my thoughts, she goes on. "I know what you're going to say, you'll miss them, they'll miss you, and if anything should happen to you they may never see you again. It's a lot to ask of you. A huge sacrifice. But think of the children. It will be their opportunity to get a first class education and I don't even want you to think about the money. Heaven knows I have more than enough of that and what good is it if I can't use it the way I want?"

There's a long pause. Toni gets up and pours herself a brandy.

"I know you can't have a drink with all that medication, right? Promise me you'll think about it, Steph, please promise."

"Ok, I'll think about it, but just the idea of not seeing them every day is more than I can bear. I mean, things are bad enough with Mark gone...You know I don't often feel sorry for myself and I don't dwell on the past if I can help it. What happened happened, and I can't change that. But it's all been a bit much today; you understand that, don't you? Let me sleep on it."

"I'm sorry, I've overwhelmed you with all this stuff. It's just.. I want so much for the kids to have it a little easier in life and whatever I can do, I'll do. You're right; we'll talk about it when you've had your sleep."

Toni's guest room is not like a guest room at all. It's more like a cozy hotel suite with a television, a little sitting area where you can look out on the garden and the lake beyond and a full en-suite bath.

I always feel at home in this room. Especially tonight, it is a haven. Everything is beautiful, everything is peaceful, far removed from the functionality of my apartment building or the cold sterility of the hospital rooms.

I fall asleep instantly. I don't even think about the kids or the decision I know I will have to make.

Nor do I think about the companion. Not even once.

Chapter 22

On the morning after the operation I find Antonia at the kitchen table with a mound of paperwork in front of her.

"Morning, Steph, you look good. How do you feel? How was your night? I looked in on you a couple of times but you were fast asleep. Any pains?"

"No, surprisingly enough, nothing at all. Must be the pills Dr. Martineau gave me, I slept right through the night. And you know what? I'm hungry, I'm actually starving."

The doorbell rings. I hear Antonia's cheery voice as she greets whoever is at the door.

"Buenos Dias, Maria", she says in her best Spanish, "Como estas?"

"Muy bien, Antonia, but we must speak English, it's the only way I'll ever get the hang of it."

"Sure, of course, whatever you say. Come in and meet my best friend. Stephanie, this is Maria, I've hired her to do all the stuff I don't like to do," she laughs.

"Actually, I've snatched her away from the country club where she used to work".

Maria is a petite Mexican woman with pitch black hair, dark flashing eyes and the sweetest smile, showing a couple of dimples in her round cheeks.

"I'm ever so pleased to meet you," she shakes my hand and turns 'round to Antonia. "Shall I get started upstairs then?"

"Sure, great, Maria. And if you could run over to the market later to get some things that would be nice. Save me a trip. I made a list. It's on the kitchen counter."

"Of course, no problem at all."

Maria has left the kitchen and I stare at Antonia.

"What was that?"

"What? Oh, you mean her English? She's trying very, very hard to learn the language, but properly, as she puts it. And by that she means the 'King's English'. She constantly watches reruns of Upstairs/Downstairs and practices the accent and looks up all the words in a dictionary. Really sweet, though, isn't it?"

"I admire that, I really do. Sometimes I wish I could speak another language. So how long has she been coming to help you?"

"Oh for a few of weeks now. I'm going to ask her to stay and be my housekeeper. Ken never wanted anyone living in the house full time; he believed that a wife should look after the household, especially if she wasn't working. Don't ask! I actually didn't mind the cooking and cleaning so much, and I had a maid service twice a month, but I drew the line at gardening. I hate digging around in the ground and having worms pop up, though I do love my garden and all the gorgeous plants and bushes and flowers, as long as someone else takes care of it all. Maria is an absolute sweetheart. You'll get to love her too."

Antonia takes out pots and pans and starts banging them about. Soon the counter is full of stuff, eggs, bacon, potatoes, oil, bread and butter.

"Ok, you said you're hungry so let's have a huge fattening breakfast. Bacon, eggs, the works, and I'll even make hash browns from scratch the way they make them at home."

"Hold it, I'm not that hungry. Some toast and maybe a soft boiled egg will do."

"You sure? Hell, no, I'm making it anyway and then we'll see how you feel about it, ok?"

"Ok, go ahead if you must."

Antonia busies herself at the stove. Grating fresh potatoes and frying them in olive oil until they are golden brown. She's piling lots of crisp bacon on a plate and cooks the eggs over easy, just the way I love them. And I actually do have the huge breakfast. Huge for me that is.

"I've never tasted hash browns like this. They're delicious."

"Aren't they? I could eat them every day. Not a good idea though, they're loaded with fat and calories. But once in a while, why not? It's like everything else. You shouldn't deprive yourself."

And with that she helps herself to another spoonful of potatoes and bacon.

"I've thought about what you said," I say when we have finished eating. I start moving a little piece of toast 'round the plate, not looking at her.

Actually, I haven't really thought about it that much, because I know in my heart that I have to do what is best for my children. And since I can't give them what I really want for them to have, what they deserve, well...

"Yes?" Antonia doesn't look up from her plate.

"It's awfully generous of you, Toni. In fact, I know of no one in the entire world who would do such a thing. Friends or not."

"Yes?" she says again, in a small voice, as if expecting rejection.

"I've decided to accept your offer. God bless you for it. I must do what's best for my kids and since I can't..."

I can't continue. I choke. And once again, I feel so helpless. Grateful and helpless at the same time.

"Don't cry, please, please don't," she rushes over and hugs me. "It's going to be alright. I've thought about it some more too and Switzerland is too far away. We'll find something here in Canada. A good college prep school. The best, in fact. Something a little closer, ok?"

"Ok. I love you Toni; I don't know where I would have ended up without you."

"Don't be daft. What's money good for if you can't spread it around? And I intend to do a lot of spreading, believe me."

I have to laugh at her. Sitting there in her pale blue track suit, hair piled on top of her head and a smidgeon of jam in the corner of her mouth, she looks like a little kid. Determined. Not caring one bit about anybody else's opinion.

It only takes a few days before she's found the perfect place; perfect in every way. A famous college located in the Ottawa valley. So it's not that far away. She's gotten all the brochures. All the information. The curriculum. The living quarters. Everything. But that still isn't enough for Antonia.

So one day she packs Adam and Bettina into her car to check out the place for herself and to make sure the kids will like it and feel at home there. It's only about a two hour drive and they're back the same night.

Well, both kids absolutely love the school. They are so enthusiastic and at the supper table they tell me all about the grounds and their rooms and the headmaster who, apparently, is a great guy. Well, it just sounds bloody perfect and in a few weeks I will have to let them go.

Antonia takes them on shopping trips to buy clothes and books and everything else they might need and even though I protest, there's no stopping her.

"Look," she says, "let me have some fun. I've never had kids to spoil, at least let me spoil yours a little. And since I'm their guardian, I can spoil them all I want, right? Why don't you come with us?"

"Thanks, Toni, I'm not really up to strolling around malls, as much as I would love to come along. I get too tired too quickly. It wouldn't be any fun for you or the children."

"You must stop calling them children, they're young adults now. Adam is almost as tall as I am and Bettina, well, she's a proper young lady and so beautiful, as beautiful as her mom."

She gives me a quick hug and they're off.

I have to smile. Yes, Bettina is beautiful. Every mother thinks that, of course, but there is a sweetness and innocence about her that actually reminds me of pictures of my Mom when she was young. Same golden curly hair, bright blue eyes, even the dimples. No, she doesn't look like me at all, but Adam does. Looks like me and his dad. Dark hair and dark eyes and he has a way of running his fingers through his hair, exactly like Mark used to do. But he has a gentle disposition and at times he seems wise beyond his years.

Looking at the two of them, you'd never think they were twins. But they have a strong bond, a bond only twins have, or so they say. They are always looking out for one another, taking care of each other. I guess losing their father at such a young age only strengthened that bond. I am blessed. In spite of everything, I feel truly blessed that I have my children.

And without Mark I wouldn't have had them, so for that there is a tiny spark of forgiveness in me toward him. But not much, you can be sure of that because he's also robbed them of their father and probably even their mother – sooner rather than later for sure.

When they come back from the mall, all excited about the cool stuff they have bought and modeling outfit after outfit for me, I am happy. Happy for them. And I know it won't make any difference to Toni if I tell her that she's spent too much; I can tell by the shopping bags that they haven't exactly gone to Wal-Mart.

It gives me a little stab though that I can't buy these things for them, and immediately I feel guilty. Guilty and grateful to see my children so excited and looking so good in their new clothes.

"Mom, are you ok? You look sad," Bettina asks when she sees my face. "Aren't these clothes the best? I didn't really want Antonia to spend so much money but every time I tried something on, she just kept saying; do you like this? It looks good on you, we'll take it. And she just kept piling stuff on the counter and the same for Adam; only I think she was more interested in the girl stuff."

Bettina describes their shopping expedition in detail and laughs because Adam had been embarrassed going into the store with two women and didn't want to try anything on but just picked out things and held them up to see whether they would fit.

"It was pretty funny, Mom, I wish you could have been there, but you know, all that's not really important. Sure, I'm happy to have all these new clothes and shoes and stuff, but the most important thing in the world is that you get better. That's all I really care about."

She comes over to the couch where I'm sitting and gives me a big hug, careful not to touch the arm with the IV in it. I rest my chin on my daughter's head and try my best to put on a happy face.

"Don't you worry about that, Princess," I call her by the nickname I gave her when she was little. "You know I'll do whatever I must to fight this thing, don't you? I'll dance at your wedding. Just wait and see."

"Sure Mom, I know you're going to fight this thing. But when are you going to tell me what this thing is? What is it? You're getting skinnier; you have an intravenous for your medication. Medication for what? Do you have cancer?"

I look at her sweet young face… I don't want to hurt her, don't want to worry her… She's my child; I'm supposed to protect her…

"No, I don't have cancer. It's a little more complicated than that and well, you're still too young, Princess."

Bettina sits next to me on the couch and pulls me closer. The smile has left her face and her eyes are serious.

"Mom, I'm sixteen; almost seventeen. I'm going away to school, I'm going to be away from you for the very first time. I need to know what's wrong; you have to tell me… before…"

"Before what?"

"Before someone else does, like Aunt Sissy or Nurse Helga, or someone. Whatever."

I take a deep breath and take Bettina's hand in mine.

"You're right, Bettina, you're old enough now and you have a right to know, you both do. Ask Adam to come in. I'll talk to both of you at the same time."

Adam comes into the living room and sits on the floor looking up at me.

"What's up Mom?"

I look at my two children and I know this will be the hardest thing I ever have to tell them.

"I know that you've been wondering what's wrong with me and probably have been wondering about that for a long time. Well, I will tell you, now that you're all grown up. You see… Your dad… Your father… He didn't just die of meningitis… Well, he did, but the meningitis was a complication that resulted from his real illness…"

I pause and take another deep breath. How will they react? Will they be horrified? Will they understand? I don't want them to hate their father… Hate me…

"What was his real illness, Mom, what?"

"AIDS," I say quickly… "Your father had AIDS, sweetheart and…"

"AIDS?" Bettina wrinkles her forehead. "AIDS? But that's, I don't know that much about it, but isn't that what you get from having sex with other guys? That's what I've heard somewhere… Gay guys get it?"

I'm surprised she knows that much, but then kids are so much more mature, so much more informed, so much more open than we were at that age.

"Not always, Sweetie, sometimes they pick it up by…" I'm talking slowly, carefully weighing my words, "by having a relationship with someone else. It doesn't have to be another man."

There! I've said it! I've said out loud to my teenage children that their father had "relationships" with other women.

Bettina's eyes are wide with hurt and surprise. For a long while she says nothing, just holds my hand and lays her head on my shoulder.

Adam is still sitting cross-legged on the floor, his face is pale and without expression. I don't know what he's thinking.

"And so," Bettina finally whispers "and so you got it too. You got the AIDS from our father. That's what's really wrong with you?"

"Yes. I got the AIDS from your father," I answer and softly stroke her hair. She's too young. They both are too young. They shouldn't be burdened with this knowing.

Bettina is quiet for a long while, she stares into space. Somehow I wish she would cry, get angry, anything. But she says nothing, just holds on to my hand so hard, it hurts.

Finally she looks up at me. No tears. Nothing. All I see in her eyes is hurt, hurt and understanding at the same time.

"I'm beginning to forget Dad," she says in a quiet voice, "if I don't look at his picture, I don't remember anything about him. Not his voice, not what we did together, like he's a stranger. And now I wish he really was. A stranger. Not my father who did this to my Mom."

Again she falls silent and the three of us sit without speaking for a long while.

Adam breaks the silence: "Mom?"

"Yes, Sweetheart?"

"Why didn't you leave him, why did you stay with him when he hurt you so much, when he made you so sick, when he could have killed you like he got killed himself?"

"It's not that easy to explain. I had nowhere to go, I could not work and I could not tell anyone what was wrong. He insisted on that. He threatened me. He was afraid, afraid that people would find out, afraid he would lose his position in the firm, but his biggest fear was what people would think of him."

"It shouldn't have mattered what other people think, should it? I mean who cares?" Bettina is raising her voice; her face has turned red with anger.

"That's right, Mom" Adam adds. His voice is full of resentment. "I mean, who the hell cares? Now he's dead and you know what? I don't care, I don't care that he's dead. All I care about is you Mom, that's all. And I hate him for what he did to you. To all of us!"

Finally Bettina starts to cry and I'm holding my sobbing daughter close and I stroke her hair and I rock her like a baby.

"Are you going to die, Mom?" she can barely get the words out, "like Dad did?"

"No, Sweetie, I'm not going to die anytime soon. Everything is going to be ok, you'll see. One of the reasons that your father died, and died so quickly, is because he refused to get help. He totally denied that there was something wrong with him, wrong with both of us. Somehow he just hoped it was all a big mistake... That it would all go away."

I pause for a minute.

"So, in a way, it was his own fault because he placed other people's opinions above his own. Had he been on medication, he may not have caught meningitis, he may have lived, who knows? But he didn't even want to talk about getting treatments and he insisted that we must tell no one, not even his parents. And so he died."

Adam doesn't say a word. He is not looking me; his eyes are dark with anger. He stares out the window, clenching and unclenching his fists.

"When I was diagnosed with AIDS," I continue, "and after the initial shock had worn off, I swore to myself that I would not sit back and do nothing. I would find help and I would make sure that you guys were tested as well, even if I had to do it behind your father's back. Turns out that wasn't necessary because in the end he died so unexpectedly and so quickly... And a few days after the funeral your grandfather and I took you into Richmond for the tests."

Again I pause and study their faces to see whether they remember that trip. But I guess they don't. They were too little.

"It was the best day of my life when both of you tested negative.

With all the heartbreak and with all the uncertainty, it was still the best day of my life."

Finally Adam speaks.

"You're sure he wasn't gay, Mom? Our dad, he wasn't gay?"

"Absolutely not. I don't think I've ever known anyone who was more of a homophobe than your father."

"Well, it doesn't matter I guess," he spits out the words, "he's dead now and good riddance. I only wish he had died before he gave the AIDS to you, that's all."

I understand why he talks like that, I understand that he's angry and so I say nothing in reply.

"I've been lucky in having found good doctors who care and a lot of support from the people around us, like Antonia and Aunt Sissy and Nurse Helga. And there are new medications being discovered every day and things look more hopeful than ever before. I promised you that I'll dance at your wedding, at both your weddings, didn't I?"

I dry Bettina's tears with the sleeve of my sweatshirt.

"You'll be my big girl now, promise? You and your brother must stick together and look out for one another, will you promise me that?"

"Sure Mom, of course we will. But I don't want to go off to school now and Adam doesn't either, I know that. We want to stay close to you and…"

Adam nods his head. He gets up and sits next to me on the other side. I put my arm around his shoulder and hold him close. There's an uncomfortable stab in my arm where the intravenous goes in but I don't pay any attention. No pain in the world could be bigger than having to hurt my children the way I had to hurt them today.

"Ok now listen to me, both of you. The best thing you can do for me is to get an education, and, thanks to Antonia, you will be able to get the very best education money can buy. So you two go off and get good grades and we'll talk on the phone every day, well, almost every day, ok? Promise?"

Adam squeezes my hand.

"Ok Mom, sure. We will promise you that... but you cannot ask us to forgive our father for what he did. Never ever will we forgive him. We both love you so much, Mom, and we'll come home as often as we can. On long weekends and on holidays and we'll talk on the phone, like you said."

By now Bettina's eyes are dry and with the resilience of youth she again concentrates on the treasures that are spread out all over the room.

And so I have to let them go.

For the first time since they were born, I will have to live without my children.

And another little piece of my heart breaks.

Chapter 23

Antonia is throwing a big going away party for Bettina and Adam. She's invited all their friends and Aunt Sissy and even Nurse Helga and Slick.

We have a barbeque on her patio with hot dogs and hamburgers, and a huge cake that has "Bye Bye! Good Luck! Adam & Bettina" written on it, except that Bettina's name is spelled wrong, missing a 't'. But that doesn't matter one bit. And everyone is having a super time and I'm so thrilled to see their happy young faces and somewhere in my heart I wish that their father can see them too. But, who knows, maybe he can?

Antonia is driving them to the school tomorrow, so we stay at her place for the night. Bettina sleeps in my bed with all the packed suitcases lined up against the wall.

My heart hurts when they wave goodbye, ready to start a new chapter in their lives. I know they really don't want to leave, I know they're worried about me, but I also know it is best for them and so I had to convince them that I will be ok, that the school is not that far from home and that we'll be talking on the phone all the time.

But the way they looked at me and hugged me and the tears in Bettina's eyes and the way her brother put his arm around her shoulder to comfort her was hard to watch and it took all my courage to keep smiling and waving and putting on a happy face for them.

I will forever be grateful to Antonia for making it all possible and for loving them almost as much as I do, but my heart hurts just the same. What if something happens to me? What if I never see them again?

I stand in the driveway and I wave and watch as Toni's car pulls away and I can't help it, I sit down on the front steps and tears are streaming down my face and I cannot stop them.

Maria comes out with a sweater and drapes it 'round my shoulders.

"Come inside, Chiquita" she says softly, "I've made you a nice cup of tea. Everything will be all right. They'll be home on vacation and you can talk to them whenever you want, right?"

I smile at her and brush the hair out of my face.

"Sure, Maria, you're right, thank you. I'm acting like a baby."

"No. Not like a baby. You are a mother," she replies in a serious tone.

"Yes, of course, I'm a mother. Join me in a cup of tea, will you?"

"Certainly, I join you. We will sit on the verandah."

It is one of those rare fall mornings when everything is bathed in golden light. Not a leaf is stirring and it's still warm enough to sit outside. So we have our tea on the verandah, and look at the beauty that surrounds us. The still lake. Birds flitting about. Squirrels gathering whatever it is they gather. And we drink our tea amid the peacefulness of it all.

"Enough shilly-shallying for me," Maria says and stands up just as the phone rings.

"Shilly-shallying?" I have to laugh. I swear, I don't know where she picks up some of the words she uses, though I know she likes to watch all the British TV shows to improve her English, and that's probably where that one has come from.

I slowly sip the tea and think about how lucky I am to be surrounded by people who care; people who not only love me, but who also love my children.

For the longest time I sit in my chair thinking, hurting, and being grateful, all at the same time. The phone rings in the distance.

"It's for you," Maria yells from the kitchen. "It's Doctor Martineau."

"Ok, I'll take it out here," I yell back and pick up the cordless extension. Briefly I wonder why she's calling me here but then I remember that I'd left Antonia's number as an alternative.

"Hello Mary? What's up?"

"I want you to come in and see me as soon as possible," I hear her sweet voice through the wire.

"But why? I'm not due for a checkup for another two weeks."

"I know. Don't you think I know that? Try to come this afternoon. Any time. It's important."

"But..." before I can continue she has hung up.

I am freaking. Totally freaking. Why does she want to see me out of the blue? It can't be good. No sense in panicking. She didn't sound really serious or anything. Just rushed. I mean if something were wrong, she would have said, right?

In the afternoon, Maria drives me to Mary's office. She grabs a wheelchair since I don't have enough energy to walk the long hallway.

"I'll be back momentarily, ok? I'll just park the car."

Here she goes again, I mean, *momentarily*, please. I surprise myself thinking about such a trivial thing as Maria's stab at the King's English. I mean, I give her credit, she tries really, really hard and it's so sweet, in a way.

I don't have to wait for more than a minute before Mary comes flying out of her office. She wheels me inside and plunks her big backside into her big leather chair.

"Well?" I ask apprehensively.

"I have news.. Good news.. Really good news, in fact."

She's rubbing her hands with glee. I don't think in all the time that I've known her I've ever seen her so excited, breathless almost.

"Good news? For me? There's a switch."

"Yep, good news... very good indeed."

She makes an impressive pause and I can see that she is totally pleased with herself.

"How would you like to have your PICC line removed?"

"Get off the IV? Oh my God. Really? Are you kidding? There's nothing I'd like better in the whole world. This thing is like an albatross 'round my neck. But how can I get off it? What about the medication?"

"Ok, settle down, I'm getting to that. As you know, Steph, I have a number of patients who are HIV positive or have AIDS. I'm working with a group of doctors in Toronto who are testing a new drug, called valganciclovir. The drug is taken orally. It's similar to ganciclovir, which is administered by a catheter, like the one you have. In other words, valganciclovir contains all the medication you're now getting intravenously, only it is taken orally. And only those patients who have contracted cytomegalovirus retinitis qualify for the experiment and…."

"Oh my God, Mary," my voice is choking, "oh my God, of course I'll do it. I'll do just about anything to get rid of this thing… and.."

"Well, the thing is, I can only select a handful of patients. Naturally the medication is in short supply at the moment. They haven't mass-produced it yet because they have to wait for the outcome of the tests. Whether it really works, that sort of thing. But a lot of AIDS patients can't wait that long, time is running out for them. I have patients who are much, much sicker than you are, Steph, but I've decided to include you in the group, if you wish, because you're still young. You won't give up without a fight.. And there are the kids, of course."

Tears spring to my eyes. I am so grateful, so very, very grateful to Mary for choosing me to take part in this study.

"You must understand that this is strictly in the experimental stages, Stephanie. There's a chance that it will not work and you'll have to go back on the IV."

"I don't care, Mary, I really don't. I mean, it's worth a shot isn't it? If it works, great. If not, I haven't lost anything. When do we start?"

"It's not quite as simple as that. First, we have to take the central line out, that's not a big procedure. In fact, Nurse.. What's her name again? The nurse that comes to your place..."

"Helga."

"Yes, of course, Helga. Nice woman, very efficient. Wait, doesn't she have a little poodle with a funny name?"

"Slick," I laugh, "she has a Yorkie named Slick."

"Oh yes, silly of me. Yorkie, poodle, they're both small. Anyway, Helga is a qualified nurse. She can remove the line in your home. I'll call her and authorize the procedure."

"Will it be painful?"

Mary shakes her head.

"No, it won't hurt a bit. You probably won't even feel it. After the line is removed you'll have to be monitored on a daily basis to make sure the pills are working and there are no complications. You'll have to go to the clinic for that."

"Oh Mary. I don't care. I don't care about that. I would stay in a hospital for a month if I had to. You have no idea what it means to get rid of this thing. I guess I shouldn't complain though; it's kept me alive all this time. But still..."

I cannot continue. I'm afraid I'll cry again and anyway, the pills may not work for me and I'll be back to square one. And then what?

I can tell from the look in Mary's eyes that she understands.

"After you've been on the pills for a while and everything seems to be working out ok, you have to go back to the clinic every couple of weeks and then every three weeks until you're down to once a month or so, ok?"

"Ok, I'll do anything you say. Anything. My God, Mary, it'll almost feel like being back to normal. So when can we start? "

Mary pushes her chair away from her desk and comes around to give me a quick hug.

"Well, we can do it in a couple of days. And the next time I see you will be for your regular examination. I don't foresee any problems there, so I'll schedule you in for the end of the month."

She pushes the wheelchair down the hallway where Maria is waiting anxiously.

"Everything alright Chiquita?"

"Oh, Maria, everything is splendid.. Unbelievably splendid indeed."

I'm not mocking her English and she knows it.. I'm just so happy looking into her beaming face.

I'm floating on cloud nine.. No more IV .. It's almost too good to be true.

Antonia is waiting for us when we return.

"Where have you been? Don't ever do that to me again," she starts before I can get a word in. She has a worried look on her face.

"What?"

"Take off without a phone call, a note, something. I was freaking out and Maria not being here either.."

"Sorry, Toni. Mary called and asked me to come over straight away.. and .. well, I didn't even think to leave a note, I didn't expect you back so early."

"Steph, it's only a two hour drive to the school. I've been back since three o'clock and going nuts thinking something has happened to you."

"Sorry Hon. I really am, but Maria didn't think of calling you either, did she?"

"I forgot my cell phone at home," Maria says.

"Well, ok then, next time please, please let me know when you take off unexpectedly. So why did Doctor Mary want to see you out of the blue? Not anything bad I hope?"

"Oh Toni, it's the best news ever. Guess what? I'm getting rid of the IV.. Isn't it fabulous? I'll be able to take proper showers again and go out in the sun and.."

"That's fantastic! I'm so happy for you, but how are you getting the medication that you need?"

Maria has made a pot of tea and brought some biscuits. We sit at the kitchen table and I explain everything Mary has told me. To say that Antonia is delighted would be a huge understatement.

"But now tell me how the trip went," I ask, "how is the school, I know, I know, you've checked it out before so I guess nothing has changed there. Do the kids like their rooms, are they nice, do they miss me?"

"Oh Steph, please. They've only been gone since this morning. Their rooms are lovely, they overlook a park and the football field and I think they'll be very, very happy there, ok?"

"Yes, of course Toni, they'll be happy. And I must go home now if you'll take me please."

"No way, you're staying here and we'll talk."

I'm not protesting too much. The thought of being alone in my apartment has been bothering me for days. What if I need something? Sure, Aunt Sissy lives just around the corner, but still it's the whole aloneness thing that I'll have to get used to.

And there's the thought of the companion... Always near... Always within reach, it seems. And though I've gotten used to his invisible presence, the thought of being alone with his heavy shadow looming, frightens me more than I care to admit.

So I'm happy to accept Toni's offer and I know tomorrow in the light of day things will look different.

I will have all day to mentally prepare for the emptiness in my apartment and I'll be ready for that, even when his presence gets ever closer with the coming of nightfall.

But I also know that I'll never get used to the feeling of dread, the fear of him catching up with me.

Tonight though, I'm free.

Chapter 24

I'm not having a good night after all, too much has happened today. Dr. Martineau's phone call that had unsettled me so much and turned out to be such good news after all. And the children going off to school, though both of them called at night to tell me they miss me already but they also love their new surroundings and I put on my happiest voice for them so they wouldn't feel guilty or something.

But it's all been a bit much. I wasn't able to eat any supper and only had a little soup, which is better than nothing, but I had to force myself to eat even that because I had no appetite.

Antonia looked a little worried. As usual, she finished a large plate of pasta with a glass of wine, even dessert. I swear, I have no idea where she puts it all, but looking at her I'm beginning to believe that her motto 'pasta makes you happy and keeps you slim' is not altogether farfetched, at least it works for her because she looks fabulous.

"You don't mind if I go to bed?" I asked when we had finished eating.

"Of course not, Hon, I'm a bit tired myself and will turn in soon. It's been a long day. Maybe I'll watch something stupid on TV before I go to sleep."

She gives me a quick hug and goes upstairs with me to make sure that everything is in place in the bathroom and the bed has fresh sheets on it. There's no need to check, of course, because Maria has seen to it all. Toni just wants to make sure that I'm ok up here on my own.

She gives me a quick kiss on the cheek.

"Try to get some sleep, I'll see you at breakfast, ok?"

"Ok, I'm sure I'll have no trouble sleeping tonight. I'm pretty tired after all that's happened."

But sleep will not come. I'm lying here wide awake and everything that's happened today is going round and round in my head.

And I know what it is that keeps me awake. I am scared. I am afraid of being alone in my apartment. I'm trying to think of what my daily routine will be like. Without the IV, things might be a bit easier though, at least I will be able to do many things that I can't do with it in place.

I will manage. I will be ok. I can always rely on Aunt Sissy. She's already asked me to move in with her but her apartment is just too small and besides, I like to have my own furniture and all my stuff around me and the children need their rooms when they come home. And staying in my place gives me a feeling of continuity, of safety and comfort, of home.

A pale swath of light filters through the sheers. The moon is full. Perhaps that's why I can't sleep.

But there's something else. Not only the feeling of aloneness but an intangible dread, an ice-cold fear of being completely abandoned.

And the companion is with me in the room. I can sense his presence and I'm afraid to go to sleep lest he takes power over my dreams. I know that that is nonsense but the feeling of dread is real. Very, very real.

And then, when I open my eyes again, bright sunlight streams through the curtains and despite the restless night, I feel refreshed and even a little hungry.

I find Antonia in the kitchen, boiling eggs and making toast.

"Morning. Did you sleep well? Come sit, have a cup of coffee and some toast, you must be hungry and even if you're not, try to eat anyway, ok?"

"Thanks, Toni. I actually am a bit hungry."

And I have toast and a soft boiled egg and a steaming hot cup of coffee.

"That's it? One slice of toast? You sure?"

"Yes, thanks, it's better than nothing though."

"Well, ok then. Let's take our coffee into the sun room. It's too chilly to sit outside but this way we can at least look out at the gorgeous morning."

The sun room is a little room just off the kitchen with windows all 'round and French doors opening out to the terrace. It's such a happy room with white wicker furniture and tons of plants.

"You should call this the Morning Room", I suggest, "I've always wanted to have a Morning Room, ever since I read Rebecca, at least I think that's where I read it. It sounds so lovely and so English."

"Well, of course Rebecca would have a morning room. She even had special vases for lilac, for heaven's sake. But, if you like, we'll call it the morning room. It does sound nice, nice to start your morning in a pretty room."

Antonia puts her feet on the coffee table and shoots a sideway glance at me.

"Steph?"

"What?"

"I've been thinking, and please believe me, I've been thinking about this a lot. I really want you to consider moving in with me."

"What?"

"Move into my house. I've asked you before and I respected your reasons for not wanting to do it then. But now, with the children at school.. Well, it's different, isn't it? So before you start up again with all your charity business, please think about it in a different way. You'll actually be doing me a favor. The house is far too big but I don't want to give it up. I love it too much, but I feel quite lonely at times, rambling around by myself, and it would be nice to have someone to share it with me.

Besides, you need someone around to make sure that you're ok, with the AIDS and all and.."

"Toni, thanks, but no thanks. I hear what you're saying and I love you for it, but if I lose my independence, I lose everything. I lose myself. If I can't take care of myself any longer it would feel as if I'm giving up... giving in to the disease that has wrecked my life. I will not do that. I will not let that happen..."

"Ok, hold it for a minute, I'm not asking you to give up or give in. I'm asking as a friend, or soul sister if you like, to look at this whole thing in a pragmatic manner..

I need your company. You need monitoring, for lack of a better word... And together we can complement each other's life. You see?"

I can honestly say that I've never looked at it that way, that she may need me as much as I need her. Well, needing is not the right word... Wanting me around and vice versa would be more like it.

Ok, I have to be honest, I have to be practical, and all that losing myself doesn't really change the reality, the way things really are. Sure, I'd like to be strong enough to fight this disease on my own but the fact is, it already has me in its grip to the point where I'm afraid to be alone because I may not be able to cope with a sudden attack of breathlessness, or fainting, or worse.

I look at Toni.

"You know something? Perhaps you're right. I think it's a wonderful idea for me to move into your house. But we have to get a few things straight from the outset.."

"Well, thank heavens you're seeing sense, Steph. Of course we have to work things out first and don't think I haven't thought about it in detail. So here is what I would suggest. You pay your share of the household expenses the same way you pay rent at the co-op, no more, no less. That way the place is yours just as with any other rental arrangement. We'll move your own furniture upstairs, there's plenty of room and you will feel more at home.."

"Well, that sounds nice but there's just one little thing, what about the children? When they come home?"

"Don't you think I've thought about that too? Give me a little credit, will you? Well, I had the coolest idea... You know the guest house down by the edge of the lake? We'll have their very own rooms set up in there. What do you think? They have their own bedrooms and a bathroom and there's a living room and a small kitchen and..."

"Oh, Toni, that's a super idea, they will totally love it. I'm so grateful to you..."

"Ok. Stop right there. There's nothing to be grateful about, it's a perfect solution that will be good for all of us. What I mean is that we will all benefit... We'll be like one big happy family and Maria will be part of that too."

"Maria?"

"Yes, I have asked Maria to move in as my full time housekeeper and she has agreed. She'll have her own living quarters in the west wing of the house. It's a totally self contained one bedroom apartment with a one-car garage attached. You've probably seen it from the outside; it's tucked back a bit. Maria works her regular hours, but will be available if we should need her for something."

"Something?"

"Steph, Honey, I've told you once before, I'm no Florence Nightingale. So if something happens with the AIDS and all, like when you need help, well, I really don't know what could happen, but she'll be here to help, see? It's perfect. Of course I had to tell her about your illness, it's only fair, but it doesn't matter to her. Maria grew up in a dirt poor section of Guadalajara where there's a lot of prostitution, and many of the women, and men, I guess, are HIV positive or have AIDS. She knows how you got it and she also knows that the risk of being infected in a home environment is practically zero.

When you first told me about the AIDS back in Virginia, I informed myself, that's only common sense and so I know that everyday contact like kissing, shaking hands or sharing cutlery or other stuff does not result in the virus being passed on. And unless there are cuts and open wounds, you know, from needles or sharp objects, where it can get into another person's bloodstream, there is no risk of infection."

"Yes, Toni, I know. I studied anything and everything I could get my hands on to find out about the risks of infection for my children's sake. The absolute best day of my life was the day the clinic called and confirmed that my kids had tested negative. You have no idea what that meant to me, I was terrified that they might have been infected at birth. Of course, it also meant that Mark got the AIDS after they were born. So much for marriage vows. But never mind that, the main thing is that the kids are ok."

"So you don't mind that I told Maria?"

"Of course not, if she's part of the household, live-in or out, it's the responsible thing to do. I would have told her myself if you hadn't already done so. And I'm glad she'll be around because she's fun to talk to and what's more, she's a great cook. I mean her quesadillas, I could eat them even when I don't have an appetite…"

"Yep, she's a good cook but you have to admit that my pasta…"

"Nobody can hold a candle to your pasta, Toni, that goes without saying."

She smiles and nods her head.

"Si, you have to be Italian to make perfect pasta al dente. So I guess we've covered the basics. I suppose we could draw up a rental agreement if you want to make the arrangement more official. It's not necessary, but I know how you are about wanting to pay your own way…"

"You're right; I don't think that's necessary. I'm getting pretty excited about the whole thing, in fact, I can't wait, when should we start?"

"There's no time like the present, is there? You give notice at the co-op, thirty days should do it. They have a waiting list a mile long, so it's not that the place will be vacant for any length of time. And in the meantime we'll fix up your flat upstairs, you know, paint it, get rid of the stuff that's in it and bring in your furniture and things."

Antonia makes it sound so simple and, as it turns out, it is simple.

I stay at my apartment for another couple of weeks and Aunt Sissy sleeps in Bettina's bedroom so that I won't be alone. And she's with me when Sister Helga shows up at noon on Saturday.

"I guess this will be the last time you see me, Stephanie," she smiles and plunks her black bag on a chair.

Her face is rosy and shiny from the cool breeze outside.

It's only the beginning of October but already the days are getting shorter and though all the bushes and trees are aglow in a brilliant display of crimson and copper and gold, you can sense the nip of winter in the air.

"Well, Stephanie, today is the big day and I'm so very happy for you that you're getting rid of the IV and moving on to oral medication. You are lucky to be included in Dr. Martineau's group and I'm totally thrilled because things look very promising. Very promising indeed. And you deserve a break after all you've been through, heaven knows."

"Thanks, Helga," I smile at her, "but you won't be a stranger will you? You must come and visit and bring Slick, even if the cat won't be thrilled. Will you promise that?"

"Of course I will, absolutely. But let's get on with it now, shall we?"

"Will it hurt?"

"Not a bit, just don't look if it bothers you."

Nurse Helga rolls up the sleeve of my loose shirt. I don't want to see what she's doing, so I look over at Aunt Sissy who is sitting beside me, holding my hand. She looks rather pale, but she stays with me during the whole procedure which doesn't take very long at all and there is no pain.

"Finished", Helga says. "That wasn't so bad, was it?"

She cleans the spot where the IV used to enter my arm and covers it with a small bandage.

"There you go, Stephanie, just change the bandage twice a day. This should heal in no time."

"Thank you so much, Helga, you were right, it didn't hurt one bit. When can I take a proper shower?"

"Tonight, I should think. So long as you dry the spot and cover it with a fresh bandage, just like you would any other small cut."

I am so happy and relieved. I keep moving my arm and it seems like a miracle that I don't feel anything. After all these months living with the constant discomfort, I feel free at last and in my heart I offer a little thank you prayer to Mary.

Nurse Helga stays for a cup of tea and talks about the antics little Slick has been up to. I know I'll miss her daily visits. She's made friends with Aunt Sissy too and they are already planning on playing bridge together, which will be great for both of them.

Antonia has a bunch of painters and workmen in the house to renovate the upstairs and turn it into my new home.

She had been right, of course, once my furniture is in place and we've hung my pictures and moved in the plants and the cat, it is cozier than I had expected. I have a large balcony off the bedroom looking out on the tall trees and the lawn and the lake, shimmering in the background. And there is a fireplace in the living room that reminds me so much of my house in Virginia.

Adam and Bettina are ecstatic about the move. Almost every day I'm on the phone with one or the other, mostly Bettina because she loves to talk, and I have kept them up to date on everything that's happening.

The weekend before my move they come home and they're busy packing their own stuff into boxes and labeling them. I am so happy to have them with me, it's been ages since they left, or so it seems. Both of them are so much more mature than when they left only a few weeks ago, but I'm probably only imagining that.

For now, the children have their own rooms in the basement of Antonia's house. Big rooms, to be sure, and there's a pool table downstairs which they're thrilled about. Toni hasn't mentioned anything about the guest house yet because she wants it to be ready first, so it will be a huge surprise for sure.

It hurts when they leave to go back to school after the weekend but I guess every mother feels the same and you have to let them go sooner or later, I only wish it were later. They hug and kiss me goodbye and tell me over and over how happy they are that I'm going to live at Antonia's.

"Now we don't have to worry about you so much, Mom," Adam says, "we know you'll be safe and happy there and it's such a beautiful house.. Nothing like the co-op, but that isn't too bad either.." he adds hastily.

My grown up boy. How much he looks like his father and how unlike his father he really is. He's so sweet and kind and very serious when it comes to his studies. I'm glad that he and his sister are at the same school and can look out for one another.

And Bettina too is changing and growing up faster than I would like. She can't be my baby girl forever, of course, but it seems there's no transition period. Little girl one day, young woman the next. And she is getting prettier every time I see her with her sparkling blue eyes and flawless skin. At least she has that from me, other than that she is the spitting image of my mom.

It takes no time at all for me to settle in and I truly treasure my new place. It is calm and peaceful, there is no traffic noise, no neighbors arguing and slamming doors, or playing loud music and partying. An oasis of peace but still close to the city and shopping and the clinic and my doctors' offices. In fact, it's only a fifteen minute drive from my old apartment but the difference is as great as living in a high-rise or a country estate.

On Friday before Thanksgiving Antonia comes home from the market and plunks a huge turkey onto the counter.

"Cripes, I could barely lift that thing."

Both Maria and I look at the bird, it's big enough to feed an army.

"Toni, are you nuts? Who's going to eat such an enormous turkey? There are only three of us?"

But she only laughs, takes off her hat and shakes loose her red hair until it dances around her face.

"Nope, I'm picking up the kids this afternoon and they're bringing a couple of friends. So I think we'll barely have enough. It was supposed to be a surprise."

"Oh Toni, I could kiss you!"

I didn't think the children would be home for Thanksgiving since they already had a weekend off for moving. But, leave it to Antonia, she wanted them to be home and home they will be.

"There's only one small problem," Antonia says and pokes the bird with her finger, "I have no idea how to cook such an animal. We have to find some kind of cookbook or look it up on the internet..."

"Internet?" Maria laughs out loud... "Internet turkey? Oh Madre mia, leave it to me. I know how to cook turkey Mexican style and it will be good, very good indeed."

It turns out to be the happiest Thanksgiving that I can remember since my life changed forever.

Bettina and Adam have brought a couple of friends, great kids whose parents live too far away for them to go home for the holiday, and we have a fabulous feast, thanks to Maria's Mexican turkey.

And I feel great. I even manage to eat, not so much the turkey but stuffing and gravy and dessert.

After dinner, the kids are eager to play pool with their friends but before they go downstairs, Antonia takes them down to the guest house by the lake for their big surprise.

I watch from the window. She had wanted me to come along but it's Antonia's surprise, her gift to the children, and after a long while they come racing back to the house totally beside themselves with excitement.

So their new home in the guest house is a big, big hit. They will have their privacy and be able to have their friends over, but they are close enough to be part of the family. We hug and kiss and take turns hugging and kissing Antonia and we're altogether thankful. Truly thankful for all we have.

Maria is standing next to us, beaming.

"We do not have Thanksgiving in Mexico," she says, "not like here, but I like it, I like it very much indeed. Feliz dia de gracia," she adds softly... "Happy Thanksgiving."

I feel very tired when I finally go upstairs to sleep. And thinking about the day, and thinking about my new life in Antonia's house, and thinking about all the love that surrounds me, I feel blessed. Despite all that's happened and all that may still happen, I'm blessed.

And the only thing I've not left behind is the companion.

He is with me still and will be for the rest of my days.

I know it. I feel it.

And I will have to come to terms with his presence.

Chapter 25

"I've decided to go to work!" Sitting down for breakfast, her hands cupped 'round a cup of coffee, Antonia looks at me across the table.

I drop my piece of toast. "Work?... Work?... You?... But you've never, I mean, in the whole of your life, you've never worked?"

She looks a little hurt.

"That's not entirely true, I worked when I was at college, worked at the library in Milano actually, and I was pretty good at what I was doing..."

I pick up my toast again. "Ok, sorry, so you worked... For how long?"

"Well, for almost six months, after school..."

"Yeah, that will do it alright, that will give you the experience they are looking for."

"Who is looking for?"

"Well, wherever you're going to apply for a job, they'll be looking for experience and..."

Antonia throws back her head and bursts into laughter. She's got a funny way of laughing, infectious, you know. She laughs and laughs until you can't help it and you laugh right along with her, even though you don't know why or what's so funny.

"Oh, Steph, you're too much ... Not that kind of work, silly. I'm thinking of opening a little boutique, something special... a little place where women can come and find little treasures that won't cost them a lot... You know?"

"Oh, I get it. I understand. You'd be fantastic at doing something like that and you'd be your own boss and can come and go as you please."

"Well, that's one reason. I also feel that I would like to add a little beauty to this world, I think every woman deserves to have that and most of them don't allow themselves the little luxuries or they can't afford them. That's what I'm after; it won't be a big money making venture, just something that's close to my heart."

I rest my chin on my hands and look at her beautiful face. She has a faraway look in her eyes, as if remembering something she'd rather not remember.

"That's really sweet of you, Toni; I mean thinking of how to make other women's lives brighter. I'm surprised that you would think along those lines."

"Why?" she turns her head and looks straight at me. "Why would you think that?"

"Well, you've always had everything anyone could wish for. The houses, the trips, the clothes, the money.." I can hear how lame that sounds.

"Steph," she takes a sip of coffee and looks into my eyes. "Steph, I've not always had money. In fact, I grew up dirt poor as a child and as close to an orphan as you can get."

Her amber eyes are dark with memories and a fine line that I've never noticed before has appeared on her forehead. A line that reflects pain - pain and sorrow.

I look down at the tablecloth and start shifting little crumbs back and forth.

"Sorry, Toni, I didn't know. You've always seemed to be so care-free... carefree and happy and I naturally assumed... I don't know what I assumed."

"Oh, don't be silly, of course you couldn't have known and I never talk about it. But you are my friend, my very best friend, my soul sister in fact. So yes, I don't mind telling you."

She pauses for a long while and takes my hand.

"I grew up in Milano, as you know, in the poorest corner of Milano, to be exact. My mother died when she had me and I never knew my father. It was shameful, very shameful even in those poor parts of town, to have a child out of wedlock and I think, my mother wanted to die. She was very young, sixteen I think, and she wouldn't have been able to handle the pressure of raising a child on her own in those days.

"So I was taken in by relatives. My mother's sister and her husband took me in and raised me. It was a guilt thing, you know, they didn't really want me but they didn't want to stick me into an orphanage either for fear of how people would talk. So I grew up without any love or affection and I only had my books and my imagination to keep me happy."

I don't know what to say. I look at Antonia's perfect features and I can't see the little girl living without hope, without love, with only her imaginary friends. It seems impossible; she's always so happy and has such a great outlook on life.

"I might as well tell you about the rest of my life in a nutshell," she continues after a long pause. "I guess I was born under a lucky star. I was always a quiet child, but happy, I always knew there was something better waiting for me to be discovered. And I loved to read, every chance I had, I had my nose in a book."

"My uncle used to take me to his job every so often because my aunt worked cleaning houses and they couldn't afford a babysitter. He worked in a publishing house, operating the printing press. I found that fascinating; fascinating to see how books are made. And I would sit in a corner somewhere and pass the time reading.

"My uncle's boss was a staunch and crusty old bachelor, mean and miserable looking with hardly ever a kind word for anyone. But he took a liking to me and always brought a shiny new book or an apple or some candy to the dark corner where I was sitting. And he made sure I got a good education. He sent me far away to a private school and on to university and he paid for everything. He never ever asked for anything in return except that I study hard, and he'd always say to me:

'Bambina, you are a beautiful girl, you will become a beautiful woman and you will have a wonderful life, but not without an education which is more important than all the beauty in the world.'

"His name was Giovanni and even though he was terribly rich, he was in poor health, I think he had TB or something like that and he died the year I finished University. He left me a little money, not a lot, but a good sum and the rest of his fortune went to some ridiculous charity. At least everyone thought it was ridiculous, but I didn't. Because sometimes, when we had our little chats in his office, he sitting by the fireplace to 'keep the old bones warm' as he used to say, and me on a little footstool next to him, he'd share his philosophy on life.

"Bambina", he said, "I've made a lot of money in my life. At one time I thought that was a good thing to do and then the money kind of made itself and there was no satisfaction in it. I've never met a woman that I loved enough to make her my wife so I preferred not to marry. But," he chuckled and took in a wheezy breath and looked at me as if we were conspirators, "I've always loved cats. As you know, I have a bunch of them and they keep pretty well to themselves. Not like people who crawl all over you when they think there's something to be had. So you'll see, Bambina, when I die…You'll see where my money will go!" And he'd cackle like an old witch but he was the smartest and kindest man I've ever known and I understood about the cats and he knew that I understood.

"So, long story short, he left most of his fortune to an organization that looked after stray and homeless cats. Don't you think that's fantastic?"

Antonia looks at me with a sparkle in her eyes. She must have loved that old man who was so kind to her and saw the spunk in the little girl.

"What a story, Tony, straight out of Dickens. It must have been so hard for you as a little girl without parents and without anyone loving you apart from Giovanni..."

"Oh no, it wasn't hard, when you don't get any love, you don't miss it. You can't miss what you don't know, right?"

"I don't know, I suppose so and here I thought that you've always lived the good life, spoiled, rich, you know? I'm sorry. I've been so occupied with myself and with my problems I've never even asked..."

"Don't be silly, how on earth could you have known? It's not as if I haven't outgrown all of that and moved on with my life."

"Yes, and then you met Ken and..."

"Yes, and then I met Ken."

Antonia puts her elbows on the table and rests her chin in her hands. The fine line on her forehead has disappeared and she looks out the window at the wide expanse of lawn and the lake far beyond.

"Well? You married Ken, you loved him, and you had a grand life together..."

"Yes, a grand life. Listen, Steph, I've never told anyone this but.. I didn't really love Ken, you know, the way a woman loves a man, and he didn't love me that way either. He liked me, he liked me a lot, even loved me in his own way, and he showered me with every luxury a woman could possibly dream of. Remember when we first met and I took you to see my horses? "

"Of course, you said: these are my best friends."

"Right. And I meant it. Ken bought me, it was an arrangement, I had the looks, the education, the European flair whatever that is, to make the perfect wife. And he offered me safety, security, and America. So I married him."

I am speechless; stunned and speechless. "But... I thought, well you always seemed to be so happy and Ken worshipped you until, well, until..."

"Yes, until the young blonde came along."

Antonia gets up to make a fresh pot of coffee and soon the soothing perk is all I hear in the silence. She doesn't say anything and I don't want to press. I know she'll tell me everything when she's ready.

"I'm ready," she says suddenly. I swear she can read my thoughts. "I'm ready to tell you the rest of my story... "

"You don't have to, Toni, if you'd rather not..."

"I know I don't have to, but I want to. If I cannot talk to you, there's no one else in the world that I would want to tell about my life."

The coffee is ready. Toni pours us a fresh cup and sits down again, heavy like. She blows a strand of hair out of her face and takes a long sip.

"I married Ken because it was convenient, it suited us both. I loved him like a brother, he has a good sense of humor and a quick sharp wit, you know? We had a lot of fun together. And, of course, he had money. Lots and lots of it."

"If you marry me in name only", he said, "you'll be well looked after. We'll have a pre-nuptial drawn up and you'll never ever have to work a day in your life."

"But," I interrupt, "didn't you want to marry for love? With your looks and intellect and your personality, you must have had dozens of guys swarming around..."

Antonia shoots a quick amused glance at me.

"Well, I suppose, but I didn't want that kind of commitment. It wouldn't have been fair to any man... you see, Steph, I cannot have children... That's why".

"Oh." I don't know what else to say. I had wondered a few times in the past of course, since Toni is such a natural with kids, almost as if she's still a kid herself.

"Oh..." I say again.

Her beautiful mouth is set in a straight hard line.

"I was raped," she continues "by a neighbor. My uncle's best friend. My uncle knew, they all knew, but they did nothing about it.

I got a terrible infection and the doctors at the hospital screwed up badly, so then I could not have children... ever!"

Antonia's voice is so matter of fact, so unemotional; I can only sit and stare with my mouth open, not knowing what to say... How to respond... Nothing!

There is a long, long pause. Antonia gazes out the window and then her eyes turn to me. "I was twelve," she concludes her story,

"I was twelve years old."

I feel like weeping but I know this is not the time to cry. All I can think of is how preoccupied I've been all the time since I've known her. It was all about my problems. My marriage. My kids. My AIDS. My treatments. And all the while she carried her past around with her and stood by my side to help me, to help my children. I feel ashamed. Shocked, sad, and ashamed.

"Toni", I whisper, "Toni, I had no idea. You always seemed so happy and without a care in the world. You should have told me sooner..." my voice trails off; I take her hand in mine.

"Perhaps," she says, "perhaps I should have, but it all happened such a long time ago. I have come to terms with it."

"You must hate and despise all the people who did this to you. That man... your family... the doctors at the hospital..."

"Well, it's a funny thing, you know. When you're that little, you just don't understand and then, when you get older you have to make a choice. Carry hate and bitterness for the rest of your days, or get over it and move on. I came to realize that none of this was my fault and I was not a lesser person for it. In fact, I came to love myself for what I'd been through and how I chose to deal with it. It's over, it's done. I cannot make it undone and I have much to be grateful for. Life is beautiful if you decide that it is!"

Her brown eyes are warm with emotion and a soft smile appears on her face.

"Over... Finito... Basta!"

She slaps the table with her flat hand. The coffee cup takes a little jump.

"Ok, Steph," she smiles "now you know. It actually feels good being able to talk about all that stuff without bitterness. And now we move on and find a little store!"

I'm still in shock but I have to respect and admire her attitude.

"Only one more thing, Toni, and we'll never have to talk about this again..."

"Ok, shoot, what?"

"Ken, I mean, didn't he know? Didn't he want to have children?"

She looks at me, a little amused.

"Hon, I thought you might have gathered by now. Ken is gay!"

"What?"

I jump up so quickly, I knock over my coffee cup and spill its contents all over the table.

"What? What do you mean... gay?"

"Gay. Homosexual. Ken likes boys!"

"What about the little blonde secretary?"

"Secretaries come in both genders. This one is male. I guess I didn't make that clear."

I plop back on the chair and look at the little coffee puddle. Toni gets some paper towels and mops up the spill.

"Sorry, Sweetie" she says, totally calm and cool. "I guess that was a little much to take in. But you see, that's why our marriage was so perfect. Ken was totally paranoid, absolutely and one hundred per cent paranoid about admitting that he was gay, especially to his father who was an old fashioned tyrant and SOB. Sorry, but it's true. So marrying me was the perfect cover and it shut up the old goat. Ken and I got along fine. We liked the same things, books, food, travel, see?"

She chuckles and looks at me.

"That's why you weren't heartbroken when he left you..."

"Precisely, that's why I wasn't heartbroken. We stay in touch, he's happy now that he can live without pretenses, now that his father is dead!"

I take a deep breath and push myself away from the table.

"Well, ok, thanks a lot for those bombshells," I say, trying to make light of the situation. "I'll help Maria with the dishes. And you better start shop hunting."

Toni gives me a big hug and kiss. "I'm glad we talked, Steph. It's good to have things out in the open... OK, shop hunting it is."

And with that she grabs her purse and coat and flies out the door.

Chapter 26

You just never know what's going to happen in your life, do you? I certainly don't know from one day to the next. Like yesterday, for instance.

I was sitting on the verandah wrapped in a huge soft blanket against the autumn chill and I had just finished my tea.

It is one of those rare mornings when I feel good, physically good, glad to be alive you know? I guess I have more reasons than most people to be glad to be alive.. Many, many more reasons.

And I now look at little things and appreciate them. Little, everyday things like perfect and ever changing cloud formations… A flower opening its petals to the sun… A mild breeze rustling in the leaves… Morning dew drops on the lawn… You know? Things.

I know these things have always been there, but I've never really seen them, never paid much attention and I'm thinking just how so many beautiful things in life are free and here for everyone to appreciate. And if, on top of all that, I feel well, physically well, then, yes, I'm glad to be alive and it's a good day.

These days don't come to me as often as they used to, when I was still normal. I separate 'normal' from the post AIDS days, before I even knew what AIDS was and that I would ever become one of its victims. Those were my 'normal' days, these are my AIDS days.

Anyway, as I said, I've just finished my tea when Maria calls from the kitchen.

"There's someone here to see you, Chiquita," she yells, "some friend of yours."

I look up and there she is. After all these years, there she stands on the threshold of the kitchen and it is as if I've seen her only yesterday.

"Nanette... Oh my God!"

"I wasn't sure that you wanted to see me," still standing on the threshold.

"But of course, oh Nanette, I don't know what to say, it's been forever..."

And then she comes rushing over and we hold each other. Hold each other and our tears mix as we kiss and hug and kiss again and I don't know who lets go first.

Maria brings more tea and biscuits and we sit and stare at each other.

She has not changed, well, yes, she's older of course and she's put on a few pounds, but she's still Nanette. Same sparkling blue eyes, same raven hair, same sweetness in her smile. I can't stop looking at her, my God, how long has it been? Let's see. Before my marriage, before my children, before Virginia, before the nightmare took over my life. Oh God, Nanette, if only I had listened to you. If only..

But I didn't. I didn't and I'm paying the ultimate price. I'm paying with my life because surely with all that has happened, with all the invasive surgeries, with all the battering about, my body won't be able to take much more.

But I know I cannot give up, I will not give up, not now.. Not ever. For as long as I have a breath in my body I will fight, I will hang on. For my children. For the people who love me. For myself. And somewhere in my mind I know with absolute certainty that I'm not ready to go, not just yet.

The companion will just have to bide his time.

"Well", Nanette strokes back her hair and blows her nose in a tissue. "Well, I don't know what to say to you. I should have tried to find you sooner, it was just..."

"Yeah, I know. I didn't try either. I didn't think you'd want to ever see me again after, well, you know."

"I understand, I didn't understand then, but I do now. I was very, very hurt and didn't think I could ever forgive you for doubting me. But never mind all that now", she continues, "it's water under the proverbial."

She stops and bites her lip and looks at me with questions in her eyes.

"So, how are you, Steph, I mean, really?"

"I guess you know?"

"About the AIDS, yes, I do know. I found out in the strangest way. Remember Helga? Your nurse? Well, she used to come to the house to help my mother in law, who was very sick before she died and she talked about you and how heartbroken she was about your situation. I mean, she didn't mention your name or anything, but I kind of put the pieces together, the way she talked about you and that you had lived in Virginia, and she mentioned certain people and all.."

"Nurse Helga.. Oh yes, of course, we don't really stay in touch any longer but she plays bridge with my aunt every now and then. Well Nan, now you know and I guess I've paid a pretty steep price for not listening to you."

There's a long pause. Nanette stares into the distance.

"What I really mean to say, Steph, is, no I didn't understand how you could possibly be so in love with someone that you would risk our friendship and take his word over mine. We were so close, we shared everything, so to me, that was the ultimate betrayal. But.."

She sits quiet for a long, long time.

"But now I do understand. I too fell in love with a man whom I would have given my life for. I loved and trusted him so totally, so utterly, so unconditionally that, many, many times, I asked myself whether I had been too harsh on you. Whether I should have just let it go. Because, no matter what anyone would have said to me when I fell in love, nothing would have changed my mind or my feelings for my husband. Nothing!"

"So you finally married? Any kids? Tell me everything. "

"No children, no.. And nothing much to tell..It's a chapter in my life that I'm trying very hard to forget. I met Lars at a party, what else? Fell madly in love.. and divorced him when it turned out that he was a wife beater in the worst possible way. Don't get me wrong, when things were good, they were very good. I stayed with him for many years, thinking it was all my fault, hoping he would change.. Hoping he would start loving me again.. And so, yes, Steph now I totally understand why you acted the way you did.. And I'm sorry.. Truly sorry. And it breaks my heart to see you like this.."

"Like what?"

"Well," she takes a sip of tea and goes on. "Well, with the AIDS, what it's done to you. I mean, you're still so pretty but you've lost an awful lot of weight.."

"Yeah, I know. Remember how we always wanted to be model thin and then ordered pizza anyway? Well, I got my wish, only not the way I wanted it to happen."

"You're so brave, Steph. Anybody else would have given up, I'm sure, I won't ask how all of this happened, but one thing, how are your children? I guess they're ok? I'd love to see them sometime.. only.."

"Only what?"

"Well, ironically, I live in the States now.. Arizona to be exact. In Sedona, just north of Phoenix".

"I've heard about that place, it sounds magical.."

"It is. Really magical. After a final brutal beating that landed me in hospital, I left my husband and I started to look for something to fulfill me.. I know that sounds lame, but I wanted something outside of the everyday rat race.. I had to get as far away from him as possible so he would never find me again. And I needed time to heal both physically and emotionally, time to finally take care of myself.

"So I turned to spirituality, of sorts.. Don't laugh, I'm not chanting and meditating all day or anything like that, but I discovered there's so much more to life.. And death, for that matter. After my parents died.."

"Your parents are dead? Oh my God, I didn't know that Nan, I truly didn't. You can be sure that I would have done anything to find you had I known."

"Yes, they died six years ago. When they first found out that my dad had a brain tumor, it was at such an advanced stage that nothing could be done.. He only lasted a few weeks after the diagnosis.."

She falls silent and bites her lip, trying to hold back tears. I put my hand on hers and I feel like weeping too.

"And your mom?" I whisper.

"Mom died three months later. They couldn't really figure out what was wrong with her but I know she died of a broken heart, as banal as that sounds. You know how much she loved Dad, how inseparable they were, like two peas in a pod, quite literally. She couldn't handle living without him and I guess she felt that I was in good hands, being happily married and all, or so she thought. Of course, she never knew the reality of the nightmare I was trapped in because by that time they had moved to Montreal and I didn't see them very often and then I was too ashamed to confide in my Mom. So.."

Nanette blows her nose again and brushes a strand of hair out of her face.

With a deep sigh, she continues: "So, Mom just sort of gave up. She got pneumonia and never recovered. And now, I guess, Mom and Dad are together again. At least I'd like to think that."

"Shortly after Mom's death I left Lars. With her gone, even though she didn't live close by, he figured he had carte blanche because now I had no one to turn to, no one to call, no one to confide in or ask for help. The brutality got worse. He was beating and kicking me like a dog. Once he tried to strangle me and another time he pulled a knife and came after me."

"Oh my God, Nanette, but why didn't you look for help, like a shelter for battered women, or go to the police?"

"It's not easy to explain. When you're in that situation, all you can do is try to survive, make yourself small and invisible until the rage is over.. Just once I told him, 'I'll call the police' and his answer was 'you won't be alive when they get here'.. And I knew he meant it and I knew I would have been dead."

Nanette stares into the distance and it is as if she can still see these scenes of horror playing out in front of her eyes.

I'm horrified; I don't know what to say. I can't imagine that sweet, smart, spoiled Nanette could be trapped in such a nightmare.

She looks at me and smiles, a tiny sad smile.

"But that's all over now; I didn't mean to go into such detail, Stephanie, I only wanted you to know that I understand, understand that a person can be so enmeshed in a relationship that they lose all reason and common sense until it's too late. If they're lucky, they survive."

"Oh God, Nanette, I'm so sorry to hear all that. But how did you get away from him if he was so controlling?"

"That was the hard part. I had to arrange it so that he would not suspect in a million years that I was about to leave. But I got a lucky break. Lars was called out of town for a week to assist on a defective oil rig, he was an engineer, you see. There was no way that he could come home unexpectedly. So, I packed up some of my stuff, took all my savings, got into my car and drove to Sedona. I was ok financially because of the money I had inherited from my parents."

"And what do you do for a living?"

"Oh, I have a little shop and sell stuff. You know, crystals, spiritual books, music... Native jewelry... That sort of thing. You don't get rich doing that, but I don't need the money. And it's what I love to do and I'm at peace. Nothing else matters."

We sit for a long time without talking. And then Nanette and I look at each other and we both realize that there is nothing left to say ..

It's been too long.. We were young then and full of dreams.. And now?

What happened to the dreams? What happened to our hopes, our innocence?

Nanette finishes her tea and gets up and smoothes down her skirt.

"I have to go now, Steph. I'm driving back home this afternoon. It was so good to see you, I wish I could help you in some way but I don't know how. I know you'll beat this AIDS thing, you'll see.."

Her voice trails off. There's nothing more to add.

I get up and give her a final hug.

"Be happy, girl," I say "Just be happy."

I think I should feel sad, I think I should be crying, but I don't.

Too many years have passed. Too many changes in our lives... In a way it's as if I had talked to her only yesterday and then again, it's as if we're strangers. And we are. We were best friends then... We are strangers now.

"Bye, Nan, thanks for coming."

"Bye, you take good care of you, Steph... And if you ever come to Sedona..." her voice trails off once again...

"Yes, if I ever come to Sedona..."

And then she's gone.

And another chapter in my life is complete. The wound has healed; we have nothing left in common, nothing left to share.

I walk into the kitchen and give Maria a big hug.

"She was a good friend of yours, Chiquita?"

"Yes, a good friend, a very good friend... But now..." I shrug.

"I fully understand," Maria says in her best English "Time waits for no one..."

That doesn't really make any sense, but we both know what she means.

Through the kitchen window I see Nanette's car disappear around the bend in the road.

Another chapter of my life has closed.

Chapter 27

Antonia will be out of town when I have to go back to have my eyes checked after the cataract surgery.

She is flying to New York for an exhibition to see if she can find some stuff for her store. Well, her boutique, actually. She's renting this small store on Main Street and she's had it completely redecorated.

Done with typical Antonia flair, the store looks like a little jewel box with crystal and plants everywhere and candles flickering in glass bowls, their soft light bouncing off beautiful mirrors in gilded frames. She has soft music playing in the background and the whole atmosphere is calm, serene, and lovely.

The things she has for sale are lovely too; exotic necklaces from India, silk shawls from Paris, trendy handbags from Florence, and beautiful jewelry from all over the place. Things you don't find in your regular department stores, things that are just a little different and unusual.

Antonia calls her boutique "*Beauty on a Shoestring*" and the name is perfect because none of the items are overpriced, so many women who are on a budget can still afford to buy stuff. In one corner of the store is a huge old-fashioned samovar with tea brewing all day long and once word has gotten around, women just pop in to see what's new and have a cup of tea and a chat.

Toni doesn't spend all her time at the boutique. She's hired Erica, a young single mom who loves the store as much as Antonia does. Her daughter comes in after school and does her homework on a little desk that Toni has set up for that purpose. Erica, of course, adores Antonia and is thrilled about having a job that allows her to have her daughter with her.

This morning Antonia is throwing things into her suitcase which lies open on the bed. Neat, she's not, at least so far as packing goes.

"Are you sure you'll be ok when I'm gone? I know you have to go for your checkup; I'd feel better if I were around for that."

"Don't be silly. You are acting like a freaking Italian Mamma. Like you said, it's only a checkup and Maria will take me to the clinic."

"Well, ok, if you're sure. I'll call you Wednesday night to see how it went, ok? You shouldn't swear so much."

She stubs her toe at the end of the bed.

"Merda! Shit!!"

I can't help myself, I have to laugh.

"Who's swearing now? Hey, buy me something nice at the show."

"Like what?" She actually thinks I am serious.

"A diamond tiara would come in handy. It'll look great with my new track suit. I'm going for the trash-to-class look."

"You're an idiot, but I love you anyway."

Antonia zips up her suitcase and grabs her coat and handbag just as the airline limo pulls up in front of the house.

"See you in a couple of days," she gives me a quick hug and is out the door.

It's a cool and windy morning when Maria drops me off at the hospital entrance and goes to park the car.

"I'll be in the waiting room when you're ready to go home, Chiquita, ok?"

I am a little disappointed that Mary isn't here to do the checkup but apparently she was called to assist in an operation. So her colleague, a youngish man, slightly cross-eyed with unruly blonde hair, is going to look after me. He has a twitch in one eye so it looks as if he is winking at me, which is a little unnerving and I wonder why an optometrist can't have that fixed.

Stupid things go 'round in your head when you're nervous. And I am nervous. I don't know why. It's just a routine checkup, right? But I have come to trust my instincts. And when Dr. Johansen, that's his name, the guy with the twitch, turns to the nurse and asks her to get another doctor to come in, all my alarm signals go off.

So then this other doctor pops in and he too peers into my eyes and he too calls for yet another guy and goes, "Have a look at this: what do you make of it?"

And the three of them are discussing my eye as if it were some kind of strange phenomenon and as if I'm not even here. I mean as if I'm not a person, just this being with a fascinating condition in her eye.

"We'd better have Dr. Martineau take a look at this," Dr. Johansen with the twitch says to the others. "After all, she is her patient and she should tell her herself."

"Tell me what?" I feel as flipping helpless as a sitting duck, with my eye clamped open and unable to move.

They ignore me, of course, the bunch of them. But then Mary comes rushing through the door and they all step aside and let her take a look. I can only vaguely make out her shape because my other eye is tearing up so much.

And she doesn't say anything at first just removes the clamp and covers my eye with gauze. Then she asks the other guys to leave and sits down heavily on a stool in front of me.

"Stephanie," she stops for a second, grabs a Kleenex and blows her nose, "Stephanie... I'm afraid this is not good."

"You mean the cataract operation was not a success? You'll have to do it again?"

Oh God, is there no end to this?

"No, it's not that. But you have developed a retinal detachment, which means your retina is moving away from your eyeball, and yes, we have to do another surgical procedure. If we don't do it, you will go blind."

"You're kidding, Mary, aren't you?" I reply, stalling for time. "You must be totally kidding, right?"

I really don't want to hear anything more. Blind, for Christ's sake. Blind, on top of all the other crap.

"You know I wouldn't joke about anything like that, now don't you?"

I bite my lip.

"Ok, I'm sorry. Explain to me what has to be done so that I know what's coming."

Mary takes hold of my hand and talks in her low, soothing voice.

"Ok, this is another type of surgery called a vitrectomy. We insert a gas bubble into your eyeball. To put it in simple terms, the gas bubble pulls the retina back into place where it's supposed to be and this prevents you from going blind."

"Well, I've done it once, I guess I can do it again," I try to be light-hearted about the whole thing but my stomach is in knots. Heaven knows it's not something to look forward to, but what choices do I have? None!

"When can we do it Mary? The sooner the better. Get it over with, you know?"

By this time my vision has normalized somewhat and I don't like the fact that Mary's face is so serious and I can see pity in her eyes. Pity and compassion.

"You're a fighter, Stephanie. I've said it before and I like that about you and we'll get you through this, ok?"

"Ok," I smile. Bravely, I think. But inside I feel my stomach twisting and turning. Oh God, don't let me get sick, not now, please, not now, I pray.

Mary is talking on the phone and then turns 'round to face me.

"Friday morning, eight a.m., ok? We'll do it Friday morning."

"That soon?" Today is already Wednesday.

"I'd do it tomorrow if I could," Mary continues, "but the operating room is booked and Friday is the earliest I can get you in. As it is I'll have to push another surgery ahead to fit you in."

I don't like the fact that it is that urgent, but I also know that she is the best there is and if she feels it has to be done right away, then so be it.

"Ok, Friday, it's a date." I don't mean to be flippant but that's all I can think of.

Maria is waiting patiently for me to return. I don't feel it necessary to tell her what happened. I'm not up to it. All I want to do is go home and try to forget about what is ahead of me. All I want is to be in my room and not talk to anyone.

Antonia returns on Thursday night, full of news about the show, about New York. I don't have the heart to tell her that I have to have yet another operation.

"We'll have to go there one day soon, you and I," she says. "You'll love New York; it's so unlike any other city I know. I mean, I love Paris, I love Napoli and Rome, and I truly adore Munich. But New York is different from any of the others. It's gritty. Beautiful and gritty at the same time."

"Yeah, that would be nice, going to New York," I reply without a great deal of enthusiasm.

"What's wrong Steph? How did your checkup go? Are there any problems?"

And so I tell her. Tell her that I may, no, will go blind if I don't have this operation right away.

"It wouldn't be much fun going to New York if I can't see, right?"

I might as well make light of the situation but Antonia has turned white and I think she might burst into tears. But she doesn't. She's strong, strong and resilient, like an Amazon of Greek myth.

"I'll take you to the hospital in the morning. Everything will be alright, I can feel it. There may be other things to consider, but we'll deal with them if and when they come up."

Friday dawns bright and cheerful. A typically crisp early winter's day when you feel that nothing bad can possibly happen. I take it as an omen and am actually fairly calm when Antonia drops me off at the hospital.

She gives me a big hug before they wheel me into the operating room.

"It will be alright," she says again. Her jaw is set in a straight line as if she's trying to force back tears.

"Sure, of course, I just wish it was over and done with. I'm a little scared," I say. "You know, from now on I'm going to do a Scarlett... No sense worrying about something until it actually happens; perhaps it won't be as bad as it sounds."

But it is. Bad. Very, very bad, even though they have given me Valium before the procedure, which has calmed me down a bit. The first time the needle didn't hurt, after they froze my eyeball. This time they stick the needle through the skin underneath my eyelid and it hurts like a son of a bitch. I can't believe that anyone can stand this kind of pain without passing out. It is horrible, absolutely unspeakably horrible.

But once the freezing has kicked in there is no more pain. I don't remember much at all, I try to psych myself out, try not to be here. Here in this chair. Try to pretend I'm somewhere else. And after what seems like forever, it is over and I am wheeled out into a room where I'm all alone.

Dizzy and sick and tired, I just lie here; face down on this hospital bed. And then, ever so slowly, the freezing starts to wear off. And I can feel the pain coming on. It washes over me, my face, my head, my entire body. Throbbing, pulsing stabs of pain that won't stop.

I don't know that I've ever felt so isolated and so alone in my whole life. It seems like forever before I feel a hand on my shoulder.

"Stephanie," Mary's soft voice comes from far away. "I know you're in pain, I know you're uncomfortable, but the worst is over. The operation was a success and with any luck you don't ever have to do go through anything like this again."

I can't even reply. The pain is too bad and I am afraid I'll choke with my head down like this, lying on my stomach.

"You'll have to keep your head down for the next 24 hours," her voice continues. "Otherwise the retina might detach again and the whole thing will have been for nothing. It's horrible, dear, I know. Believe me, I know how horrible it is, but I'll have the nurse give you something to make you sleep, if that's possible. She'll stay with you through the night and she'll call me immediately if anything happens, ok? You'll get through this, Stephanie; you are strong. I'm damned proud of you."

She says it as if she means it. But I can only make a muffled sound and no words come out of my mouth. I feel a needle go into my arm and slowly the pain goes away. It is still there somewhere, but it feels like it's filtered through cotton and doesn't touch me anymore.

What if I suffocate? I panic. I try to raise my head but I can't. And then I think, so what? So what if I suffocate? It's supposed to be a peaceful, quiet death and nothing could be worse than this.

It is a long night. A long, long night. And I can sense *the companion* nearby. Watchful… waiting. And I do not fear him.

I know the nurse is here. I know she is reading a book because I can hear the paper rustling every time she turns a page. And every so often she tries to give me a little water through an opening that is underneath the pillow that my head is strapped onto.

And then, in a soft voice, she sings a little song in a language I do not understand. A lullaby of sorts, I think. The way you sing to a child to comfort it and make it go to sleep. And somewhere during that long night, I do go to sleep, a few minutes at a time.

The nurse is gone in the morning and I've never even seen her face and I will always wonder what language that was that she sang in.

Mary shows up just before noon to take the bandages off and

examine my eyes. My body is so stiff from lying in the same position for so long, it's a relief just to be able to sit up. Mary has her back turned and before she can stop me I take my little compact mirror out of my purse and look at my face. I look hideous, absolutely hideous. The whites of my eyes are blood red and my face is swollen and bruised beyond recognition. I look like the freaking Elephant Man.

Mary hears me gasp. She whips round and takes the mirror from me.

"No time for vanity now," she jokes. "Yeah, you're not at your prettiest today but that will pass. In a few days you'll look as good as new. And the best thing is that the operation was a great success and you'll still have your eyesight, right?"

"Right," I nod and try to forget the face that stared back at me from the mirror. I mean, what the hell does it matter anyway?

"Thank you for everything, Mary," I say quietly, "Thank you for saving my sight."

"You're a trooper, Stephanie, I'm sorry you had to go through this but there was no other way. You're ok to go home this afternoon, just follow these instructions for the next few days."

She hands me a list and a couple of little bottles containing eye drops. I cannot read the list because my eyes are teary, so I fold it and put it into my handbag. The worst is over, to be sure.

"You're a mess," is all Antonia says when she picks me up, though I can see that she is shocked at the way I look.

"But what the hell, you'll be able to see and nothing else matters, right?"

I feel nauseous and weak and all I want to do is sleep. When we get home I hand Antonia the list of post-operative instructions that Mary had given me and she quickly scans it.

"No big problem that I can see, it's all pretty straightforward. The hardest part will be to keep your face down for most of the time, especially when you're going to sleep. But I know that you sleep on your stomach quite often, so maybe it won't be so bad. Other than that, we'll have to apply these eye drops four times a day and have some painkillers at hand, if you need them. We'll have Maria do the drop thing, I don't think I'll be too good at that, I've told you before, I'm no Florence Nightingale."

Despite the nausea and discomfort, I have to smile.

"I'll be ok, Toni, I'll follow instructions like a little lamb, God knows there is no way that I want to go through anything like that operation again. Ever! Still, I didn't go blind and for that I'm more grateful than anyone will ever know."

Antonia smiles back at me and hands me a small cup of peppermint tea.

"Here, this will settle your stomach Hon, and when this is all over, I mean when you're back to normal, we'll go to New York. You and I will go to New York, soon. Real soon, I promise."

And even though I am not crazy about going to New York, I know it is her way of trying to make me feel better, for me to have something to look forward to. I smile even though it hurts.

"Sure," I say. "Sure, we'll go, it'll be fun."

But as it turns out, I never get to see New York at all.

Chapter 28

You know how they always say things come in threes… Well I'm two down, one to go. Nanette's visit was one and then the operation, and three weeks later, to the day, I again hear Maria's voice yelling from the kitchen…

"There's someone here to see you… Wait, I'll see him out…"

She appears on the verandah with…

"Oh my God… Max… oh my God, I don't believe it, how on earth did you find me?"

I hadn't seen him since, well, since that day when I left Virginia, when I saw the utter helplessness in his face, knowing I had to leave, knowing I too was sick and might die, knowing that I loved him but could not stay …

He looks old… Much, much older than I remember, but he's still the same Max. Immaculately dressed… Clean shaven as usual, his soft brown eyes that are so much like Mark's, perhaps a touch sadder as if he's seen enough, too much, in fact, more than he'd ever wanted to see.

Max hugs me and looks me up and down.

"You're thin… Much thinner than you used to be… But you look healthy, all things considered…" he adds quickly.

"Thanks, Max, I'm doing ok, all things considered…" I reply and I can't stop the tears from coming.

I'm so happy to see him, so happy he's made the effort to find me…

"Your Aunt Sissy told me where to find you," he says as if he'd been reading my thoughts. "I'm sorry it took so long for me to come and see you … but you know, the way things were with Hannah, and… well…"

His voice trails off and he looks into the distance as if trying to find answers in the blue mist that hovers over the lake.

"It's nice here," he finally continues "Peaceful. I'm glad you've found a home with Antonia, glad you're not alone. I've worried about you and the children, but I followed your life as best I could to make sure you're ok. But I couldn't be there for you, and for that I'm deeply, deeply sorry and I will forever be sorry."

Maria walks onto the verandah with a fresh pot of tea, her cure-all for everything. She pours a cup for Max and me, drapes a soft blanket over my knees and discreetly disappears.

"I've missed you, Max, missed you terribly. But with all the things that have happened, all the treatments I had to take, all the problems and worries about the future, the kids, well and, to be honest, I wasn't sure that I should stay in touch, knowing the way Hannah felt about me…"

Max puts a hand on my knee.

"That's one of the things I came to tell you, Stephanie, had to come in person to tell you. Hannah… well… Hannah is dead."

He takes a deep sip of tea to bridge the stunned silence. I don't know what to say, don't know how to react, all I know is that my heart hurts for Max.

"She took her own life," Max continues with less emotion than I would have expected, "you see, she never got over losing Mark. Never. He was her life, her only child, she doted on him since he was little and with losing him, she lost the will to live."

I am stunned. Shocked and stunned. Don't know what to say.

Max looks over at me.

"It's ok," he says, "It's ok now. We had a good marriage because I always made sure her happiness came first. But in the end that was not enough, I could not help her with her grief. Hannah had her faults, heaven knows, but she was a good woman and a good mother and, I guess, a good wife."

"But how did she die?" I whisper.

"Hanged herself," Max answers. "Hanged herself in the bathroom. And the only note she left was to say she was sorry but she did not want to continue living without Mark."

My hand flies to my mouth.

"Oh my God, Max, that's horrible. It must have been awful for you, finding her like that."

"I didn't find her, I was out of town. Our neighbor found her. Came looking for her because they were supposed to go out shopping together. When I came home it was all over, well, you know what I mean. I think she might have done it on purpose, waiting until I wasn't home, I mean. At least I don't have that picture in my mind, when I saw her she looked right peaceful, almost as if she were taking a nap."

I don't know what to say to him. He seems strangely calm and strangely at ease. Again he continues as if reading my thoughts...

"I've come to terms with it, Stephanie. I knew she would never get over losing Mark. I mean, I miss him too, he was my son and I loved him but somewhere along the way you have to let go if you want to keep your sanity. And she couldn't do that. Hannah could not do that. She'd sit in his room every day. Every single day. And she talked to him as if he were there. And no matter what I said, no matter how much I tried to help... she'd turn away from me".

"Oh Max, it must have been so hard seeing her like that."

"Yes, it was, but now she is where she wanted to be all this time. With her son, at least I take comfort in the thought that it might be so."

His voice has gone quiet and again he looks across the misty lake.

"Well," he finally picks up his train of thought, "well, I've come to say goodbye as well. For a while at least."

"Goodbye? Where are you going?"

He smiles that quiet calm smile I know so well.

"All of my life I have wanted to travel," he says, his eyes lighting up. "See foreign countries. Go to La Provence and stay a while and speak what little French I know with the natives. Go to Italy and see the statue of David in person... Sit on a piazza and drink a little wine. Visit Greece and sample fresh olives straight from the trees... All the history, all the things I've dreamed of seeing when I was young..."

His voice trails off once again and there's a long, long pause. His face looks peaceful, young, expectant.

"Well, I thought I might as well do as much of that as an old man can..."

"Oh Max, you're not old, you'll never be old." I smile and take his hand in mine.

"Well, I'm in my seventies now but as long as you have your health, and thank the Lord, I have that, you can't allow yourself to get old. And that's another reason I want to go. To keep active, to see and learn new things, you know?"

"But when will you go? You've obviously thought this out in detail..."

"Yes, I have. Sold the house, and packed my suitcase. I intend to travel light, figure if I need something, I can always buy it wherever I am. And, besides, I'm not going all alone. Travelling with a friend who is of like mind."

His grin is mischievous as he shoots a look in my direction.

"You're wondering who it is, aren't you? Well, remember the lady from the library back home? The one who always gave you heck when your books were late?"

"Oh Max, of course, I remember. She only pretended to be mad and the kids totally loved her. Theresa, yes, that's her name, Maria Theresa... So you became friends?"

"Yes, that's about it. Friends, very good friends and when I found out that she too had wanted to see foreign countries all of her life, well, it just seemed to be reasonable to ask her to come along... For company, you know?"

"For company, I understand..."

"Well, the way I see it, things always have more meaning when you can share them with someone. And besides, there's someone with you if anything happens overseas, like if you get sick or something."

I get up and give Max the biggest hug. I'm so very happy for him. And he hugs me back, so hard he almost squeezes the breath out of me.

When I sit down again, he picks up the blanket that has fallen to the floor and drapes is over my knees.

"I could not leave without seeing you, without saying goodbye, and without you knowing that I've always loved you like a daughter..."

His eyes well up and he stops talking and he gazes across the water where dusk is turning the misty blue into a velvety violet.

Soon it will be night... Soon the stars will be out... Soon he will be gone...

I'm sad, very sad but happy at the same time.

"You'll send postcards, won't you? Postcards from wherever you are, to me and the kids?"

"I'll do better than that..." Max says with a wink "I'll email pictures from my laptop."

He pauses to savor the effect his words have on me.

"Laptop?? Laptop?? You have a laptop, I don't believe it."

"Yep, got it a few weeks ago and am getting pretty good at using it. Theresa helped me, which was good."

"Well, the children are going to be so impressed with their grand-pa..."

"The children... Yes, the children... I'm sorry I didn't get to see them, but then they probably don't remember too much of the time they spent in Virginia..."

"Oh, but they do. Well, the things that are important to kids, you know? Sleigh rides... Christmas... Their dad and, of course, you and Hannah. But their memories are fading and it's only when we look at pictures that things come back to them. Sadly, they are beginning to forget they ever had a father. But perhaps that's good, healthier for them, you know?"

"I'm sure it is, but I guess they'll get to know their grandfather again when they get emails from the world traveler, don't you think?"

"Absolutely, absolutely they'll remember and you'll come to see them whenever it is that you return, won't you?"

"You can count on that, Sweetheart, and if there's anything I can do for you... you must tell me, Stephanie, promise?"

Max stands up and stretches his legs. For a long while we don't talk... There's no need... He stares across the water into the ever increasing darkness... Now the stars have come out... one by one...

"Beautiful... But not the same stars as in Virginia, right, Steph?"

I nod. I remember. I remember the starlit night sitting on the verandah, holding onto to each other for comfort... Oh, I remember.

"We can't go back, Stephanie. No one can. We must make the most of what life is giving us now and be thankful for it, each and every day."

"Time to go, I'm afraid" he continues .. "But we'll stay in touch from now on, right?"

I get up and arm in arm we walk toward the kitchen door.

"Yes we will, Max... And please give my love to Theresa..."

"I will do that and you give Antonia a big hug from me. Always liked that woman, she has a good head on her shoulders, and so pretty too..."

"Oh, and, before I forget..."

He fumbles in his coat pocket, pulls out a somewhat crumpled envelope and presses it into my hand.

"What's this?"

"For you, for the children. Please, don't open it now. Look at it later. For now all I want is a big fat kiss and a big fat hug, ok?"

And he gets both, of course.

Maria is standing at the front door, ready with Max's coat.

The door closes... I hear a car engine start... And then he too is gone. But I feel that this is a chapter that is just beginning and for that reason I am not sad.

Later that evening I pull out the envelope that I have shoved into the pocket of my cardigan. Slowly I open it and stare at the cheque. A cheque for seventy five thousand dollars... And just a little post-it note attached to it.

"For you... For you and Adam and Bettina...

From Grandpa!"

Chapter 29

Last night Antonia came back from her second trip to New York; her head full of stories, her suitcase full of stuff, totally excited about her trip and the things she's bought for the boutique.

"I'll show you in the morning what I've bought, you'll love it, I'm sure. But I'm too wiped tonight; I think I'll go straight to bed."

In the morning, after breakfast, she takes me into her bedroom which is in chaos with open suitcases and shopping bags everywhere.

"These are just samples," she tells me as she's spreading the stuff out on the bed. Fancy handbags, whimsical jewelry, unique t-shirts, gorgeous scarves... You know, stuff.

"I've ordered a whole bunch of things; they'll be shipped in the next couple of weeks... Oh, I'm so excited. Don't you just love them, Steph?"

I can't help it, her enthusiasm is contagious.

"Yes, of course, I love what you've bought. Can't wait to see the rest when it gets here."

"And..." she pauses dramatically, "Close your eyes..."

I cover my eyes with my hands and wait.

"Ok, you can look now!"

"Oh my God, Toni, it's absolutely gorgeous!"

She is wearing the most beautiful white fur coat I have ever seen. And she looks stunning with her fiery hair cascading down onto the shimmering fur.

"Beautiful, isn't it? It's fake, of course, and... It's for you!"

"What?"

"Yeah, for you. You're always cold and this will keep you toasty in the winter."

She takes off the coat and helps me put it on. It's stunning, absolutely stunning, and with my dark hair flowing softly around the collar, I look almost beautiful. Like a princess. Almost.

Antonia is pleased.

"See? I knew it would fit; it's a little too snug for me. You look lovely, Steph, like a snow princess. Do you like it?"

"Oh Toni, I absolutely love it. I've never ever had such an amazing coat. And I love the lining; it feels so soft and cozy against my skin. Thank you, thank you sooo much."

"Oh, don't thank me; I'm happy you like it. When I first saw it I knew it was for you."

She puts her arm 'round my shoulder.

"Let's have a cup of tea; we'll talk."

It's a rainy day. Not the kind where raindrops drum heavily against your windows, but the kind with a misty, quiet rain that shrouds everything in a silver-gray fog.

We sip our tea in the kitchen and look out onto what little we can see of the trees and bushes. We cannot see the lake, but we can hear it. It is restless and we can hear the waves thundering onto the shore. Inside the kitchen it is cozy. Bright, warm and cozy.

Antonia puts her hand on mine.

"It's good to be home," she sighs putting her feet up on one of the stools. "Heaven knows, I love to travel, but... well, enough for a while. So tell me what's been happening while I was gone?"

"Good grief! You've only been away for a week. But yes, something did happen ... guess who came to see me?"

"Please, please, please, not the 'guess who' game... Just tell me, ok?"

"Max!"

I wait for her reaction and I am surprised that she's not surprised, not overly so, in any event.

LORENE ALBERS

"Good, good. I've always liked him… He came alone?"

"Yes. You see… Hannah died almost a year ago. She killed herself, can you believe it? How horrible for Max, I mean, I wasn't overly fond of her but still…"

Antonia is not all that shocked.

"Well, I didn't know her at all. Never talked to the woman except briefly at some function or other. She always seemed a little mousy to me, sort of shriveled from the outside in. And then, the way she treated you… I mean, after Mark being such a bastard and all and she trying to put the blame on you… Well, excuse me!!"

Antonia lets out a little snort. She does that sometimes, when she's angry, which is not very often, or when she laughs, which is very often. She snorts. Tiny little snorts like a stuffed up kitten. It's cute, but she hates it, only most of the time she doesn't even notice.

"I don't know," I reply, "I don't know whether she was all that bad. I mean, having your child die of a horrible disease. Perhaps I would look for someone else to blame too?"

"Oh, don't even go there. She knew exactly what kind of a loser her son was and just couldn't face the facts. Anyway, enough about Hannah. May she rest in peace."

Toni is still enough of a Catholic to add that little blessing, without thinking about it, I'm sure.

"Tell me more about Max? How does he look, what's he doing, surely he must be retired by now?"

"Here!"

I pull Max's cheque out of my pocket and slide it across the counter.

"What's this? Oh my God, that's a good chunk of money, Steph. Good for you! And good of Max, even though I think it's about time."

"Yes, only I can't accept that…"

"Accept what?"

"The money, I can't accept the money. Like you say, it's an awful lot and he might need it for himself, especially now that he's retired and wants to travel the world."

Antonia gets up and brings over the teapot. She pours a fresh cup for us.

"You're nuts," she says, "totally nuts. Max probably sold the house and, knowing him, he gets a good pension and I'm sure he has savings as well. If he gives you this money it means that he can afford it, he wants to do it and probably would have done it a long time ago if it weren't for… well, whatever, it doesn't matter now."

"You think?" I'm hesitant. I'm staring at the large number on the cheque. "It is an awful lot but…"

"Listen, Sweetie", Toni continues, "Max has always had a great deal of love and respect for you, and he loves the children, you know that. It would be very hurtful to him if you refuse to take the cheque. So stick it in the bank and write him a little thank you letter or a big thank you letter, it's up to you. Ok?"

I'm still not sure, but Toni is staring me down.

"I'll take you to the bank this afternoon," she continues. "You can put it into a savings or trust account for the kids, whatever you want. That way you don't have to pay any taxes, I think, but I'll check with my accountant how to best handle it, ok?"

"I don't know, perhaps you're right. I know Max did feel awful when he found out that Mark had lost all of our money with his stupid investment schemes, plus the money I got from my mom's insurance. Max couldn't help me at the time and I'll never forget the look on his face when I said good bye. He looked so… angry, yes, angry and helpless… Maybe you have a point, Toni, maybe he would be hurt if I don't accept the money. Yes, I'll email him a thank you letter!"

"You what??"

"Email, you know that thing people do on the computer? Instead of licking stamps?"

"Well, excuse me, of course I know what email is, but Max? He has a computer?"

"Yep, brand new laptop, along with a lady friend who taught him how to use it and, moreover, who is travelling with him 'round the world!"

I smile at Toni, savoring the reaction of my words on her face.

"Well, I'll be... the old devil! Good for him, I say, great in fact,"

I get up and walk around the kitchen for a bit. I can't sit in one position for very long without getting tired and cramped. I don't have a lot of padding on my butt anymore and my knees tend to hurt. Like an old woman; I swear. And then I wonder whether I'll ever get to be old enough to know what it feels like to be an old woman. Well, I guess I'm getting a pretty good taste of it already.

Toni tosses a sweatshirt my way.

"Here, put this on, you look chilled".

I smile at her. I'm lucky, you know.

In spite of all the shit that has happened, I'm still fortunate. Fortunate to live in beautiful surroundings... Fortunate to have friends like Toni and Maria who care about me... Fortunate that my children are at a good school that they love... Fortunate that I don't have the IV any longer... Fortunate that I didn't go blind... I could make a huge long list of why I'm so fortunate.

Sure, I have to take the 'cocktail' every day. Each and every day I have to swallow about sixty five pills just to make sure that nothing new attacks me. But the pills are working for me and I don't have to go back on the IV, and I've actually gained a little weight, which is great.

It's an awful lot of pills to swallow though. A pill in case I get the flu, a pill in case I catch pneumonia, which could still happen even with the pill. A pill for everything you could possibly imagine. You would be surprised at how many sicknesses and diseases are out there, just waiting to attack you. You would never leave the house, if you knew.

But, most people are surrounded by zillions of germs each and every hour of each and every day and they never get sick. They have an immune system that helps fight off any sneaky intruder before he can do any harm. But I don't. I don't have the luxury of an immune system and so every lame little bug or virus or germ can happily invade my body, knowing he's found fertile grounds and no one's there to resist him.

Still, things could be far worse. I've been relatively healthy for a while now. Relative being the operative word. My vision, if not perfect, is still intact even though I now have to wear strong glasses for reading. My breathing is not great, what with all the damage from the various times I had pneumonia, but I don't need to be hooked up to oxygen like some people. So what if I can't run up and down stairs, I manage one step at a time.

I guess that's all you can do. One little step at a time, shouldering your little bag of pills. Well, you have to take it with a bit of humor.

I turn and look at Antonia who has her nose pressed against the window, staring out at all that wetness, as if wishing it away.

"You know what?" she swings 'round…

"No, what?"

"We will go away. A vacation, just you and I, Maria will take care of the house."

I laugh.

"Sure, we'll go on a holiday. Why not? In case you've forgotten, I'm not altogether well; I don't think I can travel anywhere without knowing there's a doctor or hospital nearby."

"Ok, ok, don't you think I haven't thought about that? We'll go to Florida, we'll stay in the condo, and believe me, there are plenty of doctors and plenty of hospitals around. I mean ninety percent of the residents are geriatrics; they wouldn't be caught dead knowing there's no hospital nearby. Pardon the analogy!"

"I don't know, I mean, it sounds lovely. I would have to check with Mary and I may not be able to cross the border with the AIDS and all…"

I can hear myself talk. I can hear myself making excuses. And I wonder whatever happened to the carefree little adventurer that I used to be, not all that long ago.

I mean, what's the worst that could happen? I catch pneumonia… I go to the hospital… I die… Whatever.

It could happen here, it could happen in Florida.

And suddenly I'm excited.

"Yes! Yes Toni, let's go! Let's go to Florida!"

And that's the last thing I remember.

Chapter 30

I do not know where I am. I'm floating round and round in an endless void, it is dark but not totally, more like an indigo blueness, a calm and icily strange environment.

I can hear and feel and sense a heavy heartbeat pounding and echoing all around me. It must be my own heartbeat, pounding, reverberating, bouncing off the walls that enclose me.

In the far distance, at the peripheral of these walls I hear the screaming of an ambulance siren. I hear labored breathing, I think it could be my breathing, but I can't be sure. I can't be sure of anything; I may not even be alive... I feel the bouncing of the ambulance, the lifting of the gurney, the slamming of doors to the emergency room, but I'm not there.

And far, far in the distance I hear a young woman sobbing. I know it is my child sobbing but I can't see her, can't reach her, all I can do is feel her pain while I'm floating in this void.

As if through a fish-eye lens I see a room, dimly lit with an eerie bluish light, with people all around an operating table and on that table is my lifeless body. I feel strangely disconnected from that form, as if it has nothing to do with me. I try to focus on what's happening, I see surgeons and I see blood and I see nurses handing instruments to the surgeons and I see a big gaping hole in that body that is mine but doesn't seem to belong to me any longer. And I see all this off in the distance, distorted, with no emotions attached to what's happening. No emotion at all. And I try to move closer, but I cannot, and the images start to blur and the silence around me gets thicker and a gentle force moves me away from these images below.

And I can sense a presence. I can feel the presence that has been with me for so long. It is the presence of the *companion* and he gives me nothing but comfort and love. And now I want to stay with him, want to go with him wherever that may lead.

But again I'm listening to my child crying and I yearn to be back with her. And I feel hot electricity surging through my body that is lying lifeless on a bed far below me. And I see the body responding and I'm back in it and the pain is excruciating. And my child is crying. And I leave the pain behind and am again in the void.

Two days, they tell me, for two days you were on the brink of death. Two days, forever eradicated from my waking memory.

I see Antonia's tear streaked face, I hold my daughter's hand, I see the pain in my son's eyes and still I don't know what happened.

"You collapsed, just like that. One minute we talked about Florida, the next, well…" Toni fills me in on the lost time.

"Turns out it was an aneurysm. I freaked, as you can imagine, totally freaked, but Maria kept her cool. She called 911 and they came within minutes… and altogether we were lucky. Lucky that the top cardiologist in Canada was on call that night, lucky that they were able to perform the surgery immediately… Oh my God, Steph…"

"And you went and got the kids?" I can only manage a whisper.

"Maria did, I couldn't leave the hospital not knowing what was going to happen to you."

The surgeon enters the room, followed by a nurse who motions everyone to leave. He's taking a long time examining my body, removing the bandages and checking the wound, adjusting all sorts of little things on the instruments I'm hooked up to while the nurse holds up a little bottle so that I can drink a tiny bit of water through a straw.

"Touch and go, Stephanie," the doctor says, "but you're going to make it, you'll be ok. It's going to be a bit of an uphill climb but not too, too bad. The good news is that you're able to freely move your feet and hands, so there's no paralysis and you'll be as right as rain in a couple of weeks."

Nurse Phyllis always used to say that. Only I wasn't, right as rain that is, not that time.

"Was it because of the AIDS?" I have to whisper, because my voice is gone.

"No, the aneurysm had nothing to do with your illness. It can happen to anyone and no one really knows why. We'll put you on medication and perhaps blood thinners and do an ultra sound in about six months."

I get better so quickly, the doctors are surprised.

"You are a fighting little devil, aren't' you?" The surgeon laughs when, a few days after the operation, I'm able to walk up and down the hallway. With a walker, mind you, but still.

I have a hard time remembering his name. He has saved my life, and I cannot remember his name. It is long and has a lot of o's in it, so I think it's probably Greek.

"Don't worry about it," he had said the first time I tried to address him by name. "I'd tell you my first name but it's even longer than my family name... Just call me Doctor Joe, or just Joe."

And once again I think how blessed I am. Another angel has touched my life and he just wants to be called Joe.

So as I said, I'm recovering in no time at all and I'm able to leave the hospital after only two weeks. Mind you, I've lost about five pounds which is half of the weight I had slowly gained in the last couple of years, but I'm alive and I will be home long before Christmas.

And as it turns out, it's the best Christmas ever, except that Maria won't be with us for the holidays. She's flying to Guadalajara for a couple of weeks to see her brother and his wife and their new baby. Antonia has given her the airline ticket as a Christmas present along with an envelope containing a bunch of pesos, a big bunch, I suspect, and an adorable outfit from her store for the little baby.

Of course, Maria is worried that we won't be able to manage without her.

"Who is going to cook the turkey for the festivities? And who will bake cookies and decorate the house... and..."

"Don't you worry about that, Maria," Antonia laughs. "Aunt Sissy has volunteered to help and I understand she cooks up a mean turkey. Probably not as delicious as your Mexican bird, but I'm sure it will be great."

"Well, if you think you can manage, I'm pretty excited about seeing my brother and his family and, of course, the little one."

Bettina and Adam arrive by bus a couple of days before Christmas, and even though we talk on the phone every other day, I'm ecstatic to have them at home. It's only been a few weeks since I've seen them last but already they look so much more mature and grown up and I suspect that Adam is actually shaving.

And then, at noon on Christmas Eve, an airline limo pulls up in front of the house.

"Oh my God," Toni yells from the hallway, "It's Maria, what the hell...?"

Maria walks into the lobby and sets down her suitcase.

"I'm sorry, Chiquita," she says and hugs Antonia, "One week was enough, I simply couldn't miss Christmas with my family, my real family."

"But what about your brother and the baby?"

"Oh, they understood. They fully understood that I wanted to leave early to be back home, and home for me is here..."

"Oh, it's so good to have you back, Maria." I give her a big hug and we sit down to a steaming cup of coffee and buttery toast.

"Yes, Chiquita, and it feels good to be back. It was a nice visit but long enough. My brother is well and the little one is adorable, but I don't belong there any longer. It is not home anymore, I was like a stranger in a strange land, to quote Heinlein."

I look at her, amazed.

"You have read that book, Maria?"

"My taste in books is very diverse, Chiquita," she says and smiles like a sphinx. "I read anything and everything, it helps me grasp the intricacies of the English language," she adds with a flourish.

I have to laugh; you just have to love Maria and her determination.

"I know what you mean, Maria," Antonia adds, "I don't feel at home any more when I go to Italy, but then I don't really feel this is my home either. It has nothing to do with the country you're in, but only the people you're with. And so I would have to say that this is home not because of its geographical location but because I am with the people I love... and I love Stephanie and I love you and Bettina and Adam, you all make up the family that I never had... and yes, that makes it home!"

And so we celebrate Christmas Canadian style. On Christmas Eve we all go to midnight mass in the church just around the corner because Antonia says it wouldn't be Christmas without it.

I'm not Catholic and the kids have no opinion one way or the other, but it is very festive in the little church, ablaze with candles and filled with beautiful choir voices singing Christmas carols.

And we walk home through the freshly fallen snow and 'all is calm and all is bright' just like the song says.

On Christmas morning we open our presents, sipping hot cocoa that Aunt Sissy has made.

I've dipped into my savings and bought a beautiful gold mother-daughter heart with three diamonds in the middle for Bettina and a gold bracelet for my son.

Antonia, of course, has gone all out, even though I had asked her not to spoil the kids so much.

They both get new laptops and the very latest cell phones and for Adam there are hockey sticks and jerseys since he plays on the school team and for Bettina a smart riding habit and boots.

I look back and forth between Antonia and my daughter. They look like a couple of conspirators.

"It was to be a surprise, Mom," Bettina smiles. "I've been taking riding lessons at a stable near the school and I love it so much, I can't begin to tell you and Antonia is taking us up to Ballinafad to see the horses and I get to ride Ophelia who's my favorite..."

"She has that from me," Antonia offers.

"What? She's not even your child..." I have to laugh.

"I know, but she might as well be. Born horsewoman, you should see her, well, you will. I'm so proud; I think she should train for the Olympiad."

It makes me happy to see how well the two of them get on, how they both have this love of horses and can't stop talking about them.

I had had a hard time finding a gift for Antonia though. I mean, what do you give someone who has everything?

So I hand her a little box, wrapped in gold paper and I'm a bit startled when she starts laughing after she looks at the gift. I mean, I had spent so much time trying to choose a photo of the two of us and I had it mounted in a beautiful silver frame. I love this particular picture. We're on the golf course in Virginia and we have our arms 'round each other and we are both smiling for the camera. How happy and carefree we look. It's a great shot, so why is she laughing?

But when I unwrap Toni's gift, I understand. She has given me the exact same picture in a crystal frame. We smile at one another.

"Great minds... Right?" she laughs, "we can keep one of them here and one in Florida when we finally go. It's best to spend the dreary months there... So maybe in January..."

"Yes, let's take another stab at going and January sounds like the perfect month to escape, " I agree.

Toni had been right about Aunt Sissy's cooking too. Her turkey, Polish style, is delicious. She and Maria have outdone themselves in the kitchen and so we end up with a meal that has a bit of both worlds, Polish and Mexican.

I can't remember the last time I ate so much.

After dinner Bettina puts her arm around my shoulder, "Here, Mom, I've got a little present for you."

"But we did all that this morning?"

"I know, this is special, just for you."

She hands me a little book, you know the kind you make notes in, only fancier. And in it, in her neat handwriting, day by day, she has reported her activities at the school and after school, her thoughts, her dreams and aspirations.

"I wanted you to be part of my life, Mom. The way you would have been if I were living at home and I could talk to you every day."

I look at my beautiful grown up girl who looks so much like my Mom and I wish that her father could see her now, wish he could see both his children and be as proud of them as I am. So yes, my feelings toward Mark have softened over the years. Despite all the hurt and heartache and despite the fact that I'm battling an illness that there's no cure for, as yet. Despite all that.

He was my one and only love and that is hard to forget and even though he's hurt me more than any person should ever hurt another, I also remember the good times. And I know that, in his own way, he had loved me too and he certainly had loved the children.

I hold the little book close to my chest and hug and kiss Bettina.

"I'll treasure this to the end of my days."

"Which won't be anytime soon," she jokes to hide her emotions.

And just then the door bell rings and Adam runs to answer it. I look at Antonia who shrugs her shoulders. She's not expecting anyone, I'm not expecting anyone, then who..?

We hear Adam talking in the hallway and then...

"Merry Christmas, sorry to barge in on you guys like this but..."

"Oh my God, Max, oh my God, I'm so, so happy," I laugh and cry at the same time as he holds me close.

Toni is grinning from ear to ear.

"Well, if it isn't Santa Claus himself..." she smiles and then I realize that she knew all about this unexpected visitor.

Adam and Bettina are sitting on the couch, looking at the man who is a stranger to them. They were little when we left Virginia, they don't even have any recollection of their father, never mind their grandfather.

Max walks over and shakes their hand.

"Allow me to introduce myself, I'm Max, your Grandpa!"

They smile at him politely and a little hesitantly.

"I understand that you're shocked, and I'm sorry to drop in on you guys like this, but... It's Christmas and I wanted to be with what family I have left in this world."

And then Bettina jumps up and gives him a hug.

"Thanks for coming, Grandpa, we're happy to see you even if we don't remember..."

"Yes, of course, thanks for coming." Adam adds though he doesn't hug Max but only shakes his hand.

Both kids warm to him immediately. He tells fascinating stories of his travels and has the pictures to prove them on a little USB stick. Imagine that! Max has a USB.

"Why didn't you bring Theresa?" I have to ask.

"She stayed at the hotel, didn't want to come uninvited you know?"

"Oh but you must bring her next time, she'll be amazed when she sees the children..."

Adam scowls, Bettina just looks amused. I really must stop calling them children.

"I will, definitely, I'll bring her next time... But we're off again tomorrow to Iceland! I've always wondered what it's like there... cold, I suspect."

And before he leaves the house he hands a sealed envelope to both Adam and Bettina.

"I almost forgot to give you your cards," he smiles "open them after I have left."

And then he is gone but I know he'll be a major part of our lives from now on.

"Look at this, Mom; I've never seen one like it, looks fake." Adam and Bettina hand me Max's Christmas card, and in each one is a brand new thousand dollar bill.

As I said, it's one of the best Christmases ever.

It is late and I'm exhausted when I head upstairs to my rooms. I'm exhausted but happy and grateful.

And the *companion* did not appear tonight even though I don't fear him any longer. I think I'm beginning to understand who or what he is.

It's more of a feeling than a knowing, but I think he's around to protect my soul. And perhaps I should be grateful for that.

Chapter 31

Sometime during the night I hear a phone ringing in the distance. I hear Antonia answering it and a little while later there's a soft knock on my door.

"Steph? Sorry to wake you, I've just had a call from Ken's partner, something terrible has happened, Ken's in the hospital and... Oh Stephanie, it sounds really bad. I have to fly out to Edmonton first thing in the morning. I'm so worried about him. He's like a brother to me, as you know..."

She's shivering, looking totally lost, like a little kid.

"Would you come downstairs and have a cup of tea with me? I can't go back to sleep and I need you to be with me..."

We have our tea in Antonia's bedroom where she's starting to pack stuff into a small suitcase.

"What happened, Toni?"

"Ken's been in an accident but I have the strange feeling there's more to it than that. Hans-Jorgen, that's his partner, wouldn't say. But of course, he's in shock, as you can imagine."

Antonia is on the computer, looking for the first flight out to Edmonton which is at seven o'clock. She calls the airline and books a first class ticket. There's just enough time for the limo to take her to the airport, half an hour's drive away.

I'm trying to go back to sleep but I'm just lying there, staring at the ceiling, thinking of Toni and how hard it will be for her if Ken is seriously injured or worse. I don't know him well at all. The few times we've met it was either a social occasion or on the golf course when

Mark and I played with them as a foursome. But other than that, I never really got close to him.

Mark was friends with Ken though and they got on very well and I was glad about that because it meant so much to Mark's business.

Ken has always been very pleasant, kind and pleasant, not putting on airs because of his success and money, you know?

So yes, I'm sorry that he's in hospital.

Antonia calls in the afternoon. It is worse than they thought and it looks as if Ken is not going to survive the night. His partner is devastated, falling apart. They've been together for nearly six years now and, apparently, they love one another deeply.

"I'm going to have to stay here until this is all over", Antonia says, "oh my God Steph, never in a million years would I wish this on anyone."

And the next time she calls, Ken has died.

"I was with him, Stephanie, we both were, Hans-Jorgen and I. It was very peaceful in the end and he was not in any pain. We had a chance to talk and I..." she breaks down and cries. "I'll have to stay a few days longer, legal stuff to look after and helping Hans-Jorgen cope a little, as much as that's possible. But I'll call you when I know for sure. Oh God, all I want is to go home. Are you ok? Thank goodness Maria is with you..."

"Don't worry about us, Toni, just look after yourself, ok?"

"Sure, I'll let you know when I'll be back."

Turns out Toni is gone for a full two weeks. When she finally comes back on a Friday evening, she looks drawn and tired. Her face looks older and the fine lines on her forehead seem to have deepened. Toni hugs us both, Maria and me.

"Thank God that's over. Just pour me a stiff Scotch, would you Maria? All I want to do is sleep for days."

I don't ask her for any details. She'll tell me what I need to know when she's ready. And the next morning after breakfast, she's ready.

We've finished our toast and Toni puts the plates into the dishwasher and pours another cup of tea for us.

"Let's sit in the sunroom," she carries the tea and I follow her.

"Sit," she pats the sofa cushion next to her... "Sit down, I'll tell you the whole story about Ken and what happened and why he did what he did..."

"Did? What do you mean, did?"

"Well, you see, the accident... It was not so much an accident... it was a suicide attempt."

"What?"

"Ken tried to kill himself. It all came out during the endlessly long night when we sat with him in the hospital, Hans-Jorgen and I. He told me that Ken was HIV positive and had been diagnosed with ADC."

"Oh my God, Toni, did you know that Ken...?"

"That he was HIV positive? I don't know, I kind of suspected something like that because of remarks he'd made in the past about HIV not being a big deal, that it could lead to AIDS, but not necessarily and once he said to me.. *'it shouldn't make any difference to you, Babe, we live like brother and sister, so it wouldn't affect you in any way'*, and he said it as if it was a joke or something. So yes, at times I suspected that he may be positive... but.."

"I see," I reply, even though I don't see at all "but what is ADC? You said he was diagnosed with ADC?"

"Well, I got all this from Hans-Jorgen. ADC is short for AIDS Dementia Complex and, as the name implies, you gradually lose your faculties. Apparently, it affects many people who are HIV positive.

At first, Ken started to forget little everyday things, like he'd leave the kettle boiling, he'd forget where he left his car keys, he'd go from one room to another and not remember why, stuff like that. Then it got so bad that he had to make detailed lists every day and tick off the stuff he had already done."

"That's awful, Toni, how very sad for him and his partner."

"Yes, it must have been very hard on Hans-Jorgen. You didn't know Ken that well but he was always in great shape, worked out all the time, and was sharp as a tack when it came to his business. Naturally, he did all kinds of research on ADC and he must have been devastated knowing what lay ahead. He was getting morose and surly and fell into deep depressions for days on end.

"I guess he just couldn't face the future. So one evening he told Hans-Jorgen that he had to stop by the office to pick up something or other and when Hans-Jorgen wanted to go with him, he refused to take him along."

Antonia pauses for a long while, and looks out onto the snow-covered lawn.

It's a beautiful winter morning. The sun has broken through the mist and the slanting beams of light are dancing on the freshly fallen snow, making it glisten like a myriad of diamonds. The air is icy and all the trees and bushes and blades of grass are frozen in glassy stillness. The whole scene is breathtakingly, achingly beautiful.

Antonia continues in a soft voice.

"You know that the Saskatchewan River runs through Edmonton and there are many lookouts and spots where couples, or anyone else for that matter, go to enjoy nature ... and that's where Ken went. He drove to one of those lookouts high above the river, but he didn't stop for the scenery. He just kept on driving. Some passerby saw the whole thing and called the police. They found his car at the bottom of the embankment, he was badly injured and well... You know the rest. The police are treating it as an accident; the road was covered in ice and extremely slippery..."

"Oh my God, Toni, that is so awful. I didn't know Ken that well but he was such a good guy. How very tragic for his partner..."

"Yes, very. Hans-Jorgen is heartbroken. They've been together for years and he was prepared to stay with Ken through his illness and support him as best he could.

"Turns out he didn't have to see him gradually go downhill; perhaps that's a good thing. I don't know. It's hard to make sense of what motivates people. Well, at least he is looked after financially. Ken has left him a sizeable amount of money which should last him for the rest of his life, and the rest of his fortune, which is considerable, was given to me. That's why I had to stay there for a while, meetings with lawyers, stuff like that."

I feel a shiver down my back, but I'm not cold. It's just a strange foreboding, as if there's more to this story, something she hasn't told me.

Our tea has gone cold and, as if on cue, Maria appears with the trolley carrying a fresh pot and the little samovar to keep the tea hot.

"I thought you both might want a fresh cup," she smiles, "And I will take my leave now to run some errands."

"Be careful, Maria, it's slippery out there," Antonia warns.

"Oh I will, don't worry. In any event, it's not that far to the market."

She grabs her coat and shawl and is out the door.

Toni pours another cup and leans back with a sigh. She looks at me sideways and continues the story.

"There's something more in this whole scenario that concerns you, Stephanie, something you must know."

"Me, why on earth? I had nothing to do with Ken, I mean, I'm very, very sorry that he died but…"

"Yes, I know you had nothing to do with Ken, but Mark did."

"My Mark?"

"Yes, your Mark."

"Well, I know they were friends, good friends even, but what are you getting at?"

"Stephanie, you know that I love you like a sister and I would never ever do or say anything to hurt you, don't you?"

"Of course I know, but…"

"Well, there's something that I never told you and I feel guilty about that, but now I think that you should know."

"What is it, Toni?"

"Well, way back when we still lived in Virginia, before we moved to Canada, well… "

"What? You can tell me, what is it?"

"Ken told me that he had seen Mark in some gay bar in Richmond, not once, but several times. I never mentioned it to you because I didn't think much of it at the time, you know how guys are, they do stupid things like going to strip joints or gay bars just for a laugh or whatever…"

I'm surprised, not shocked but surprised. Mark never ever mentioned anything like that but then he hadn't mentioned his various indiscretions either, had he? So why would he tell me that he'd been to a gay bar or a strip joint? So yes, I'm surprised but only because he'd been so homophobic, it seemed improbable that he would frequent such places, even for a lark.

"Ok, Toni, I understand. It's a guy thing. But it happened a long time ago and you and I weren't as close then as we are now. So yes, I understand why you didn't mention it to me. Let's just forget it; it has nothing to do with our friendship now."

"I'm happy you feel that way, Stephanie, and you're exactly right. I thought it was a guy thing too. Of course, I knew that Ken went to these bars quite frequently. But there's more… "

"More? Like what?"

Toni pours a fresh cup of tea and takes tiny little sips of the hot liquid.

"All this came out much later, after Mark had died and just before Ken left for Edmonton to live with Hans-Jorgen. It seems that Ken and Mark's friendship was much closer than I had thought. They weren't involved or anything like that, or so I thought, but apparently, Mark confided in Ken that he had mixed feelings about his sexuality, that he was torn and didn't know which way to turn, that he loved you and the children and didn't want to hurt anyone...And that he was thinking of ending his life. Stage a hunting accident or something like that."

Toni sets down her teacup. Her hands are trembling slightly. Tears are welling up in her eyes.

I just sit on the couch and I cannot move. My mouth has gone dry, I cannot speak. All I can do is stare at my best friend who has carried that knowledge with her all these years. I do not feel betrayed, not really, I know exactly why she has never told me this before and probably never would have if Ken hadn't died.

Some secrets you carry to your grave because there's no point in sharing them and hurting another person that you care deeply about. I understand all that and I probably would have done the same thing if I were in Toni's shoes.

But still, I cannot speak and just sit and try and catch my breath.

"Stephanie?" her voice is small and seems to be coming from far away, "Stephanie, can you ever forgive me for not telling you all this sooner? There seemed no point at the time to hurt you further because Mark had already died, except now..."

"Now what?"

"When Ken lay dying, he told me that he and Mark actually did have what he called a *little fling* that didn't last very long but that's how their friendship had started... and.."

"I see," I can sense how cold my voice is, "you knew all this and now you feel it necessary to tell me? Why?"

I get up and start pacing back and forth. I don't know what to think, what to say... I'm upset, I feel betrayed, and I don't know why on earth she's never mentioned any of this disgusting business to me before. She's supposed to be my friend, for God's sake, my best friend.

"I feel it necessary because you are like a sister to me, I feel it necessary because it is the truth and you must know the truth and I feel that you're strong enough now to deal with the way it really was.

Besides, I had absolutely no knowledge of the fact that Ken and Mark had been involved. It never even crossed my mind.

Ken told me about it in the hour of his death and I have no idea why he told me. Perhaps there was still enough of the Catholic in him that he needed to confess, even it if wasn't to a priest. Heaven knows, I could have lived quite nicely without that confession.

You have known me long enough, Stephanie, long enough to know that I would not have kept such a secret from you but would have told you straight away; especially when you told me that Mark had AIDS...

But the only think I knew at the time was that Ken had seen him in this bar, that's all and I'm disgusted and pissed off with Ken, with Mark, with that whole sordid business."

Antonia has pulled her feet up on the couch and is resting her chin on her knees. She's looking at me with tears in her eyes, her lips are pressed together in a hard straight line, and I can see she is hurting, hurting as much as I am.

I'm starting to shiver. I grab a little blanket from the couch and sit down beside Toni. And now I start to cry too, the kind of tears that just come, the kind of tears that stream warmly down your face, that won't stop, ever.

I'm not crying for Mark, I'm crying for me. I'm crying because I lived with him all those years and never suspected anything, I'm crying because he must have suffered so, but what he did to me was far worse than his god dammed suffering. He made me a victim and he took my life away from me and there is no way that I can ever forgive him now, not even beyond the grave.

How naïve I had been. How very young, how very trusting. Not in a million years would I have suspected that Mark had these feelings and tendencies. That he was torn inside.

And now I wonder, wonder whether Max or Hannah knew. No. She would have denied to the high heavens that there was 'something wrong' with her precious son. Much easier to blame someone else for his philandering. Heck, she'd probably have blamed me too if it turned out that Mark was gay or bisexual or whatever. But Max? He was much more worldly, more realistic, he had a keen eye for phoniness and deception. I wonder. But then, if he had suspected anything, would he have told me? I know he wouldn't have wanted to hurt me and perhaps he had kept his suspicions to himself, if he had any in the first place.

I'm trying to remember whether I had ever suspected that Mark could like men in that way. But I only ever had fleeting thoughts after the AIDS diagnosis and even then I had pushed them away immediately because I felt disgusted with myself for even thinking in those terms. I remember the times when he had not wanted me to touch him, or cuddle, or have sex, and he would turn away from me and feign sleep. And even at those times the thought had never entered my mind. What a child I had been, what a romantic fool thinking that my husband loved me and all was well in the world.

In retrospect it would be easy to look for tell-tale signs, subtle nuances, little happenings and incidents, but I cannot go there. It is of no use now and it will change nothing.

I wish things were different, I wish I did not have AIDS, I wish my husband had loved me instead of dying and leaving me to raise our children... I wish all these things but the reality is that things were not different; they are as they are and I think I'm stronger for it and I will make the best of my life as it is now.

Antonia is sitting quietly beside me. She knows all this is a lot for me to digest all at once and she knows we're both victims in this.

I turn toward her and hug her and together we cry, each for our own reason, each for our own pain, each for our own memories. But we are together in this and we'll support each other forever and ever. We both know that and there's nothing to forgive between us because what she's done, she's done out of love.

I finally let go of Toni and sit up straight. Toni blows her nose and brushes back a strand of her fiery hair.

"I wasn't sure how you would react, Steph... There were times when I was close to telling you but then, well, it wouldn't have changed anything."

"You're right, Toni, a long time has passed since Mark died and there are times when I hardly think of him. Only when I look at my children, I remember stuff, because Adam looks so much like him but his character is so different, and Bettina, who looks so much like my Mom... Well, I'm blessed with these kids... and I guess that's the only thing I'm thankful for when it comes to Mark. There is no need to tell them any of this. It's in the past; it has nothing to do with them. It doesn't change anything. And yes, Toni, I do understand why you never told me, it's for the same reason that my children will never be burdened with any of this."

"Well, that's that then. Now there's nothing between us that has been left unsaid... Except..."

"Except what? There's more?"

Toni looks at me with a tiny little smile.

"Yes, there's more, but it's not a bad part. You see, when Mark found out that he had AIDS he told Ken about it. I think that Ken wasn't overly surprised and had a pretty good idea who it was that had infected Mark, but he never talked about that. So, when Mark confided in Ken he asked him to take out an insurance policy for you and the children because he himself would not have qualified with his condition, you see."

"And? What has that to do with me now?"

"Well, Ken did take out a policy for half a million dollars and you and the children are the beneficiaries... So, you now have some money and don't have to worry about the kids and you can forget about feeling beholden to me, although I think you're over that."

Now I'm speechless. I get up and leave the room, Toni looks

alarmed and a little scared. I walk over to the hall closet and grab our coats.

"Here," I toss Toni's coat over to her, "Let's you and me go for a walk. We both need the fresh air, don't you think? And it will give me a chance to find out how warm and cozy this beautiful coat really is."

We slip on our boots and arm in arm we walk down the snowy path toward the lake.

There is no wind and the air is frosty and alive with zillions of sparkling ice crystals. I know they call it diamond dust and it adds the most magical shimmer to our winter walk.

We look at one another and smile.

There is no need to talk any more.

Epilogue

So you see if it were not for my friend Antonia, I would not be sitting here on the beach in the Florida sunshine. I would not be staying in this beautiful condo up on the thirtieth floor, looking out over the ocean that stretches as far as forever.

Way below I see the private beach that hardly anyone ever goes to, except for me.

It's the middle of February, so most of the condos are empty. Many belong to Canadians and Americans who live up north and only come down to escape the bitter winter months. Just like I do. Well, we... Maria and I.

Maria is here to keep an eye on me in case something happens and she's doing the cooking and cleaning and shopping. She loves it and I'm so happy to have her with me.

Toni comes down every so often, but she only stays a week or so. I guess she gets bored and wants to go back to her boutique that she loves so much and make sure everything is running ok. When she's down here in Florida, Toni tans almost instantly, nice, evenly bronzed. I'm not so lucky, my skin is too pale now and I have to be careful not to get too much sun or I'll get a rash. Another stupid side effect of the AIDS, I bet. But not an important one. So I walk along the beach wearing a huge sun hat and long sleeved filmy tops.

There are a handful of Jewish women from Toronto who meet every morning at the pool. Their voices are shrill and they talk loudly, as if they're afraid of not being heard.

Every morning they meet, standing waist-high in the pool. Talking about Aunt Ida and her bad back, about Harry who scored big in the stock market, and about all the other husbands who are working away at their jobs so that they, the wives, can enjoy the winter months in Florida.

In all the weeks I've been here, I've never once seen them actually swim or go near the beach or into the ocean. They just stand there in the pool, up to their waist in water so they won't mess up their hairdos, and they talk.

And they are nice enough. Friendly even. Every time I walk by with my beach chair they say good morning, or good afternoon, as the case may be. And I can feel them looking at me as I walk down to the beach, wondering who I am, what I'm doing here by myself.

I don't like the pool. I want to feel the sand between my toes, feel the heat rising up and burning my soles, and walk close to the edge of the water where the sand is wet and as hard as cement and cools my feet.

I look at the waves, washing in and receding, following an eternal rhythmic force and I look at the tiny birds dodging the waves and making a run for it. And they never get caught. I don't know what kind of birds they are. Sandpipers, I think. But I can't be sure. They run and run and run and they never leave the ground, they just run and run and run...

And then I think about my Mom, more and more often I think of her. I see her in my beautiful daughter who looks so much like her.

And now that I have grown children myself, I think how hard it must have been for her, raising me on her own, giving me a good education, providing a lovely home... And not a word about my father. That was her secret, her love, her life, her destiny.

Sometimes I think I can I hear her laughter in the wind; I see her smile in the sunset; I feel her being here with me and I will always know that she's around. Her soul is around, her spirit is around.

And then I think about all the things that have happened in my life and I try to make sense of them, but I cannot.

I don't think that much about dying any more. It's going to happen. Death is coming closer and closer. Definitely closer to me than to most people my age.

But I've seen it... I've seen death. I've dealt with it. I've dealt with it but I've not made peace with it. I don't think that anyone ever does. If somebody says they have, I think they're lying. But I don't think about it that much. It comes when it comes. Probably sooner, to me.

Sometimes though I just walk along the beach and I don't think about anything at all. I remember how I used to panic every time I got sick, when I had a cold or a sniffle. I'd be paranoid about people with colds coming near me, as if they shouldn't be more paranoid that I could infect them with something much more dangerous than a cold... But that's not even an issue any more.

People come near me... they have a cold... I get a cold... Well... I'll live with it. At times I have to be rushed to the hospital. I know that will happen again. It all depends on what it is that attacks my body, which is defenseless. But I'm not paranoid about that anymore either.

I haven't given up or anything like that. Somewhere in the back of my mind there's this little voice that keeps whispering: you know what? There could be a cure; a cure could be just around the corner.

Everyone who has an incurable illness has these thoughts deep down, otherwise they couldn't go on. Well, they could go on but they wouldn't want to go on. A little sliver of hope flickering in the background. In the deepest part of your being you know, you absolutely know, you're not going to die, not just yet anyway.

I guess another thing to be thankful for, an important thing to be thankful for, is that I've never developed these odious black sores that are quite common with AIDS victims. Remember the guy in the movie Philadelphia? Tom Hanks? How he had these tell-all sores that freaked everyone out? Well, that was a movie, but nevertheless, many people who have AIDS get them, sometimes all over their bodies.

I'm glad I don't have these sores anywhere and you can be sure that I watch for them. In my mind, every little pimple could potentially grow into an AIDS sore and I don't think I could stand it, waving the AIDS flag for all to see.

I guess if I haven't developed them by now, I probably won't ever get them. The doctors aren't too sure about this. In fact, they're not too sure about anything at all. For all intents and purposes I should have been dead long, long ago and so they pat themselves on the back because they've kept me alive with these wonderful new drugs for so long and I guess they're right, to a degree.

And every so often during my walks, my thoughts go back to the last holiday I spent with Mark and the kids. Walks along the endless beach, looking for sea shells, building sand castles, all of us together. But I stop myself, you know? What's the point in dwelling on a shattered life, shattered dreams, a shattered future?

I have learned to be strong, even learned to be a bit cynical or perhaps that's not the right word, more accepting of what is and not wishing for something that is not. Yeah, that's it.

If you cannot accept what is, then you don't have a chance, you'll be feeling sorry for yourself and spend your life in misery, making everyone around you miserable as well.

So yes, I've accepted my condition, accepted being alone, widowed, without a man, with limited mobility, with limited health. But acceptance does not mean giving up, not by a long shot, not ever. It simply means not crying over spilt milk and getting on with it.

So for now, let me walk along the shore with my *companion* by my side, my steady shadow who has become my friend.

Let me enjoy my little sandpipers, let me enjoy the peace of the ocean... the thrust of the waves... the hard glitter of the sun as it splinters into a thousand brilliant pieces when it hits the water.

Those are my joys.

For now, anyway.

CPSIA information can be obtained at www.ICGtesting.com
Printed in the USA
LVOW122219180413

329662LV00001B/12/P